Looking for Utrillo

A Novel in Three Movements
by
William-John Deerin

 *PUBLISHING*

First published in 2014
by White Craw Publishing
Biggar
United Kingdom

ISBN 978-1-291-78121-2

Typeset in Palatino Linotype
Cover Art and Design copyright © William-John Deerin 2013

William-John Deerin was born and brought up in Airdrie, Lanarkshire. He worked in a variety of factories and steelworks before successfully attending Jordanhill College of Education and Queen's College, Glasgow. After graduating he spent the next 30 years working in local government before retiring in 2009. He currently lives with his wife, Caroline, in South Lanarkshire.

His poetry has appeared in a number of anthologies and he is the editor of *Stepping into the Avalanche*, an anthology of poetry and prose by writers James Robertson, Matthew Fitt, Gerry Cambridge, Linda Cracknell and Aonghas MacNeacail. A volume of his own poetry, *A Starling's Eye*, was published in 2005.

He now spends his time between painting and writing poetry and short stories, and he has recently begun writing song lyrics. *Looking for Utrillo* is his first novel.

This book is dedicated
to my friend and fellow traveller
Jim Ness
and to my wife
Caroline

A story should have a beginning, a middle and an end... but not necessarily in that order.

Jean-Luc Godard

1st Movement

Romeo and Juliet
Nina Rota

2nd Movement

Nocturne #19 in e minor
Frederich Chopin

3rd Movement

Metamorphosis # 5
Philip Glass

1st Movement

Romeo and Juliet
Nina Rota

Preface

The story you are about to read is a companion novel to the art history, *Utrillo: The Man Who Loved Walls* by John Gil-Martin, first published in 1998 by Reid & Seymour, London & Boston. This account of John Gil-Martin's year in Paris researching the history of painter Maurice Utrillo was written three years later but is only published now after the resolution of considerable legal differences concerning publishing rights.

The origins of *Looking for Utrillo* lie in a book tour that John undertook shortly after *Utrillo: The Man Who Loved Walls* landed on the bookshelves. An Australian journalist from Melbourne's Morning News asked him what it was like to live in Paris for a year while researching his book. There and then the idea took root and John began to write about his days wandering round universities, libraries, art galleries and museums in the French capital.

At first John wrote about the research only, then gradually, bit by bit, more personal details began to emerge. The first manuscript was serialised in the monthly journal, The Edinburgh Review. This was mostly the research that he had done.

An article in the Toronto Quarterly included some details of his relationships during his research. It was obvious to many of John Gil-Martin's friends and colleagues that a book was beginning to emerge from these early musings. At first John refused to undertake such a project, then quite unexpectedly a piece of good fortune occurred that sealed the deal; John broke his leg in a fall while hill walking in upstate New York. With time on his hands he finally put together his memoir of that time. No names have been changed, nor have the places where the events were played out. What you are about to read is John's final account of his time in Paris.

Fiona Shaw
Soho, London
2011

1

The night I met Yvette

A very small degree of hope is sufficient to cause the birth of love.
Stendhal

I am living in an apartment overlooking the boulevard Garibaldi near its corner with Pasteur. The rooms are small but adequate for my needs; enough space to write and a small room to sleep in. I prefer rooms that are relatively bare; too much furniture demands attention, and I have no desire to become attached to their needs.

A little balcony permits me a view of the Eiffel Tower if I lean far enough over. Sometimes at night when I have run out of words to write I sit there and watch the cars race along the boulevard with red brake-lights flashing in one direction while on-coming headlights fill the night with halogen threats. Across the street is the métro Sèvres-Lecourbe. This is important to me as I usually only travel by métro.

This is a part of the city I know well. I like its ordinariness, its lack of fuss and conceit and the fact that it holds no special attraction to the visiting world. People here can get on with their lives without the daily disruption that you get further along in Montparnasse or up in Montmartre. Here, you can go about your business in relative peace. Most of all it is a part of Paris with little or no pretension; a village within a city; a village where life is lived in the open.

It's been ten months since I arrived in Paris, just overthree-quarters of my allotted time here. The weather suits me. Everything I need is in this city. Everything I want is here too. I have learned to recognise the difference between the two. Everyone should live in Paris at some time in his or her life; it is the most stimulating of all the great cities.

This is not my first stay in this section of the city. I spent a year here some time ago as a post-graduate student at the nearby Pasteur Institute. I discovered during my stay then that this was a quarter of the city where normality existed, where every day was manageable, where every day was a workday.

These conditions appeal to me now as my work is such that I require long periods of peace and quiet. Because of this and a natural inclination – I confess to having become a creature of habit – I am now said to be a man set in his ways.

This is borne out by my custom of dining whenever possible at the Bistro de la Gare on boulevard du Montparnasse. I prefer not to eat at home. I see no purpose in it when so many excellent restaurants are nearby. Nor, for that matter, do I like the lingering smell of food once I have eaten. I prefer the rooms where I live and work to be scent free.

The walk to the restaurant also helps me to think. I try and walk every day just for the purpose of thinking. The exercise helps burn off the toxins that cause me to worry. Sometimes I go along rue de Vaugirard, the street where William Faulkner and F. Scott Fitzgerald and his wife Zelda lived. At other times I go up Pasteur then cut across to boulevard Montparnasse at the railway station.

The restaurant is a favourite place of mine to eat. The food is very good and I enjoy its atmosphere; it is one of the few restaurants that I have dined in where diners laugh out loud and often. The décor is Art Nouveau and reminds me a little of Charles Rennie Mackintosh but with softer more diffused lines in its motif.

When I first visited the restaurant on a regular basis the waiters thought I was an Englishman, and on occasion made a few derogatory remarks with regard to some news item or other they had read in the newspaper about some trivial matter in politics. I told them I was British but not English. This confused some of them at first but gradually, with a little assistance from me, they came to realise that a person could be British and not necessarily English. They seemed not to comprehend that a Scot, or a Welshman for that matter, could be British: a common misunderstanding I have often come across elsewhere in Europe and in North America also.

On my way back from the restaurant I generally walk down the boulevard before turning left into rue de Sèvres and along past Hópital Necker. This brings me out at the intersection under the iron bridge at Sèvres-Lecourbe; a busy junction at which one needs to be heedful. Some evenings, if the weather permits, and long after I've returned from the restaurant and my work has come to a stop for the evening, I have a gaelic coffee in the little café-bar near the corner of rue Lecourbe, where I sit on a barstool staring out at the dark empty night in a scene reminiscent of one of Edward Hopper's pictorial dramas.

The routine of this activity creates a sense of familiarity for me, but more importantly it gives me a feeling of belonging, which in turn generates a sense of respect for where I am; an attitude which, I have found on my travels, is often reciprocated. Now, as if proof is needed, many of the residents and shopkeepers that inhabit the routes I walk recognise me and greet me politely as I pass. Occasionally one or two will engage me in a little light conversation. I tell them I am a writer. No one is surprised. I tell them I am writing a biography about the painter, Maurice Utrillo. This information usually brings about one of two reactions: some look blankly at me and shrug their shoulders while those who know of him ask me why I am not living in Montmartre where he spent most of his life. I tell them I prefer staying in Sèvres-Lecourbe. This pleases them. This pleases me.

It was during one of my evening walks along the boulevard and down from the restaurant that I met Yvette Carné, a beautiful and delicately made woman, who seemed to appear from out of nowhere. It had been a while since anyone could take me by surprise but, that evening, Yvette Carné managed to catch me well and truly off-guard.

There was a slight chill in the air that evening so I had carried a jacket to the restaurant. After leaving the bistro I took my favoured route north with thoughts in my mind of a research visit I was to take soon in Pierrefitte. The traffic was particularly busy at the junction with boulevard des Invalides as I stood with others waiting to cross. Up till then nothing out of the ordinary had happened that evening. I was just a guy waiting to cross a street.

'A gentleman would give a lady his jacket on a cold evening like this.'

'Pardon, Madame.' I turned to look at the woman now standing next to me. I caught her beauty straight away. My recognition of her beauty must have shown in my expression as she laughed a little laugh as if acknowledging a reaction she had experienced from men in the past. She then surprised me even further.

'My name is Yvette and I'm going your way — well, as far as the hospital. I work there.'

This was a new experience for me. I felt completely disorientated. An older couple standing behind us, who had observed this little episode, laughed at my awkwardness. I tried to remain dignified.

'And how do you know I am going past the hospital, Madame?'

'Because I've seen you go that way often. And I know you are a writer. What I don't know, Monsieur, is your name.'

I passed her my jacket, which she hung loosely across her shoulders. It sat like a giant oversized tweed coat on her and made her seem even more petite than she actually was. This amused me. The traffic lights changed in our favour. I felt relieved. We crossed over, still talking.

'Thank you'. She said on receiving my jacket. 'And are you going to tell me your name, Monsieur?'

'Before I tell you my name, Madame, will you tell me how you know that I am a writer and where I am going? You have me at a disadvantage.'

'Oh, that is easy. Monsieur Bourdan told me. You know him. He owns the little fruit shop where you buy your apples. I too buy my fruit there. It was he who told me you are writing a book on Utrillo.'

'Oh, I see. I am a man with no secrets. I can't even buy some fruit without strangers getting to know about it.' I was beginning to feel a little more like myself.

'Ah, Monsieur, but we are not strangers. I have told you my name— Yvette, Yvette Carné— it is you who is being strange.'

This made me laugh. It held an innocence I found appealing. I turned towards her.

'Do you always speak to men you don't know, and a foreign one into the bargain? Isn't that a little dangerous?'

'How else will I get to know you?' Her face was an expression of logic. 'Anyway you don't look that dangerous to me.'

I was finding myself being more and more drawn to her each time she spoke.

'All right, you win. My name is John Gil-Martin and I like to think I am a little dangerous.' I was smiling. I had managed to get myself back on to level terms. We approached the entrance to the hospital.

'Thank-you, Monsieur John Gil-Martin. Your jacket.'

I took hold of my jacket and slipped it over my arm. She turned and smiled, her eyes still sparkling.

'We will no doubt meet again, don't you agree?'

Before I could answer her she had stepped through the large wrought-iron gates into the courtyard of the hospital and disappeared into a door marked PRIVE.

I stood for a moment staring at the door, the novelty of the last few minutes forcing a wry smile on my lips. 'Well that's a first.' I told myself. 'Did that really happen?' I turned and started walking towards the café-bar on the far corner. I needed a drink. I began to laugh.

Over the next few days I wondered when I would meet Yvette Carné again. She had said as much at the gates to the hospital. Would I just have to follow my daily routine and hope she would appear one evening out of the shadows? I had no alternative but to wait and see. My brief encounter with her had intrigued me. I found myself at times recalling our few moments together, repeating the few words we had spoken to each other, looking for a meaning where there probably was none to find. I was bemused, but not enough to stop me from my work. Each day I went about my research, tracking down the haunts and habitats of Maurice Utrillo, while in the evenings, as I made my way back from the bistro, I found myself looking around the streets in the hope of seeing Yvette once more.

I asked after her at the fruit-shop, but M. Bourdan said he too had not seen her lately. He told me he had wondered when Yvette and I would meet. 'She likes you. You both like Utrillo.' This surprised me, as she had made no mention of her interest in Utrillo during our conversation. She knew I was writing a book about him. She acknowledged this. I assumed M. Bourdan would have told her about my interest in the painter from one of our brief conversations, but what encouraged me more was her telling the fruiterer that she liked me. Here, there was hope. On one or two evenings I lingered, without loitering, at the entrance of the Hôpital Necker where I last saw her, daring her to appear one more time, wanting her to appear. She didn't.

2

A shadow in the park

There is no person who is not dangerous for someone.
Marie de Sevigne

At least twice a week I walk along rue Lecourbe to the small park in place Saint-Lambert. Here I try and sort out my thoughts and enjoy the sun on my back at the same time. Often I just sit and let my eyes drift, seeing nothing in particular, but enjoying what is all around me, especially the stylish façade of the apartment buildings that surround the park.

I prefer to be in the park when there are no children present as their noise upsets my desire for peace and quiet. The park entertains a few men and women I see regularly. On the far bench to my right a dark haired man sits reading a folded newspaper. This is his normal attitude. I guess he is in his late forties as there is grey in his hair and he is a little overweight. Occasionally he scribbles a word or two on the paper. Then he makes a brief conversation on his mobile phone. At first I assumed he was working on a crossword, or more probably, looking for a job, but now I am not so sure. Why do your business in a park? His bench is too far from me to hear any conversation but, from his general posture and the way he speaks into the phone, I get the impression he is giving out orders to a subordinate. In my scheme of things I have moved him from 'job hunter' into the mysterious ranks of some kind of gambler or private 'dealer.'

On the bench directly across from me sits Marguerite,

another regular. I call her Marguerite as she reminds me of a woman I knew many years ago by that name; a French woman too. She sits with her knees spread too far apart for it to be considered ladylike; nor is she an old enough woman, for that matter, to be excused her immodesty. The other Marguerite, who was a copy-typist at our college, did the same. She would sit on a low wall near our faculty with her elbows sunk into her knees, her chin cradled by her hands, while we boys sat on the grass nearby. We were too embarrassed to look in her direction but every so often she would shout something to us and we had to look over to her, trying not to notice but blushing furiously. Marguerite would roar with laughter at our discomfort. Today, this Marguerite sits in her usual way, legs apart, elbows resting on her knees, her hands gripping an open newspaper.

Pierre, the postman, always sits on the bench to my left. I am not guessing he is a postman as he wears the yellow insignia of La Poste and carries a large waterproof satchel over one shoulder, even when sitting. I wonder if he ever takes it off, or if he wears it that way even at home? I have never seen him without a cigarette in his mouth, and he chain smokes while he sits on the bench. He is a ready advert for the cigarette Disque Bleu, his preferred smoke. I assume that he is resting in the park after making his deliveries. I like Pierre, if that's his name, as he always gives me a wave when he or I arrive in the park.

At the far end of the park, on the path leading onto the street, there is a bench partly secluded by trees and bushes. Here sits a woman who seems only to dress in black, or maybe the shadow she sits within confuses the eye. She is too far away for me to make out any discernible features. I imagine her Spanish and beautiful. She is always here when I arrive and seems to spend all her time in the park reading books. A part of me wants to go over and introduce myself to her. But I realise that to do so would destroy the mystery I have conferred on her, so I leave her to her books and the mystery lingers.

The bench nearest to me on the opposite side of the gate normally hosts the casual visitor. These are mostly girls from the nearby shops who come to the park to have their lunch, or deliverymen who take a break for a cigarette. Most casual visitors only spend ten or fifteen minutes on the benches. The regulars spend at least an hour, usually two.

Rarely do the regulars acknowledge each other. Only Pierre the postman makes the effort. It would seem that we prefer to keep our distances; each to his or her allotted place in the park, visible but anonymous. Only once did I see one of the regulars outwith the park; it was the 'dealer.' He was with a beautiful blonde woman who was wearing a white PVC coat and red scarf. She managed to make her attire seem dressy; a lesser woman would have looked cheap. They were coming out of Montparnasse Station as I entered. I nodded, smiling towards them but the 'dealer' seemed to deliberately look away from my direction. I dismissed his action. No crime was committed. He would have his own reasons for doing this. Men like the 'dealer' always had their reasons. This was borne out the next time I went into the park. He was sitting on his usual bench, mobile phone in one hand, paper in the other. He looked over in my direction and made a short waving gesture with his rolled-up newspaper. I took this as an acknowledgement we had met in circumstances he preferred not to be seen in, and nodded back to him in what I considered to be in a conspiratorial manner. He was apologising in his way. No words were spoken but the rules were now clearly understood.

The 'dealer' wasn't the only one of the regulars to bring a

degree of mystery to the park. No doubt an encounter that came my way would have been duly noted and pondered on by the others. One day I was sitting on my usual bench not far from the Lecourbe entrance on a hot afternoon, a week or so after I met Yvette Carné, when my thoughts were disturbed by someone addressing me.

'It is you! Isn't it! John Gil-Martin. How are you?'

I turned to see a smallish man in a light cotton suit standing on the path. He was dapper and tanned. I didn't recognise him.

'You know me, Monsieur?' I asked.

'Of course I do. You attended the Institute Pasteur about ten or eleven years ago. You may not remember me, Emile Renouf, from the Microbe Research Department. I saw you the other day on rue de Vaugirard, but I wasn't sure if it really was you.'

'Of course you are!' I stood up immediately. 'Forgive me for not recognising you, Emile.'

'Yes, it's been many years.' He shrugged his shoulders. 'We have changed no doubt. We are a little older, yes? You are back living in Paris?'

'For the moment, I have some work here.'

He sat down. This was a situation I should have anticipated. My apartment was close to the Institute. Yet for some reason I hadn't considered this when I leased my rooms. I just wanted to be based, for my time in Paris, in an area I was familiar with.

Emile had been one of the lecturers I attended during my studies at the Institute. That was twelve years ago to be precise. He was thinner now than when I first met him. His black hair had turned grey but he still had the looks that turned many a female student's head when he entered a room.

We continued to talk, keeping our remarks pleasant and general. A warm breeze ricocheted off the trees behind our bench. We began to relax a little in each other's company. Eventually I told him I had given up my research after leaving Paris; that my life had taken a number of changes in direction and that my interests were no longer scientific.

I found myself opening up to him, telling him about aspects of my life that I had told to few others. I'd always considered myself immune to the 'stranger on a train' syndrome. Apparently not so, for here I was, singing like a nightingale.

I told him I had been married; but for a short time only as my wife died of a cancer early in our marriage. He listened politely and seemed sympathetic but quickly wanted to know why I was back in Paris. Maybe he was uncomfortable at hearing such personal details and wanted to stay on more neutral ground, so I told him about the book I was writing and that I was now a full-time writer of art biographies and histories, and had been for some time.

He said he wasn't surprised and had suspected that I would change career. I was, apparently, too much of a romantic to be a scientist. I questioned to myself how he could make such an assertion, but let it pass without comment. It may have been true, he may have thought me 'too romantic', but I didn't think Emile Renouf best qualified to judge any of my leanings.

Our conversation opened up a number of inner passageways that had been closed by me for some time. Emile's presence acted as a key to doors into my past that I had kept firmly locked for over a decade. As we spoke I grew annoyed at myself for believing I could return to Paris – and here especially, to this quarter – and think that incidents in my past that were of significance to me would no longer have any relevance in my life. I was angry at my stupidity, at my own self-delusion. I should have known I would meet my past head-on by coming back to Sèvres-Lecourbe. Meeting Emile was, in one way or another, unavoidable. Now it was only a matter of time until one of us mentioned Thérèse.

We both knew this was a sensitive matter, to be spoken of carefully and, for me, best if he brought up the subject, as this would keep any talk between us on equal grounds. But Emile didn't; he was as elusive as I remembered him twelve years earlier.

'How is Thérèse, Emile? Is she still around? Do you still see her?'

I cursed myself. Now I had said it and had made it sound too plaintive: this would, if I remembered correctly, let Emile take the high moral ground he so enjoyed walking on.

His expression never changed; his voice remained deep and controlled. I suspected he had expected the question at some point in our conversation.

'She left the Institute about ten years ago, but she drops by every so often; at fundraising events and the likes. Claude divorced her. Did you know that?'

'No I didn't. Is she all right?'

'As far as I know she gets by. She's not the woman she was; time takes its toll, even on a brilliant and beautiful woman like Thérèse. Claude saw to it that she had enough to live on. He could have done nothing and no one would have blamed him. I don't think it would have mattered to her if he had given her nothing. She seemed not to care. A by-product of being in love, if I'm not mistaken! I suppose it meant more to Claude. She was the mother of his children. Such things matter to men. You agree?'

I thought I detected sarcasm in Emile's voice. I nodded in

agreement but kept my look fixed on his face.

He smiled. 'But that is all water under the bridge, is it not? And here in Paris we have plenty of water under our bridges!' At this Emile stood up. 'Anyway I must go now, John, as I have much to do. Let's meet again soon and catch up.'

We shook hands. I said I would call the Institute and arrange lunch.

'Oh, by the way, John: it is now Professor Renouf; I got Claude's chair. He died not long after you left. Did I not mention that? Yes, it was cancer too, like your wife. Now you and Thérèse have something more in common. Please call me. I'll look forward to it.'

I was taken aback at this news but tried not to show it. Emile had a habit of being ambiguous in his speech, especially when speaking in English. It was typical of him. He was usually the kind of man who asked a question but rarely answered one, unless it suited his purpose to do otherwise. At the Institute he was considered an enigma. No one knew much about him. I remember Thérèse saying she thought he came from Ambois in the Loire valley and had taken his first degree at a provincial university. He had studied for his doctorate at Pasteur, under Claude's supervision. She thought he lived in an apartment overlooking Montparnasse Cemetery. Other than that she knew little else.

I watched Emile stroll across the park and speculated if anything other than promotion had happened to him in twelve years. If it had, he would never tell me. I wondered if the next time that he met Thérèse he would mention to her that he had come across me. I was never sure what Emile would do at the best of times, nor did I know where his allegiance lay in what had happened between Thérèse and me. As far as I knew he wasn't a particular friend of Claude or Thérèse for that matter, but there again he and I were never that friendly either. I suppose you could say he was his own man. It was typical of him to leave just when I wanted to hear more about Thérèse, but I knew I couldn't appear too eager, especially to someone like Emile. Emile always knew more than he let on. This was the man's style. He drip fed information to his students. Control was everything to him.

The park no longer held my interest. The other regulars had slipped away during my conversation with Emile, so I made my way back to my apartment, looking into the occasional shop along the way, my thoughts flitting through memories of times shared with Thérèse.

Back at my apartment I forced myself to concentrate. I had much work to do. I'd collected a substantial amount of information on Maurice Utrillo and was conscious I needed to start bringing some of this material together and putting it into a shape that would satisfy my editors at Reid & Seymour, back in London.

3

The Doctor at Pierrefitte

There is no Utrillo, only a world of Utrillo
Daragnès

My interest in the life and art of Maurice Utrillo started long before I came to Paris. Like many children and young people growing up in the city of Glasgow, rarely did a summer or winter pass without a visit to the magnificent Kelvingrove Museum and Art Gallery in the city's west-end. It was here that I saw my first Utrillo, my first Vuillard and my first Lépine. As crowds huddled on the steps in front of Dali's 'Crucifixion', I could be found staring deeply into the magical world of the post-impressionists.

Of all the artists I had read about Utrillo captivated me the most. I read of his tormented life, his alcoholism, his ridicule, and somehow in my teenage angst felt I understood the alienation that had befallen him. Looking back I recognise that his paintings of long narrow streets, leaden skies, blind corners and culs-de-sac, more often than not devoid of the townspeople who must have inhabited them, reached out and touched my own youthful feelings of insecurity and distrust. My interest in Utrillo stayed with me long after my disaffected youth had passed. His paintings of the streets of Montmartre still fascinated me, but then so did the paintings of Derain, Bonnard and Matisse.

Within the first few weeks of arriving in Paris I did much of my research in the Bibliothèque Nationale and at The Musée de l'Art Moderne de la Ville de Paris. I was grateful for the assistance given to me by these institutions and spent many hours in their research facilities reading a range of documentation, much of it material of little interest to the general reader, but important to the researcher when referencing and cross-referencing times and dates of events. With the help of staff at both institutions I was able to identify further places to visit to aid my research.

One of the other museums I visited at this time was the Musée du Vieux Montmartre; a must for any research into the life of Utrillo, as the painter lived for a time in the house at the museum's entrance. This area of Montmartre was Utrillo's stomping ground. The streets around the museum are littered with references to Utrillo on their walls, each claiming some association or other with the painter. A little way down the hill from the museum sits the Lapin Agile, the bar where the painter and his cronies did most of their drinking. I spent a few evenings soaking in the atmosphere of this infamous bistro, an experience not to be missed by anyone wishing to get a feel for past times in Paris.

It was during my second visit to the Musée du Vieux Montmartre when a surprising but thoroughly rewarding occurrence took place. I was looking bemusedly into a glass case displaying a photograph of Utrillo next to one of his mother Suzanne Valadon, who was completely naked (I don't think of myself as a prude, but the placing of these two photographs together disconcerted me), when I was interrupted by a member of the museum's staff, a tall, attractive, but rather stern woman whom I placed in her late thirties or early forties. I remembered I had spoken to this woman briefly during my first visit to the museum. I had explained to her that I was writing a history of Utrillo for a publishing house in London and was looking for any facts on the painter that she or the museum could furnish me with. If I also remembered rightly she showed no interest in me what-so-ever as she went about her duties, so I was quite surprised by this turn of events.

She told me she remembered me from my previous visit and wanted to give me the name of a certain Dr Jean-Paul Bricard as someone to talk to about the life of Utrillo. She insisted that he would be able to explain everything I wanted to know about the painter. It was also her opinion that, if Dr Bricard did not know something about Utrillo, then it wasn't worth knowing. She would phone ahead and let the doctor know that I would be in touch.

I accepted her assistance rather warily, if not a little puzzled by the change of heart on her part. At no time in my research, so far, had the name of Dr Bricard appeared and I was a bit sceptical about how this doctor could assist my work. However, I had nothing to lose and took her advice (and the details she provided me with) and later made arrangements to meet with the said Doctor.

As it turned out, Doctor Bricard was a retired psychologist who lived in Pierrefitte-sur-Seine, some thirteen and a half kilometres from Notre-Dame. There is a regular train service to Pierrefitte-sur-Seine from the Gare du Nord. I caught an early train so that I would have time to spare in case I had difficulty finding Dr Bricard's home. The train was busy and I was lucky to get a seat. The journey was uneventful and I was soon at my destination.

I was given directions to the Doctor's house at the train station. It was nearby, so I took my time. As I walked along rue du Général Moulin in perfect sunshine I wondered what the town would have been like when Utrillo lived here as a boy.

(Utrillo lodged in Pierrefitte and the neighbouring town of Montmagny with his grandmother when he was ten years old, in a house owned by his then stepfather, Paul Moussis. I had intended to visit the town for my research before I knew Dr Bricard lived there). The population had increased tenfold since that time and was now apparently a healthy twenty-three thousand (so it said on the information board at the station).

I found the Doctor's house without much difficulty. It was as described by the men at the station – a large dilapidated stone built villa sitting in an overgrown garden with a rather worse-for-wear 1973 Citroën DS in the driveway – quite fitting for a retired doctor, I thought. A row of cherry trees lined both sides of the drive, forming a pleasant little tunnel. As I passed his car I realised by its condition that it had never moved from that same spot for years; its tyres were flat and had nearly melted into the tarmac underneath.

I emerged from the tunnel and found myself standing in front of a small glass porch which was strewn inside with dusty coats, old crinkled boots and a variety of walking sticks and umbrellas, none of which appeared to have been used in recent times. I wondered what was ahead of me and rang the bell with a little trepidation.

The doctor answered the door and ushered me in without much ceremony. He was frail and a little unsteady on his feet. I could see instantly that he'd been a handsome man in his youth but time had left its mark. He sported a large white moustache that was impeccably groomed but a trace of stubble on his chin told me he wasn't a regular shaver. I was guided slowly into a poorly lit room littered with hundreds of papers and books, mostly lying around in piles. If there had been any order to what lay in front of me, then it was long forgotten.

'Forgive the mess, Monsieur Gil-Martin. One gets more

careless as one gets older. Anyway, I think there are always more important matters at hand than tidying up one's study. Here, have a seat…'

The doctor cleared a sheaf of papers from a chair that looked like one Van Gogh would have painted and pointed for me to sit. He sat himself down in an old green leather chair behind a large mahogany writing desk strewn with an arrangement of documents, letters, newspapers, books, pamphlets — what looked like medical reports— and dirty tea cups.

'So, you're looking for Utrillo, cher ami! You have taken on a chalice, if you don't mind me saying so, not only poisoned but also dipped in the greatest curse known to modern man – alcohol – the elixir of death and despair.' He leaned forward as if to share a secret. 'No one can find Utrillo. He exists only in the shadows that lurk in places no decent man or woman should ever enter. His life was such that even he did not know that he had lived it. We are all too late to find any truths; even the pathetic Maurice could not distinguish the truth from the fiction that surrounded him. He lived his life for the most part in the gutter; a clump of bone and rags that at some time or another blocked every sewer in Montmartre. Leave him in the sewers, cher ami, find yourself someone worthier of your time and energy. Leave what belongs to the shadows in darkness.'

I hadn't expected this and didn't have a prepared answer to counter the doctor's rather prosaic assertions. I smiled, nodded my head in some kind of weakish agreement and began to look around me. I had expected him to regale me with stories of the great man's art. I was a little lost for words. The doctor returned my smile then laughed. He then chuckled like a child. I realised this was his little joke.

On the walls of the study were photographs and portraits

of some of France's finest artists and writers. The doctor caught my glance. 'All alcoholics, each and every one! There's Utrillo over there by the mirror, the prince of them all, probably the greatest drinker of all time, certainly in Paris during his adult life and even when younger. He drank ten litres of wine a day; a condition that led him to be known by the nickname Litrillo. How he lived for seventy-two years is a mystery to me and to modern medicine.'

On the wall directly across from the rogues gallery was a single photograph of a smiling man with a whisky glass in his hand. I was curious why this man had been kept separate from the others. Doctor Bricard smiled. He guessed what I was thinking.

'Ah, cher ami, you're looking at the man who led me to drink in the first place. That gentleman is the great Doctor Magnus Huss; hero to some and spoiler to others. It was he who first suggested that alcohol was at the root of a number of pathological disorders; that alcoholism was in itself, so to speak, a disease. This was back in 1853 when my profession thought drink was a panacea to the working classes, a tonic against all life's ills.

'It took many years for the work of Dr Huss to be recognised in France; after all he was Swedish and we French can sometimes be a bit insular when it comes to matters close to our hearts – or, in this case, our livers.'

I watched the doctor as he walked over to a tall cabinet next to the room's only window. 'Would you like a cognac, cher ami? It's not too early for you, is it?' I nodded for him to pour me a glass. I was surprised that he drank at all after what he had said, but I felt in deep need of a drink. My interview was going to be interesting.

'I came here as a young Doctor in the 1940s to work at the

Centre Médico-Psychologique Avicenne. The war had just ended. I was recently married and wanted out of Paris, and this seemed as good a place as any to come to. The Centre had gained a good reputation and I was keen to further my own research. Utrillo was still alive then, but spent most of his days in a controlled trance manipulated by that delusional wife of his, Lucy Valore. I don't know which one was the madder. She kept him locked up in his château, only permitting certain people in to see him. He still painted but the paintings were naïve, childlike, crudely executed. It is no wonder Utrillo is the painter whose work is the most copied or faked. His early work, and those done just prior to his death, was the work of an infantile. Anyone would have been able to copy such poor work.'

'Did you ever meet him?'

'No, not really. I saw him once in the city; it was springtime. He was being chauffeured in a limousine along the place de Clichy. It must have been his last year, but we will come to that later, cher ami.'

Dr Bricard settled down with his brandy in hand and without any encouragement from me began to speak of Utrillo in a voice that was both erudite and reflective. I could feel myself being drawn into another world. This was the world of Utrillo that no reference book could ever convey. The Doctor's voice was as mellow as my second cognac. I felt as if I was floating back in time to a Paris long lost and never to be found again. This is what he told me.

For more than thirty years Maurice Utrillo was one of the most important figures of contemporary art in Europe. Such was his renown in the early 1920s that Pablo Picasso and the Lithuanian painter Chaim Soutine regarded him as the greatest painter alive at that time and one of the greatest of French artists. Critics spoke of his genius. The world clamoured for his art…

Remarkably, Utrillo survived the ravages of his lifestyle for 72 years. No-one who knew him, or heard of his escapades with his soul mate, or drinking partner, the Italian artist Amedeo Modigliani, would have predicted such a life span. How Utrillo kept going when friends like Modigliani passed on due to tuberculosis and the abuses of drugs and alcohol is anyone's guess. He was an enigma to every doctor who treated him.

Utrillo was a dipsomaniac of the first order and possibly the most infamous alcoholic known in France. He had been disintegrating both mentally and physically since the age of eighteen when he entered the asylum of Sainte-Anne at Sannois for the first time. Sadly, he would return there often. His reputation as an alcoholic was profound; it was said he kept a partly eaten sour pickled herring in his jacket pocket to suck on when he needed to revive his taste for more drink.

While his paintings were desired by one and all, his company was not. He was shunned by all but a few. His drunken antics on the butte brought derision from the locals. Night after night he would be attacked by youths out for a bit of fun. They would leave the drunken sot beaten and naked in the gutter for the gendarmes to find and take to the nearest station, where his poor mother would be fetched to take him home.

Of the artists of his time only 'Modi' Modigliani held him in sincere friendship – possibly also Chaim Soutine, if that was possible for such an intolerant man, and the Bulgarian painter, Jules Pascin, who later in 1930 cut his wrists and hanged himself in his studio. It is possibly significant that all of these men who befriended Utrillo were foreigners and Jews; outsiders who may have recognised, consciously or subconsciously, the alienation that kept Utrillo apart from his own society. Such was the degeneration of these artists that they became known 'les peintres maudits', the dammed painters. Some would suggest 'the accursed painters' was a more apt interpretation of the term. The likes of Picasso and Derain, whilst acknowledging Utrillo and his cohorts' brilliance as artists, kept their distance most of the time.

But forgive me; I am getting ahead of myself. Let me take you back to the part of Utrillo's life when my professional interest in him begins; to the time when the artist, as a boy, emerges as a lost soul, an innocent destroyed by demons, a shadow of humanity devoid of all dignity and control.

By the age of thirteen Maurice Utrillo was a drunkard and was to spend the greater part of his life gripped in the clutches of alcoholism. (There is a story that claims US President Ulysses S. Grant was a drunkard by the age of eight.) In a ten-year period from the age of eighteen he had eight separate commitments to one form of mental institution or another. In 1915 he spent eight months in an asylum for the 'really insane' – we French like to make such distinctions. On a few occasions he would escape from the hospital he was in; at other times he would commit himself voluntarily. There were times when he recognised his need for professional support, but these occasions were rare. More often he would be beside himself in rage, tormented by the disease that was destroying him. On one occasion he tried to kill himself by banging his head against a prison wall. Yet throughout the turmoil of it all he never stopped painting.

It seems bizarre, mon cher, but it was his craving for drink that led directly to Maurice Utrillo becoming a painter in the first place! His mother, Suzanne Valadon, an artist in her own right, and at a loss with her son's violent addiction to Apero and Gros Rouge, tried the advice of a doctor she knew by encouraging Maurice to take an interest in something physically therapeutic. By doing so, the doctor and his mother hoped the activity would distract his mind from the cravings for drink.

Suzanne offered to teach him how to paint, which he reluctantly accepted. He probably had no choice in the matter; it would be that or a life in sanatoriums. Alas, as a solution to his chronic alcoholism the plan resulted in failure. Maurice continued to drink and drink and drink. What it did do, however, was to give the young montmartrois another passion in life, and for the next twelve months Utrillo immersed himself in drawing and painting. He worked feverishly on his canvasses and during this time produced a total of 150 paintings. Most of these early works were crude derivatives of Impressionism, which was popular at that time. Maurice held Camille Pissarro and Alfred Sisley in high esteem; especially Sisley, becoming obsessed with the painter for a time. For Utrillo, obsession was a way of life...'

Dr Bricard suddenly stopped talking and seemed to rest for a few moments. His breathing was heavy and every so often he would let out a sigh. I waited, not sure whether to speak or not. His eyes were closed but I could tell he wasn't sleeping. Then just as suddenly as he had stopped he began speaking once more.

Somewhere in this room I have copies of medical records that concern the diagnosis and treatment given to Utrillo in a number of institutions in and around Paris during his lifetime. It was my intention to write a thesis on my research into the medical practice provided to one of France's greatest artists, thinking the care given to him would be exemplary. All I found was pages of arrant nonsense; the ramblings of doctors unfit to treat a boil let alone a mind addled with wine. I am afraid our understanding of alcoholism at that time was still subjective and influenced by social attitudes and prejudices. In fairness we knew little then of how alcohol affected the brain and most treatments involved abstinence and diversion... now I am rambling, forgive me.

For six more years Utrillo laboured at his painting, during which time he produced some fine canvasses. We can assume with some degree of certainty that many of these paintings were produced under the influence of alcohol. It has been said by some that all of his paintings were produced while he was drunk. I doubt if this is entirely accurate but it won't be far from the truth. Of far more importance, however, was the emergence from this early pursuit of Impressionism of a style and technique that was to take him through his 'Impasto' period from the years 1907 to 1911, into the 'White' period of 1912 to 1914, and international recognition.

Now I am beginning to talk like an art critic and not a doctor. Yet, Utrillo's progress as a painter is of interest to me as a doctor. How does such a man with all his failings manage to develop, not just the skills to paint masterpieces, but to develop the intellect required within himself to understand the process of merging great creative thought with the necessary craft to achieve magnificent results? We tend to think of alcohol as a depressant, a debilitator of progressive thought; certainly if taken in copious amounts over a protracted period of time, in the way Utrillo consumed it. Yet here lies the contradiction that has frustrated my life's vocation: he defied such fundamental tenets! Once again I digress too far from what you want to hear. I'll continue.

His frequent use of zinc-white, often mixed with common house-plaster in his paintings, was the reason the 'white' period got its name. Two other periods followed this highly successful time: these were known as the 'Architectural period' which ran from 1915 to 1919 and the 'Colour period' in 1920. These divisions of his art are completely arbitrary as one could find examples of paintings belonging to one period appearing in another.

Utrillo's reputation as a great artist rose considerably as his paintings began to be recognised by the critics across Europe. By 1920 he had become a legendary figure, internationally known. This *was also the year that his great friend Modigliani died. In 1929 the French Government awarded him the highest honour it could give to a citizen of France — the Cross of the Legion of Honour.*

When I left Doctor Bricard's home it was late afternoon. I felt a little light headed from the brandies I had consumed but awash with a feeling of achievement and satisfaction as I made my way back to the station. Much of what the doctor had told me was already known to me; what made a difference, however, was how the doctor put it together. He had the ability to inform without making it sound like a lecture. It was as if he was narrating a story he knew by heart, a story he was fond of telling. And while I was unsure of some of his theories on alcoholism, I looked forward to my next visit to Pierrefitte-sur-Seine.

A slight breeze had got up and the branches of the trees along the avenue brushed against each other in a gentle embrace. The doctor had agreed to meet frequently as there was much to discuss and I was keen to explore the deeper significance of Utrillo's behaviour – and his love-hate relationship with his mother. My research so far had identified writers who only touched briefly on this complex relationship, as if it was not a proper subject to discuss. I was keen to hear Dr Bricard's thoughts on this matter.

4

Thérèse Dumard

The first symptom of love in a young man is shyness; the first in a woman is boldness.
Victor Hugo

My accidental meeting with Emile Renouf in the park had, to some degree, disconcerted me. Not so much about seeing him, which I am ambivalent about, but our conversation had brought the name of Thérèse Dumard firmly back into my mind. What threw me was that it was I who had raised the subject in the first place. Prior to my recent return to this city, my affair with Thérèse Dumard during my post-graduate time at the Institute had long drifted deep into my subconscious and rarely came to mind. I would be lying to say I didn't think of her when I made the decision to take this work on, but somehow I dismissed the possibilities of us meeting again. Yet, in saying that, I realised I had made no attempt to visit the Institute or the parts of the city she frequented.

Thérèse and I had been deeply in love; passionately so. The unexpectedness of our affair made it all the more exciting. It was my first real love affair and with an older woman too. Life didn't get much better. It was good while it lasted, and I had fond memories of the time we spent together but had long since moved on.

I hadn't known what fall-out had taken place until Emile mentioned she and her husband had divorced. I had returned to Scotland shortly after we split. I assumed from what Emile had said that our brief affair had contributed to their break-up. Did she tell him? Or did he find out some other way? Was our romance really to blame, or had she taken another lover and had that led to her marriage break up? I knew I was wasting my time speculating on things I couldn't know. And then there was the news of Claude, dead from cancer...

I cursed Emile for his sleekit ways. I should have gotten him to tell me more. Where is Thérèse now? Had she remarried? Was she still living in her house near the Luxembourg Gardens? What I did know for certain was that thoughts of Thérèse Dumard were firmly in my mind, and I knew I wanted to see her again irrespective of the consequences.

For a year I attended the Institut Pasteur: the cradle of Microbiology, Immunology and Molecular Biology that straddles rue du Docteur Roux. I was one of a dozen foreign students undertaking post-graduate research. Everyone in the Institute referred to us collectively as the 'Foreign Legion'. We liked the nom de guerre; it made us feel a bit special.

It was the Institute's practice to allocate its foreign students to the tutorial patronage of Dr Thérèse Dumard. This was mainly due, I was told at matriculation, to her ability to speak five European languages. She was an attractive woman in her early thirties, with style, eloquence, poise and a figure that aroused my more lubricious interests. I was immediately taken by her. Everything she did, she did in her own way. Her every movement was, it seemed to me, unique to her. I was highly impressed by her and not a little smitten by her charm.

She delivered her lectures in a small annexe to the rear of the main lecture theatre. The room looked out on to a small grassy knoll where a few almond trees clustered around its base, each one as straight as Aaron's rod. This was to be our main learning centre for the duration of our time at the Institute.

When Dr Dumard had something to say that she felt was particularly important she would walk to the back of the small room and address us from there. She contended that students concentrated better when listening to a disembodied voice. I found it a little distracting at first, but liked the Pythagorean eccentricity that lay behind the thought. She always spoke in short sentences. Again she would enlighten the class that brevity in speech had more impact than long-winded rhetoric. Whether Dr Dumard was correct in her assertions mattered little to me; what was important was to get through the post-graduate year and back to Glasgow and hopefully to a research post at its Royal Infirmary.

At least once every month during the summer months the doctor invited the class to her home in rue Guynemer, a luxurious apartment that looked down into the Luxembourg Gardens. Her study was spacious with two large desks and enough chairs and stools to seat a small orchestra. She shared her home and its study with her husband, Claude, who happened to be Professor of Microbe Research at the Institute. Thankfully the professor was never at home when we were in attendance, as he carried a reputation among students of being arrogant and difficult.

The walls of the study held an array of oil paintings, watercolours and sketches by some of the most prominent artists in France during the last century; artists of the calibre of Raoul Dufy, Pierre Bonnard, and Jean Gorin. They even had landscapes by my fellow countrymen, William Gillies and William Johnstone.

A large window gave an excellent view across the

gardens. On very warm afternoons we would leave the study and sit in a quiet and shaded area of the gardens. It was after coffee one afternoon early in the term that Doctor Dumard asked if we would use her Christian name when we were at her home. She spoke softly.

'I would like you to call me Thérèse. Here we are all adults and equals together, are we not? And thankfully while we are in this house we are not bound by those stuffy protocols the Institute is so proud of. And, anyway, is not one doctor enough in any house? So, if you please, call me Thérèse here and when we are in private conversation.'

This concession went down well with me and my fellow students as we enjoyed visiting her home and the freedoms it provided. Few of us had lived in such splendour. Now for a short time we could relax in harmonious surroundings and enjoy the familiarity and generosity of our host.

Usually a few of us would meet after lectures in one of the many bars and cafés that litter the Left Bank. As most of the class could speak English we used this as our common language. Those who couldn't speak English had our commentaries translated by the one or two of our group that could speak their language. This meant that we had a fixed seating arrangement that, wherever we went as a group, accommodated our conversations.

One late Friday afternoon, not long after we had been to one of Dr Dumard's tutorials at her home, a few of us were having a drink in La Dome. For some unknown reason our usual seating arrangement had been disrupted and I found myself sitting next to Frieda, a young German woman from Düsseldorf who ordinarily would sit next to Lafcadio, one of our non-English speakers. We were in high spirits and enjoying the atmosphere in the bar when Frieda commented that she thought Dr Dumard paid me special attention.

'What are you talking about?' I answered back more defensively than I had intended.

'Haven't you noticed? She always brushes against your shoulder when she passes behind you. She always looks at you when she stands in front of us. It wouldn't matter one iota if the rest of us weren't there.'

'Don't be so ridiculous,' I retaliated. 'She looks at all of us when she is speaking.'

'Not from where I sit she doesn't!'

The others began to agree with Frieda. Each told of an occasion when they too thought she had been over-familiar with me.

'See, I told you. She never takes her eyes off you all the time she is speaking. Now do you believe me?'

'It's just a coincidence,' I said, shrugging off their protests and laughter at my predicament.

'Just wait,' said Frieda, 'you'll see.'

I was aware that some of what my fellow students said had happened, though I'd considered any contact made by the lovely Doctor as mere encouragement; a nudge to remind me to pay attention. At no time had I considered her intentions otherwise. It never crossed my mind that there could be any other interpretation. She was a mature lecturer and I was a student. To me she was unattainable. Yet I now hoped what my fellow students had said was true, even if only in some small part.

The rest of the evening passed, thankfully, without further comment being made about whether Dr Thérèse Dumard did or did not show me a little of her affection. We spoke about our projects, our homelands, our national differences, but most of all we spoke about ourselves, our likes and dislikes, how much money we had to spend in Paris and what we would do when we returned to our homes. Through all of this I kept thinking about what Frieda and the others had said. I felt the rise of excitement in my gut.

It rained on the following Monday. It was the first day it had rained that I could remember since arriving in Paris for my studies. Torrents of rainwater ran down the grey streets like rivers in spate. Only a few of us turned up for lectures, each of us soaked through to the skin. I would have turned up in any weather, as I had decided during the weekend that I wanted to put Frieda's theory to the test. I wasn't sure how I was going to do it, but I needed to know if she and the others were right. The possibility had haunted me, filling me with a sense of possibility and no little dread as well.

We did our best to dry ourselves with whatever we could lay our hands on. The small anteroom next to our lecture room had little in the way of drying materials. We emptied a cupboard of its paper towels, rags and dusters and were drying ourselves to the point of indecency when Thérèse came in. She was just as wet as we were. 'I'm surprised to find anyone here,' she told us as she began to dry herself with a handful of paper towels. 'Apart from the British. You are used to being wet, are you not? You are all very foolish to come out on a day like this.' She was laughing. 'Look, go back to your residences. We can't continue in this state. We'll catch our deaths, sitting here in these wet clothes. We'll make up for today, tomorrow.'

As the others left I decided to hang back, more in hope than expectation of anything happening. I still didn't have a plan, but being in the same room as Thérèse seemed to be the right place to be. I kept on drying myself repeatedly, wondering what to say or do next. I could feel the adrenalin surge through me. I had a gut full of clenched fists. This was certainly more than I had bargained for. I could smell her standing next to me. It was an aphrodisiac. My desire for her was now hurting. I wanted this woman so badly my whole body was going into spasm. I had to force myself to do the most simple of movements without shaking.

Occasionally we touched or bumped each other as we got ourselves ready to leave. Unavoidable contact in a tight space? Thérèse always apologised. My throat dried up. Did she mean to touch me? Was it a sign for me to act? Was my imagination playing tricks? All of a sudden the clock was ticking against me. She would be gone in a few moments.

I was about to abandon the situation as panic set in and any thoughts of seduction began to evaporate in the confined atmosphere of the anteroom. I wasn't confident enough to control the situation. I needed more time, more proof of her feelings. I was about to say goodbye when she said, 'I know we're both wet through, but would you have time for a coffee, John? We could go up to staff refectory. It's usually quiet at this time and with today's weather it'll probably be empty. At least it will be warm and dry and we'll get a seat to ourselves. I've been meaning to talk with you for a while but never get round to it. That is… if you don't mind.'

She stared right at me. I wanted to clear my throat but couldn't.

'Sure, why not? A coffee would be good.' I couldn't think of anything else to say. I was sure that if I tried to say any more it would have dribbled into nonsense. Still, at that moment I could not have been happier. *Why not, indeed?* I thought to myself as she led the way from the annexe to the main building.

She was right; the refectory was nearly empty. We got our coffees and sat in a corner that held a couple of lounge seats that felt warm as we eased into their soft cushion. Thérèse spoke quietly in a voice that was both conspiratorial and open. She was relaxed yet conscious of her surroundings.

'I'm glad we have this chance to speak. As I said earlier I have wanted to talk to you for some time now, but the moment never seemed to be the right one. So much of our time is spent talking about research that we never get time to talk of anything else. This is why I try and take my students to my home. I much prefer an informal relationship with my students. After all, we are all adults irrespective of our positions in life.'

For a while the conversation concentrated on her views on status and position. She seemed to be saying that it wasn't all it was cracked up to be and that there were more things to life than pomp and circumstance. I could only agree, having had neither. I got the impression that she wanted affirmation that her views were accepted by me. We sat quite relaxed in our lounge seats. I was feeling much more comfortable now with her company. I wondered if I could say something that would let her know I was interested in her without letting her know I was interested in her. That way, if she was offended, I could say that she misunderstood what I meant. I could see she was going to say something so I decided to let the moment pass and wait for another chance later in the conversation.

'I was wondering if you would like to come for a meal one evening. I mean with me in my home. I thought you might like to do this. I thought it would be enjoyable for both of us. You could tell me all about Scotland – I was there a few years ago, at the festival in Edinburgh. It was a joyous time. And I am told you play the piano. We have a Steinway in the library that my husband often plays; you could play it for me. I love listening to the piano. I would be pleased if you could come.'

I was taken aback to say the least by her proposal. I had half expected some mention of my project work or my progress with my dissertation, but not this. Not only was I caught off guard but also the electricity surging up through my body was scrambling my brain. This was absolutely incredible; my dreams answered. I was definitely keen to say yes – oh yes, dear gorgeous, sexy lady – oh yes. An evening with the lovely Dr. Thérèse sounded absolutely fine by me. Then from the height of ecstasy a rush of doubt flooded my dream. Did she mean only me or were others going to be there? Maybe she was going to invite the class; but if she was, why didn't she do it when we were all together?

'I'm not sure Professor Dumard would appreciate me playing his piano, and your other guests might not approve either. And I haven't played on a Steinway before,' I added for good measure. 'I might be too nervous.'

Thérèse looked at me for a few moments before answering. I wondered if she was thinking my reply was too contrived; that I had sounded too Machiavellian for my own good. I cursed myself for sounding glib. Then she smiled.

'My husband will be in Toulouse this Wednesday and Thursday, and I have no plans to invite anyone else to dinner. Does that answer your question? I can dine with as many guests as I want whenever I feel like it. But, on this occasion it is only your company I want. And if you need to practise on my piano, you can do so when I am in the kitchen. Is that okay?'

I nodded in tacit agreement, then sipped my coffee. Thérèse did likewise. I was sure there was no other way to read the situation. We were going to spend an evening together. She had made this perfectly clear. This was the first time I could remember when a woman had been so direct with me. She knew what she was saying. I couldn't believe my luck.

'Let's get out of here,' she suddenly said. 'It is too crowded for me.' The refectory was nearly empty.

When we left the refectory Thérèse said we should go our separate ways. I was to be at her house for seven on Wednesday night. If for any reason there was a change of plan, she would leave a message for me on the students' noticeboard. She then walked over to the Institute's main building and entered through its central doors. She didn't look back. I stood for a moment gathering my thoughts. It took a second or two before I realised it had stopped raining.

I spent most of that evening in the residences talking to Lafcadio, which was difficult, as his English was quite poor, I had no comprehension of his mother tongue, and his French was virtually non-existent. Slowly, as the evening progressed, I managed to build a picture of where he came from and a bit of his background. He had been raised in a village about forty kilometres east of Krakow. His parents had been killed in an industrial accident of sorts and he lived with his unmarried aunt. He had an older sister who lived in Warsaw, but he hadn't heard from her in years. He had got a B.Sc. from Krakow University and had come to the Institute to bolster his credentials.

It took about two hours to glean this information from him, and some other sundry stories that made him laugh occasionally. I laughed too, not wanting to offend him. He seemed pleased with himself and pleased with me for listening. I assured him that I had enjoyed our evening together and we would talk again another evening.

I had no classes to attend the following day, so I decided to take the day off. If truth be known, I didn't want to see

Thérèse at the Institute and give her the opportunity to cancel our arrangement. I would worry about classes on Wednesday when the time came. To fill my day and keep me suitably occupied, I decided to visit two of my favourite arrondissements in the city: Montmartre and Pigalle.

5

An evening in Pigalle

The charms of the passing woman are generally in direct proportion to the swiftness of her passing.
Marcel Proust

The 18th arrondissement lies against the boulevard Périphérique to the north of the city. From this boundary the area known as Montmartre unfolds down to the district of Pigalle. Its most visible artifice is the basilique du Sacré-Cœur, a fanciful pastiche of indelicacies by its architect Paul Abadie that can be seen high on the butte from various vantage points across the city. My purpose in being in Montmartre was not to view its architecture but for a different need altogether.

Every journey needs a starting point and I knew where I wanted to begin this particular journey. From the Metro I made my way along the narrow streets to the place du Tertre. The square was busy. On every side of the historic square artists of varying abilities proffered their wares to the squeezing passing trade, the majority offering quick charcoal portraits to vain and easily-led tourists. The scene was more like a circus than an art fair. I squeezed past some Americans who were trying to knock down the price of a still wet painting of the Moulin Rouge and went into the nearest bistro.

I spent the best part of the afternoon in the cafés and bistros that surround the square. I ate and drank well while enjoying the conversation of strangers. In one café a forlorn montmartrois was explaining to a sceptical English couple that it was in the streets around place du Tertre in 1871 that the Communards built the first barricades to defend the people from the king's forces, and that in 1873, in an attempt to appease the city's population for the death of over 10,000 Communards, the Government built the basilica of the Sacré-Cœur.

At around five o'clock I wound my way down the zig-zag of well-worn streets on the south side of the butte into Pigalle, to the boulevard de Clichy, and took myself into a little art-house – not far from the metro at place Blanche – that specialised in French and German films, mostly erotica. The film showing was of no interest to me. My purpose in being there was to close my eyes for an hour or so in sleep, which, due to the amount of wine I had consumed that afternoon, I managed quite comfortably.

When I came out of the cinema it was dusk. Street lamps buzzed and an array of coloured lights decorated the townscape. I inhaled deeply. This part of the city has a scent all of its own at this time of evening: an exotic mixture of roasted tobacco, sweet perfume and strong liquor; a wonderfully sweet and potent aroma. I hadn't been out of the cinema five minutes when the first approach of the evening was made. She was a small thin girl with badly bleached hair and too much mascara. She wore the bare minimum of clothes and kept a cigarette in her mouth when she spoke. She looked cheap, very cheap, too cheap for my liking. I thanked her for her interest, but refused. She wasn't pleased. She sensed I was looking for business and was annoyed I was looking for someone better than her. She harangued me for a few seconds then moved quickly away when she spotted another potential client walking towards us.

The streets were still a cocktail of tourists, pleasure-seekers and the various inhabitants of Pigalle. Soon most of the tourists would leave the streets, vanishing into the restaurants and theatres recommended in every Parisian guide book, and thereafter into taxis and coaches that would take them safely back to their hotels situated in the more refined and respectable parts of the city. This is the time, for me, when Pigalle becomes really interesting, and on occasions a little dangerous. For the time being I was happy enough just to watch the comings and goings on the darkening streets. There is a certain time of the evening when the locals begin to shut up shop, knowing there is no more business to be had, and retire behind closed doors. The fruit-sellers take in their boxes of unsold produce, stallholders clear away their trinkets and beads, beggars drift into the shady world of secrets and shadows. This is the time when the small one-roomed bars begin to fill with the lost and lonely, and street corners echo to the muffled laughter of women. I decided to stand under a lamppost at a corner not too far from one of the small bars, lit a cigarette and waited.

She said her name was Micheline, but I doubted it. I had hardly finished my cigarette when she appeared from out of the shadows looking for a light for her cigarette. Her accent wasn't right for Paris and I guessed she had moved to the city from a village or small town that she had outgrown or had outgrown her. What pleased me instantly about her was her smile. Her face broadened out when she smiled and her cheek bones lifted, making her eyes appear a little oriental. We quickly understood we had common goals for the evening. A deal was struck before the match I lit her smoke with hit the ground.

We turned into a narrow lane that ran behind the bar. It was strewn with garbage and reeked of fouling vegetables, as well as human and animal sewage. For a moment I imagined I had stepped back in time to an age long past, into a skinny street in Edinburgh where disease pervaded the stagnant air and the odds on survival were minimal. It was hard to believe this was the late twentieth century, in Paris of all places. The only light available to us, as we walked along the stench-strewn thoroughfare, was that which escaped from the few unshuttered windows of the toxic houses that ran along one side of the lane. Every so often I would hear voices emanate from behind a window; sometimes angry, sometimes plaintive, occasionally the cry of a child. I was becoming slightly alarmed and wondered where I was being taken to. Was this a trap? Was Micheline a moll? Was I a naïve lamb going to the slaughter of a pimp and his henchmen? I began to regret my actions. This was certainly not somewhere a stranger should stumble into.

Then we were inside one of the decaying buildings, climbing a narrow stair onto a landing. The walls were scarred with decades of graffiti. A putrid smell filled my nostrils. I had no idea what it was or where it came from. This wasn't what I expected. I was about to say that I wasn't sure about going on when Micheline stopped and opened a door facing us. It too was covered in graffiti; most of it gouged out with a blade or chib of sorts. We entered into a small dank unlit hallway, no more than two metres long, where another more substantial door faced us. This one had two opaque glass panels on either side of the central frame. I could see the shadow of someone moving about on the other side, probably a child; then a larger figure, possibly a man. I was about to ask her if this was her home, but thought better of it. Even if it was, it wasn't any of my business anyway. Micheline ignored the facing door and turned immediately to her right where she pulled back a roughly sewn sack screen to unveil a small door, no more than five and a half feet in height. She quickly unlocked this door and ushered me in. I had to stoop almost to the point of bending to enter through the doorway.

Once inside, I stood in darkness until Micheline found the switch that turned on a bare wall light. It took a second or two before the room filled with sufficient light for me to see it was tiny and sparsely furnished. Apart from the bed there was only a chair and the smallest of tables at the side of the bed. As my eyes adjusted, I noticed the room was devoid of any colour whatsoever. Nothing had been painted unless you consider a dirty grey to be part of the spectrum

I wondered if the room had been once part of a larger one and partitioned off for Micheline to use for business purposes. This presupposed that the shadowy figure I saw through the glass door was aware of the goings-on in this little room and party to its function. I dismissed the thought; each to their own needs.

Micheline quickly gestured for me to get undressed. When she spoke it was in a near whisper. I took this as confirmation of aforementioned conclusions. I did as she said. She too began undressing and threw her clothes over the chair. She was perfunctory in her every movement. I was a little disappointed. I had hoped that she would have let me undress her. I let my clothes fall on the floor before joining her on the bed. For the next few minutes she let me explore her body. She remained mostly impassive to my touch only uttering the lightest of sighs when I reached deep inside her. After a few moments she whispered, 'Are you ready?' before lithely manoeuvring herself into our agreed arrangement.

On the Metro home, I recounted my day's activity and was pleased with how it had worked out. My time with Micheline had allowed me to burn off some of the sexual tension I had been feeling lately. When I reached Pasteur station I was tired but content, and confident that my evening with Thérèse would be fine.

6

Romeo and Juliet

Lust's passion will be served. It demands, it militates, it tyrannises.
Marquis De Sade

The Wednesday lectures passed without incident. I saw Thérèse on two occasions, but we didn't speak. Only Frieda asked me where I was the day before. My cursory reply – 'I had business to attend to.' – kept her at a distance. Later she gave me photocopies of the lecture notes she had taken for the day before. I thanked her for her consideration. We chatted briefly about nothing in particular. She didn't mention my truancy again.

Rue Guynemer follows the contour of the Luxembourg Gardens along its northern perimeter. It is a handsome street with elegant houses and an air of wealth and success. Thérèse's home stood in front of the Garden's gates, near Frédéric Bartholdi's small study of the Statue of Liberty; one of three studies Bartholdi made before sending his monumental edifice for erection on Bedloe island between the harbours of New York and New Jersey.

The view from Thérèse's window captured the area of the Gardens that held dense foliage. Beyond the trees, the Gardens opened up into a spread of parkland where the people of this part of the city walked, talked, cycled, jogged, read books, sailed model boats, picnicked, played tennis and made love under skies of varying hues, all but for a few days each year.

I arrived on time. Thérèse answered the door quickly and greeted me like a long lost family member. I admired her ingenuity. Her ploy would mollify any interest by neighbours. She led me into the drawing room where drinks were waiting for us. She had done her homework. A bottle of The Glenlivet stood proudly next to two filled glasses. She handed one to me. 'Slàinte!' I said, taking the glass from her. 'A votre santé!' she replied with a sly smile. I gulped my drink down and wondered if the Gaelic was one of the many languages she could speak. I let it pass.

'I missed you yesterday. Did you come to the Institute?'

'No', I said confidently. 'I had to arrange for some money to be sent over from home, and the banking system in France confuses my bank in Scotland, or vice versa. I had to make a few phone calls to Glasgow to explain the arrangements I wanted put in place. I lost the will to return to the Institute after about an hour of talking to people who don't want to do anything other than in their way. I stayed and had some food and a drink near the Bourse.'

I hated making an excuse to Thérèse, but knew it was necessary; a needs-must situation. She didn't question my reason but excused herself to attend to matters in the kitchen.

The room was filled with a variety of magnificent art pieces. Sitting on a small regency-style rosewood table was a statuette of a pageboy by Chiparus. On the imposing mantelpiece, amid gilt-framed photographs of family members, sat an empire-style portico French decorative clock. On the walls hung paintings by Soulage, Hélion, Rego and Béreny; all artists I knew from my youthful visits to art galleries back in Glasgow.

In a corner near the window stood the most elegant Hamburg Steinway model with brass hardware and red plate trim. I had seen photographs of this piano in shop brochures; now here was the real thing sitting patiently in front of me. I placed my drink to one side and sat at the piano. The action of the keys were sensitive to the touch; a sign of an often-played instrument. I guessed that whoever played this magnificent instrument did so with consummate skill. I wondered who that might be. Thérèse had said that her husband Claude played, and as far as I knew there was no one else living there. I assumed it wasn't her. I played my favourite piece at that time: Romeo and Juliet, a short work by the Italian maestro, Nino Rota. The room filled with romance.

The meal Thérèse cooked was exquisite. Her conversation was light but always intelligent and interesting. I hoped my own words and thoughts were comparable but knew there were times when I sounded awkward and clumsy. At the end of the meal, Therese poured a brandy for each of us from an exquisite Egberta decanter and suggested we take our drinks across to the Gardens and stroll along the lane to the pond where, if we were lucky, we might catch a glimpse of a few late modellers sailing their small boats and yachts in the quiet of the evening. It was as if she sensed I was feeling a little uncomfortable as the end of the meal approached and was offering a little respite from my inadequacies. If that was her thinking, she was right. What would I do now? Sit on a sofa and make a schoolboy pass at her? I was glad to agree. Maybe she was pleased too.

Thérèse slipped her arm through mine as we walked into the park. This was hardly the actions of a lecturer to one of her students. A soft warm breeze sifted through the trees. Every so often Thérèse squeezed my arm as she emphasised some point or other she was making in her conversation. Her touch made me feel desired. We stopped for a moment, sipping our brandies, laughing at some silly remark I had made. Then, with no hint of what was to follow, Thérèse leaned into me and kissed me gently on the lips. Everything I held precious surged through my veins. Her kiss opened a flood of emotions from deep inside me. My arms smothered her as I pulled her into me and kissed her passionately. For a few moments we were lost in our embrace; then, as if she had just remembered something important, she pulled away from me.

'Let's go back to the house, John. I need my privacy.'

I eased my arms from around her. She was right, we couldn't – or, more accurately, she couldn't – be seen acting in such a way with a man who was not her husband, and so close to her home, and not with a glass of brandy in her hand.

'Of course, I'm sorry. I shouldn't have done that. It was stupid of me.' I said this a little too apologetically. She smiled at me with a smile I'll never forget. 'Let's hurry back.' she said. 'I need you at home.'

'Play something for me John. Please! Play the tune you were playing earlier when I was in the kitchen. It was so beautiful… and a little haunting too, don't you think? I thought it beautiful. Play that, please.'

I drew my fingers lightly over the keys, trying to find the right touch. The notes began to fill the room with Rota's little masterpiece. I looked over at Thérèse. She was lying across a sofa with her legs tucked under her. She had wrapped a sheet around her when we left her bed. I felt a rush of adrenaline surge through me as I thought of her naked body as she lay beside me a few minutes earlier.

Any worries I'd had earlier that evening evaporated the moment I slammed the door shut on our return from the Gardens. We turned and clung to each other in the hall for a few moments as if we were old friends meeting after a long absence. I thought that Thérèse might be having second thoughts; questioning herself as to the wisdom of her actions. Then, much to my delight, she looked up, smiled and reached for my lips with hers. We kissed passionately, our mouths pressed hard together. The moment became urgent.

I followed her to her bedroom. It was obvious from the moment I stepped into the room that she slept alone. There were no indications anywhere of a man's presence. I had hardly had time to say to myself that she and Professor Dumard must sleep in separate rooms when she said, 'I sleep here alone, John. My husband has a small room on the ground floor.' She said no more. I nodded that I understood and, surprisingly, considering what was about to happen, wondered how many other men had been led to this room.

We spent the next hour pleasuring each other. Thérèse was a passionate lover. For the first time in my adult life I felt I was making love with a woman and not to a woman. There was honesty in our lovemaking; a sense of mutuality. Thérèse was not embarrassed in any way as I moved her body in ways to satisfy my desires. I looked down upon her intimately, touching her once-secret places. Eventually we fell together, side by side, spent but satisfied, our bodies glistening with warm moisture.

We arranged to spend the next evening together. Thérèse wouldn't let me spend the night with her. She said it was important to her that I left. As much as I wanted to stay, I respected her wishes and left. Appearance is everything. Maybe it was more than that. This sort of situation was a new experience for me, and there was a new set of rules and etiquette to learn. And, whether I liked it or not, I would have to put up with these changes for Thérèse's sake and that of my own desires.

I strolled back along rue Guynemer, every so often punching the air around me like an athlete who had just won the race of his life. This was what it was all about. No doubt a few of the men and women that passed by me guessed the reason for my singular happiness, but I couldn't help myself. I kept seeing Thérèse's naked body in my mind's eye: those wonderful breasts, her whiter than white thighs... My beautiful, delicious Doctor, who could twist and turn that magnificent body of hers like a serpent and leave me in a state of ecstasy.

The next evening went much the way of our first evening together, but without Thérèse's excellent cooking and the walk in the park. We made love from the moment I arrived till well into the night, stopping only when Therese wanted me to play Rota's Romeo and Juliet for her. She too was becoming engrossed with its captivating melody. To this day, I associate her with that delightful piece.

We met whenever and wherever we could. Sometimes Thérèse would know of an empty room or study in the Institute that we could spend some time in; seeing such a beautiful woman naked in such settings brought out the more base instincts in me. My love-making became more ardent, much more physical than emotional. I considered these times as my treats, when it was more sex than love; the kind of sex that men enjoy more often than their partners.

Other times we would take the metro to a part of the city where we could walk freely. Best of all were the times when Thérèse's husband, Claude, was away overnight giving a lecture in some provincial university or college. Even after months of being together, Thérèse would not let me stay overnight with her. Nor would she entertain the idea of staying-over in a hotel while Claude was out of town. The thought of it, she told me, made her feel cheap.

We continued our affair throughout the rest of the year. I loved every moment we spent together. I had never met a woman like Thérèse before. She was the perfect woman, both in and out of the bedroom. We laughed a lot, telling silly jokes to one another, but finding truth and respect from each other too. We became a couple, a partnership of equals; two minds but one heart. We began to look for each other at all times. Occasionally one of us would let slip the name of the other in our conversations with friends. Keeping our love secret became more difficult with each day.

After lectures one wet afternoon I was walking with Frieda, my fellow student from the 'foreign Legion', when she challenged me directly about Thérèse. Her outburst took me by surprise.

'John, tell me the truth. Are you seeing Thérèse? I mean, are you having an affair with Dr Dumard? Don't lie to me now. Are you? You've been acting strange for weeks. You never come out with us anymore, and going to lectures now is like listening to a private conversation between her and you. Whenever we go to her house at the Gardens you walk about it as if you owned the place. Are you sleeping with her? Tell me, I want to know.'

I didn't know what to say. Why did she want to know? What business was it of hers who I slept with? Deep within me, I wanted to tell the world that I was in love with Dr Thérèse Dumard, but knew I couldn't. My hesitation was all Frieda needed.

'I thought so, you bastard! I hate you!' She looked genuinely distressed by her assertion. I still hadn't spoken.

'You fool, you stupid fool! Are you in love with her? Does

she love you? No, of course she can't. She's just using you. She's a middle-aged woman having a fling with a half-wit. You men are so stupid. You think with your…' She didn't finish the sentence.

'Can't you see she's just using you?'

There were tears running down her cheeks. I hadn't realised that Frieda felt this way. Never at any time had I suspected she had any concerns or feelings towards me. We were friends, just good friends who got on well together, or so I thought. It took me a moment before I realised she was not only angry but jealous. I had always assumed her bossy ways towards me were more to do with her German upbringing than her attempt at disguising any feelings she might have towards me. I couldn't think of an answer that would explain the situation to anyone's satisfaction. I didn't want to confirm her suspicions – I couldn't do that – but I didn't want to add to her anger and frustration either.

'We should only cry in the rain,' I said with an attempt at a smile. Her pain was real and I felt it.

'Or in the shower,' she snivelled, trying to laugh while rubbing the tears from her eyes.

'I'm sorry, John. I shouldn't have said what I said. Forgive me? It's just that I don't want to see you hurt – honest! Thérèse probably takes a new lover at every new intake. I've read about women like that.'

'That's not fair, Frieda. You don't know anything about her.' I was angry that she could say such a thing.

'I'm sorry. I'm sorry for everything I've said. Please forgive me. I've been so stupid.'

She held her head to one side and looked like a little girl apologising to her father for letting him down. I put my arms around her and snuggled her into me.

'You've nothing to apologise for. You did nothing wrong. At least you had the courage to express your feelings. I didn't know you cared. You never said.'

'Let's leave it here, John. You love someone else and I am going back to Germany soon. It'll all pass in time.' She shook her head from side to side. I knew from her speech and intonation that she was hurting and that she did not want to further her pain by discussing the matter. I put my arm around her shoulder and began walking toward the residences. Only a few minutes had passed but already the sky was brightening.

It was always my intention to return to Glasgow when I concluded my studies in Paris. Frieda had reminded me that our departure was fast approaching and the 'Foreign Legion' would return to their homelands. We had not discussed it. That is, Thérèse and I had not broached the subject, as there always seemed to be time for this later. I now realised that we, Thérèse and I, needed to discuss what we should do.

On the river Seine there is a small island that lies close to the left bank. Two bridges, pont de Bir-Hakeim and pont de Grennelle, connect the island to both banks of the river with a third bridge, pont Rouelle, carrying rail freight over the island. The island is called l'île des Cygnes. Here, of a morning, the playwright, Samuel Beckett, would stroll while plotting out his day's work. Here, facing the oncoming river, stands another Statue of Liberty, and by far the most impressive of all the studies made by Bartholdi.

For quite some time Thérèse and I had met on this small island on Saturday mornings. We would sit, one at each end of a bench, and talk gently to each other. Our conversations were always low key, as if this was a time to relax and leave the pressures of our relationship across the bridges. Here, on the island, everything seemed possible. It was a magical place for us. We could even joke that we were like the characters in Beckett's plays, our only freedom existing in our own minds. It was here that we agreed to meet to discuss our future.

We sat on a bench in the middle of the island, as was our custom. So, too, was our crossing onto the island, each of us entering by a different bridge. The only difference on this occasion was that we sat close together, our hands clasped. Thérèse made no attempt at small talk.

'I don't want you to leave, John.' She squeezed my hand. 'I need you here. I need you now. I always want to be with you. What we have shared these last few months has made me realise what I want in life. You make me happy; Claude doesn't. He has become a stranger to me. I don't even exist to him. He has his life and I want mine. If I have to, and you want me to, I'll come to Scotland with you. I'm in love with you. We just can't go our separate ways. Surely you know that.'

I wanted to hold her in my arms and tell her we could work something out. The last few weeks had been hellish for both of us. But I knew I had to go home, if not for my sake, for hers. She had too big an investment in her marriage to Claude; and even if we could be together, we would surely grow to resent each other, as neither of us could give the other what they needed. She had her children to think of. They were young teenagers at boarding school. She couldn't abandon them. I tried to explain this to her.

'It's not that straightforward, Thérèse. There are other matters to consider, and I have to go to Scotland at some point. I'm expected back now that the course is over. I have people to see and promises to keep; and, anyway, it will give both of us a chance to think things over. Once I'm settled back in Glasgow, we can talk about what we want to do. You have so many responsibilities here; your work, your children, your friends. Let's be sensible about this.'

It was if I had stabbed her through the heart. My attempt to get her to see reason was the last thing Thérèse wanted to hear.

'I love you! For God's sake, doesn't that mean anything to you?'

'Of course it does. But it doesn't mean everything else has to take second place to it. We're adults and we have to deal with problems like adults. Why are you so pessimistic about this?'

'Can't you see why? This is my chance at happiness. To be truly happy with a man I love. I thought you loved me too. You've said as much these last few months. I just know, from the bottom of my heart, that if you leave me now, I'll never see you again. I don't know why I feel this way, but I'm as sure of it as I can be about anything.'

'There's no logic to any of this Thérèse. I need to go home to see my family. You told me before you couldn't come to Scotland with me, even for a holiday, because Claude would be suspicious. Now you are saying you want to leave him, and your children, and move to a foreign country. I live with my parents. I don't think they would be too impressed if I turn up on their doorstep with my lecturer on my arm. We need to think this through. You are putting me in a no-win situation. Whatever I do is a sacrifice to your emotional blackmail. I won't be put in a corner like this, Thérèse. I'm going home to see my family. I need space to think about us and where we go from here. Anyway, I have my plane ticket already. I fly out on Tuesday.'

These were the last words I said to Thérèse. She rose from the bench in anger, turned and cursed me before quickly walking off towards pont de Bir-Hakeim. I wanted to shout after her but couldn't; too many people were sitting nearby. I watched as she ran across the bridge. She didn't look back, in anger or otherwise.

I told myself I should go after her and tell her I'd stay, but again I remained quietly seated. I had underestimated her feelings and depth of love. My emotions kicked me hard as I sat there wondering what would happen now. Had I said the right things? Had I done the right thing? This was not how I wanted to close this chapter of my life. I had just rejected the woman I loved more than anything in the world and felt terrible for it. I was no longer in control of my circumstances and felt disorientated by Thérèse storming off. Nothing was tangible anymore. I didn't know what to do.

Looking around me, I began to realise that some of the other people seated on the nearby benches had overheard some of our argument. One old woman was shaking her head while another stared hard at me. I rose and began to walk towards pont de Grennelle. As I passed the nearest bench a man's head leaned back and I heard him greet me jovially. It was Emile Renouf!

7

The sweetest darling

Life begins on the other side of despair.
Jean-Paul Sartre

My second visit to Doctor Bricard's home was just as illuminating as my first. He greeted me like a long lost friend, fussing after me and making sure everything was to my satisfaction. The day was hot and humid but he insisted we sat in his garden under the shade of a cherry tree he had planted when he bought the house in the mid-fifties. He no longer used the expression 'cher ami' but called me John as if he had been doing so all my life. I felt flattered.

The doctor poured a cordial that he insisted his mother had taught him how to make when he was five years old. Like all these elixirs the recipe was a family secret. It tasted delicious. After our pleasantries, which were quite lengthy, I told him about my research and how I had found the information he told me at our last meeting was borne out in a number of texts I had come across. He sat smugly in his wicker chair and gave me a look that made me feel foolish for doubting his word, and more so for telling him.

We drank a few more cordials and let the day's warmth ease over us. Once again Jean-Paul (he now insisted I call him by his Christian names) began to speak of Utrillo without any prompting from me. He would begin his monologues by saying 'You know…' and off he went. I thought of taking notes but decided against it. We were in conversation, not a lecture.

The atmosphere was against it.

As a young counsellor I was fascinated with the developments that were taking place in differential psychology during the forties, fifties and sixties. This work made me very curious about Utrillo, whose behaviour was certainly different from the norm by anyone's definition. I began to use the information I had on Utrillo to see if I could allocate a behaviour or set of behaviours by biological determinism. Did he have heritable traits or had the socialisation process of his close environment impacted in ways that led to his anti-social behaviour?

At that time I was working with youngsters who were exhibiting what is euphemistically called now 'challenging behaviours'. Many of these children presented in what I considered to be a fashion not unlike the young Utrillo, who could be docile one minute then sparked into a rage the next; a fairly common trait or behavioural pattern found in young people with depression and, in some cases, a form of autism often now associated with artistic development.

The fact that I was living and working in an area where the young Utrillo – or Valadon, as he was called then – lived for a short time didn't do me the favours I hoped for. By that time his reputation had taken on the status of legend and even here in Pierrefitte it was impossible to separate fact from fiction. Anyway, let me tell you a little more about the young Utrillo.

From an early age young Maurice presented signs of distress. As a child he was docile, nervous and extremely shy, even morbid. He kept to himself, spending entire days withdrawn into himself. Even when playing with other children he would be quieter than the others would be, always unsure of himself. His shyness often provoked the local bullies into beating him: an experience he often faced even as an adult. He rarely smiled and it is said that he never seemed to laugh.

His repressed emotions were often expressed in outbursts of petulance and violence. When challenged at home he would often throw a temper tantrum, tearing up his school exercise books, or threatening to break everything around him, or to kill himself by jumping out the window. His grandmother said of him at this time, 'He's a sweet darling, but I wonder what he has in his blood. He frightens me sometimes'.

It is doubtful that we will ever know precisely why the young Utrillo behaved in the way that he did. What we can be reasonably sure of is that his upbringing played a significant part in his disintegration. Bear in mind we are all products of our childhood.

Maurice was a thin, small boy for his age. He is described as having a pretty, diaphanous face with blue eyes and dark hair; the child of an eighteen-year-old unmarried girl who regarded his birth as merely one of a number of varied incidents in her life. The young Maurice was frequently neglected by his mother. She left him for long spells in the charge of her own mother who lived with them, while she spent many days and nights away from the family home, quite often on the third floor of their apartment building, in the studio of Toulouse-Lautrec, where she was the artist's model and lover. Their romance was passionate if not somewhat bizarre. There is a story that one evening, before dinner, Lautrec asked Suzanne Valadon to take all her clothes off and sit with him at the dining table just to see how his housekeeper would react to seeing a naked woman sitting there. Suzanne immediately stripped off her clothes but kept on her shoes and stockings. The housekeeper, I believe, was mildly put out at first but then went about her duties as if nothing unusual had occurred. It is an interesting story that illustrates how liberated Suzanne Valadon was from the norms of polite society. No doubt the young Utrillo was aware of his mother's many comings and goings during this time. She was not a woman who kept her love life discreet.

It has been suggested that when Utrillo was in his early teens, and by now an alcoholic, he was only exhibiting the traits of his absent father. Many intimates of the family believed this to be a youth named Maurice Boissy, who worked as an insurance clerk, but who was by disposition and inclination a libertine and chronic alcoholic.

Maurice's grandmother deeply resented the circumstances she found herself in. She hated Boissy, turning him away from the door on the occasions he dared come near, and the young Maurice was a constant reminder to her of the predicament her daughter's dissolute lifestyle had put her in. (Maurice's mother had a long liaison with Boissy lasting several years, and she gave birth to another child, a boy, who died in infancy.)

No one knows with any certainty who was the father of Maurice Utrillo. His mother never said. She is alleged to have told friends that she couldn't remember, citing, 'maybe Degas or Renoir.' Others have suggested Toulouse-Lautrec or Puvis de Chavannes. There is no record of Utrillo ever having knowledge of who his father was. However one incident regarding his parentage did cause a great deal of disquiet for the young Utrillo and lingered long into his adulthood.

When the boy was eight years old his mother's then lover, Miguel Utrillo, a journalist from Barcelona, offered to give the boy his name. Up till then Maurice had been known by his mother's surname of Valadon. Miguel Utrillo had had an affair with Maurice's mother in 1883; the year of the boy's birth. Whether he was troubled with guilt or was acting out of friendship we will never know, but in the town hall on the rue Drouot, on January 27th 1891, he signed the necessary papers.

Unfortunately for the young Maurice he resented this act of support. He adamantly wanted to keep the name he was known by. His animosity to this change of name was not a childish whim. Eleven years later when he signed his first paintings he daubed the name Maurice Valadon onto his canvasses. Later he amended this to M. U. Valadon, then in 1910, when he was 27 years of age, he settled on the name Maurice Utrillo V, the signature we know today.

Whatever the reasons were that made Maurice Utrillo the dipsomaniac he became, the same reasons also played their part in producing the artistic genius – however short-lived – that he also became. His alcoholism and his genius were entwined. Maybe his friend and fellow artist, Amedeo Modigliani, best summed up Utrillo's life, when he said of him, 'He is the greatest painter in Paris…he can drink more than anybody.'

So you see there are so many vulnerable factors in Utrillo's life that could have played a part in his degeneration that it is difficult to point to one aspect in particular and say 'Here it is, this is why he became the man he did'. Becoming an alcoholic was the fate of many men and women at that time. Nor was it a phenomenon of Paris. London too had its Gin Palaces, as did Berlin, Moscow and every other city in Europe for that matter. Alcohol was cheap and came in many forms…something for everyone, you might say! What alcohol did for Utrillo was to exacerbate the strange traits that were already there. This too is not uncommon. Many men have it within themselves to do hurtful and evil things. More often than not they perform these debauched acts when fuelled by alcohol. But we all have a darker side that exists below the surface; thoughts that we keep under lock and key. We should all stay away from too much alcohol if we want to keep them locked away.

Utrillo's behaviour was extreme; beyond the experience of most montmartrois. Everyone that came across him thought him strange. Yet he inspired love too; not too muc,h but love none-the-less. We will talk again, John. I am a little tired. Maybe the next time we will speak of Suzanne, his mother, and her part in her son's rise and fall.

On the train journey back to the north of the city, I thought a lot about what I had heard that day from Jean-Paul. I liked how he added a professional dimension to his narrative.

It made me think more deeply about Utrillo, both as a painter and as a man. What must it have been like to be this tragic human being? What was his level of insight into his life's circumstances? Was it too late to find answers to these questions? I suspected that this would be the case.

8

The art of attrition

An art book is a museum without walls.
Andre Malraux

From my balcony I can see the men of Sèvres-Lecourbe gather on the small piece of dusty ground that lies on the eastern corner of boulevard Pasteur. There they play pétanque under the cool shade of a few chestnut trees. The younger men laugh and jostle with each other. They argue over everything and anything. They whistle at pretty girls passing by.

The old men sit quietly on small metal seats, dragging deeply on cigarettes and pipes. They have the language of the wise: a smile, the occasional gesture, a wave of the arm, a shake of the head. As the day draws on, all the men begin to sit beneath the trees and talk becomes more earnest. Points of view are exchanged, sides taken; then laughter once again. After a while a woman's voice is heard calling out a man's name. This signals an end to their activity. One-by-one the men disperse with handshakes, fingers being pointed and promises being made.

It was on an evening like this, when some of the men were still lingering beneath the trees, that I heard another woman's voice call, 'Well, John! Is this how you waste your time?' The voice came from nearby. I looked around, expecting it to one of the men's wives, but saw no one. 'Look down! I'm here.' I leaned over the railing of my small balcony to find the sparkling eyes and radiant smile of a young woman looking up.

It was Yvette Carné.

I felt a rise of emotion flood through me as I looked down at her on the street below. She was still smiling and shaking her head from side to side.

'Well, are you going to say hello, or are you just going to stare?'

'I'll be down in a minute. Wait there. Don't move.'

'I won't.'

I clattered down the stairs like a schoolboy, missing out two or three steps at a time; then, composing myself, I opened the door calmly and walked to the pavement. She was still there.

'Gosh, you were very fast. Did you jump down the stairs?'

'Of course not. There are fewer stairs than you think there are.'

I felt stupid the moment I uttered the words. Yvette laughed.

'See? I said we would meet again, and here we are. Were you wondering where I had got to?'

Her directness threw me for a moment. This was something I wasn't used to. I found myself wanting to say, 'Of course I bloody did, you gorgeous woman.' What came out was, 'Well, I did wonder where you had got to, but only once or twice.'

'I don't believe you. I know you missed me. Monsieur Bourdan from the fruit-shop told me. He said you came in one day and asked if he had seen me.'

I made a mental note to have words with our M. Bourdan.

'Now come with me. You can buy me a coffee.'

'You could come up to my flat if you'd prefer.'

She slipped her hand under my arm and began to walk to

the small café on the corner.

'I prefer café coffee… For now anyway.'

We sat at a window seat and ordered café noir. Yvette said she had been to Limoges. Apparently she had family that lived in the nearby town of Bessines-sur-Gartempe, a small market town in the Haute-Vienne. She had enjoyed the trip. It was a bit like going home, she said. The area was where her mother's family originally came from. Her mother and father had moved back to the area only a few years earlier. I asked if she would like to live there. She was quick with her reply.

'Oh, no! It is where in France we store all the depleted uranium. It is not a nice landscape; all concrete and steel.'

Her voice was a little strained and bitter. I changed the subject back on to safer ground. There is something attractive about a woman who can sit at ease with a man she hardly knows and talk in a relaxed way. Most of the women I had known up till then would say very little about anything and nothing about themselves. Anything they did say seemed less of a conversation and more of a negotiation. It was as if they would be 'letting their side down' if they didn't stay on guard; as if they were talking to their natural enemy. Yvette Carné struck me as a woman who would be comfortable in any company. I was enchanted.

As we spoke I began to think I had heard the name of Bessines-sur-Gartempe before today. I couldn't put my finger on it, but I was sure the name meant something to me. Maybe the Tour de France had passed through it. I put it out of my mind. I would think about it later. I wanted to give Yvette my full attention as there was every likelihood of her vanishing at a moment's notice.

'I have been checking up on you.' Yvette said. 'It would seem you are famous, Mr John Gil-Martin.' She was laughing.

'You have written a famous book, *The Art of Attrition*, about the life and works of Palance Strenver and Harlo Maguire; two very strange American painters, it would seem, if the newspapers are to be believed. You will have to tell me all about your time with them. Did the 'Harlo' one really try to kill you? And the other one, he tried to sue you when the book was published. What did you do that made them want to do these things to you?'

'How did you find out about all of this? I thought that episode in my life was only known to people in the art world.'

'A colleague in the hospital told me. I happened to mention I had met this very handsome writer who was in Paris doing some research on one of France's forgotten artists, when she said she knew of you. She had been working in New York at the time and remembered all the publicity that surrounded it. She said the newspapers were full of it. She remembered your name because it looked so unusual. She is dying to meet you. I told her you were spoken for, maybe…'

'Flattery will get you everywhere, Miss Carné. You work the male ego very well. I must remember that in any future dealings with you.'

We flirted for a few minutes more and never once did I get the upper hand in any of our exchanges. She asked me to tell her the story of what happened in New York.

'Well… Firstly, writing *The Art of Attrition* was the making of me. It gave me credibility in the art-publishing world. It was worth all the hassle that went down and, believe me, there was a lot of hassle. But it wasn't as bad as the newspapers said it was. The media made much more of it than what really happened, as they do!'

'But the 'Harlo' one of them shot you! Were you not badly hurt? ' Yvette was captivated by what she had been told by her

70

friend. I could see the excitement in her eyes. Since the moment we sat down she hadn't touched her café noir.

'Let me tell you what really happened.' I hoped I sounded reassuring. 'The incident with Harlo Maguire was much of my own doing. I had spent weeks with him, calling in every day at his lower east-side studio in Manhattan, listening to his stories, going through the correspondence he let me see, viewing the hundreds of canvasses that he kept in his loft. He was so helpful to me that I relaxed totally in his company and felt we had established something of a friendship.

'I had deliberately chosen to write about each of the painters separately as I knew they no longer communicated with each other, unless by mutual insult. They had been great friends at one time and had made their reputation together as collaborators, but I had been advised by the publishers not to mention the other by name when interviewing them. Unfortunately, I didn't see the curved ball coming and asked Maguire one day about the women in his life. He had something of a reputation with the ladies, did our Harlo. And I could see why, even as an older man, he would be so.

'He wore his dirty blonde hair long and pushed back from his forehead. He was a handsome man in a rugged way, like Nick Nolte, and wore black shirts and white slacks every day. When he ventured out of an evening, he would slip a red scarf round his neck and don a heavy grey herringbone coat. He looked the part – poet, painter, musician – and had that casual but cultured look that only artistic middle-aged men have. I was a little envious.

'I was curious about his womanising reputation. During the time I spent with him there were never any overt signs of a woman being present in his apartment. I never heard any telephone calls that involved a woman and he never spoke of any women. He laughed when I broached the subject.

'"I wondered when you would ask me about that," he said. "Let's get a drink or two and I'll fill you in."

'When he said this I didn't expect the drama that was to follow. He listed a number of women he had slept with. He rhymed off their names matter-of-factly, as if they had no more importance to him than his grocery list. I had heard of most of them. Some were actresses, some were singers; others were writers and broadcasters a few were society ladies. I began to think that he had slept with most of the women in Manhattan.

'Then he began to retrace his steps, so-to-speak, and gave a little too much insight into each lady's more intimate preferences and concessions. He could see I was shocked, which made him reveal even more intimacies. I was beginning to wish I had never asked the question when the tone of his voice changed and, with an expression which I took for disgust, he spat out the name of the wife of a well-known television producer. He poured us both another large bourbon.

'"I loved that woman, I really did – the bitch!"

'He scrunched the words out of a twisted mouth.

'"I would have done anything for her. I trusted her completely. We were meant for each other. Her husband was a waste of time. He was putting it about with every stupid actress he could lay his hands on. She told me she would divorce him. We talked about moving up to the Hamptons, converting an old barn or something. I would have eaten dog shit if she had asked me.

'"Back then I worked closely with a fellow artist I had known for years. No doubt you know who I am referring to – that piece of garbage, Palance Strenver, my so called 'friend and collaborator'. We were working on a triptych. It was planned to be our final co-production. Boy, was it just!

'"I came home one afternoon from a meeting at the 42nd Street Gallery. The door to the flat was unlocked, which wasn't unusual if Strenver was working in the studio. I let myself in, expecting to see traces of him; he was an untidy bastard. There was no sign of him. I went up to the loft and found them in my studio – her and him – my so-called 'best friend'. They were working up a sweat on each other like two dogs in heat."

'I pictured the scene his words were describing, but said nothing. I could understand his sense of betrayal if I ignored the irony. I could hear the anger in his voice. Then something he said brought my concentration back into the room.

'"I should have shot the pair of them. Shot them like the dogs they were."

'He was standing up now and waving a revolver around his head, aiming the gun at imaginary prey all around the room. I had no idea where the gun had come from. Then he pointed the gun in my direction.

'"Scary, isn't it? This would have stopped the traitors in their tracks," he said.

'He had hardly said the words when I heard the loud explosion of the revolver firing, and simultaneously felt the shock of compressed air against my ear. I reacted by crouching and bringing my hand up to my ear, expecting to feel blood. The bullet hadn't hit me.

'Harlo was shouting that he was sorry, he hadn't meant to pull the trigger. He didn't know the gun was loaded. Was I all right?

'I automatically turned round to see where the bullet had hit. There was nothing obvious to be seen; everything seemed intact.

'I regained my composure. I was standing again, but still holding my hand to my head as if to reassure myself that I too was still intact. I decided to leave immediately and grabbed my jacket from the hat stand at the door, put it on and made to leave. Harlo was still apologising. He wanted to check my head. He wanted me to stay and have another drink. I would feel better with some more drink in me. We could still talk. I left.

'Harlo was at the door shouting for me to come back. A few neighbours had come into the hallway to see what the cause of all the commotion was. I could hear them saying things like "I thought I heard a shot," or "Has he killed someone?" Then someone said "That guy's been shot. Look at his jacket."

'I checked my jacket to see what the neighbour was pointing at. Sure enough there was a hole in my jacket. The bullet must have passed through the back of my jacket as it hung on the stand. I assured everyone that I had not been shot; that it had been an accident. My pleas fell on deaf ears as the neighbours grew more excited. Then a woman screamed, "Look, he's got a gun."

'Sure enough, Harlo still had the revolver in his hand as he stood at the door. He waved his arms in protest but this only made matters worse. One of the men standing near Harlo made a grab for the gun. A struggle broke out for a moment before a shot rang out. A breath or two later, the man straightened up with the gun in his hand. Then Harlo composed himself. He looked disgusted at this latest humiliation. At least no one was hurt. The hallway was empty.

'The incident made the New York TV news that night. There were views of the apartment building. Neighbours interviewed told reporters what they were doing when they heard the first shot. Some thought they heard more than one shot initially. The man who wrenched the gun from Harlo's hand was interviewed. At least he played down his part in the melée. Most of the people interviewed said they were shocked that the artist had tried to kill someone. The news reporter said that the artist in question, Harlo Maguire, had been released from police custody but was not available for comment. No one gave an accurate account of the incident.

'Two policemen had arrived at the apartment within minutes of the second shot being fired. Harlo, his neighbour and I explained what had happened. The matter didn't end there however, and the three of us had to go 'downtown', as the police referred to their precinct station, to make a statement to clarify matters. No charges were filed and we left to go our separate ways.

'The media hounded me for a few days after the 'shooting'. The less I said the more they made up. Then Harlo re-appeared a few days later to assure everyone that the matter was a silly little mishap. He never explained why he had a revolver in his hand in the first place.'

'Did you go back to his studio after that?' Yvette asked, her face filled with concern.

'Only once or twice, when I had to see a letter or something; our relationship wasn't quite the same after that. More often than not we met in a small Japanese restaurant round the corner from his studio to discuss any biographical detail. He was apologetic every time we met. I think that at the end we parted on reasonably good terms. To be honest the incident did no harm to either of us. When *The Art of Attrition* was published a few months later the media resurrected the shooting story which no doubt helped sell a few extra copies.'

'You were very fortunate, John. Accident or not, you could have been killed. And to think: after all of that, the other one tried to sue you.'

Yvette had done her homework on me – or her colleague had. I was impressed. It felt good that she was taking an interest in me and my work. I explained briefly that Palance Strenver had tried to sue me on grounds of me besmirching his reputation by including his life and work alongside that of Harlo Maguire. Strenver claimed Maguire was an inferior painter, and therefore the association placed his reputation and the value of his work in disrepute. The matter was dropped after the New York Times ridiculed the lawsuit as the action of a desperate artist no longer confident of his abilities. If I remember correctly, he tried to sue the New York Times for its article. He was that kind of man. I was glad I had interviewed him before the episode with his ex-collaborator. I could do without him trying to shoot me as well.'

'And the women, John; can you tell me their names? The ones he slept with. Would I know them too?'

I was quite surprised by this request. It hadn't occurred to me that Yvette would enjoy gossip of this nature, but she re-assured me that French women were much the same as their sisters elsewhere. A little gossip was good for one's self-esteem, she explained; it made a woman feel good to know that other women made silly indiscretions too. I promised I would tell her all their names sometime later, as it would take too long to tell her all the gory details. She made me cross my heart. So much for confidentiality!

I was about to ask about her interest in Utrillo and why hadn't she mentioned it to me earlier when she suddenly stood up and said 'I have to go now. There are sick children waiting for me.'

'Of course,' I replied, a little taken aback at her abruptness.

'Don't worry, John Gil-Martin.' She was now walking to

the door. 'We will see each other again; you'll see.'

'Yes, but when…?'

I was too late. She was out the door and waving back as she crossed into traffic. She had done it to me again.

I walked back towards my apartment and told myself I would be ready for her the next time we met. I had no idea when this would be. It seemed to me she was a lady who liked to deal the cards but keep her own hand close to her chest. She had a bit of explaining to do, and I was determined she would do it. There would be no escape next time, whenever that would be. I smiled. I wanted this woman and I knew she knew it too.

9

The man who loved walls

Art is a collaboration between God and the artist, and the less the artist does the better.
André Gide

I became a frequent visitor to Dr Bricard's home over the next few months. Not only was Bricard a source of knowledge and considered opinion on the life of Utrillo; he had become a friend too. I liked his easy ways and nothing was a problem to him. He never asked me to talk about anything he sensed I was uncomfortable with. He had the ability to change a subject in mid-sentence if he thought he had touched a nerve. Not that he ever did. Our conversations were always amiable, even when they strayed into matters personal to both of us. I admired this in him. No doubt it was the result of decades of practice in his chosen profession. Even so, it was a welcome skill that others could learn from.

On my latest visit we didn't talk of the mysteries of Utrillo's mother, Suzanne Valadon, as he had suggested at one of our earlier meetings. For some reason he never quite got around to it. He didn't strike me as a man to forget his promises, so I didn't question his decision to elaborate on Utrillo and his challenges. I was happy to receive the information in any way that it came. Dr Bricard was always a delight to listen to. He told me the following story in his soft and captivating delivery.

Utrillo didn't like many people outwith his very small group of family and friends. He didn't trust people at large and kept out of their way as much as possible. It never occurred to him that they did not trust him either due to his irrational behaviour. Quite often he would go out in the evening when the streets and quays were quieter and paint from some secluded corner, lurking in a shadow. More often he would stay in his studio and paint churches and street scenes from postcards his mother would purchase from the markets.

The postcards were of scenes he knew well. Streets that he had walked along since a boy. He knew the butte of Montmartre better than most, having scoured the backstreets, lanes and alleyways that most decent people avoided. Utrillo used the postcards as a template or guide to measure out perspective on to his canvas or board. He measured the distances between buildings, their height and depth. He kept a ruler, plumb line, square, compass and protractor near his paintbrushes. Often he just used the postcard as an aide-memoir to jolt his memory about a rail or pipe or window he had forgotten about.

Utrillo's frequent use of postcards led to an incident that scandalised the art world in the early spring of 1939. The event was known as 'the Utrillo affair' and came about when custom officials in New York demanded additional tax duty from the owners of the Carmine Gallery, that was to exhibit 40 works by Utrillo, because the paintings were inspired by postcards.

The authorities classified the paintings as manufactured items and therefore exempt from duty free import which original art works attracted. In other words the paintings were regarded as reproductions. Utrillo was fifty-six years of age when this happened and an international figure in the world of art. The incident resulted in great crowds flocking to see the work of the 'cursed painter'.

This was not the first time Utrillo had experienced this type of criticism. In 1922 his work was exhibited at the gallery of Paul Guillaume. The exhibition was a great success for Utrillo and brought him fame as well as controversy. Some critics argued that he copied postcards and by doing so could not be considered a professional artist. Such accusations brought about a famous riposte from his mother.

"My son produced masterpieces by inspiring himself from postcards: others think they produce masterpieces, but all they do is postcards."

Early paintings were mainly scenes without people or people placed far into the painting to be insignificant. Whether this was due to his distrust of his fellow man and – more particularly – women, or his great love for the texture of walls and buildings, we can only guess. People began to appear in his paintings around 1910. The figures were often gross caricatures. The men were small and insignificant, the women large, ugly and with broad hips.

It was around this time that Utrillo, for some inexplicable reason, began to shout and swear at pregnant women in the street, often chasing them out of his way. There is no record that he ever physically harmed any of these women but it must have been a frightening experience for those caught up in his rage. We don't know if he continued this pitiful practice all his life. I suspect it was for a short time only. There is no record of occurrences of this nature happening later. I would suggest that such behaviour belongs in an irrational cerebral episode that existed, possibly due to his damaged understanding of motherhood, bearing in mind his own upbringing. This is of course a subjective posit; no one ever thought to ask him why.

Essentially Utrillo loved the feel of plaster, often adding it to his paint to create a rough texture to his paintings. Plaster of Paris was in abundance, as it had been mined in Montmartre long before the village became part of its neighbouring city. It is said that when Maurice Utrillo was a boy he would sit in the Café des Oiseaux in place d'Anvers on his way home from school, with the local workmen *who encouraged him to drink cheap wine. Many of these men would be builders of what we know today as the 18th arrondissement of Paris. Whether Utrillo got his love of buildings and the materials that made them from the coarse workmen in the Café des Oiseaux, or whether he simply appreciated the stillness, familiarity and beauty of the town houses that surrounded him, the fact remains that no other artist, before or since, painted the streets and churches of Paris quite like Maurice Utrillo.*

10

An exchange of histories

Truth is more valuable if it takes you a few years to find it.
Renard

When I contacted Emile Renouf we agreed to meet for lunch at the brasserie La Coupole. He arrived late, apologising profusely. His morning had not been his own. The Institute made so many demands on his time. Still, he was here now and pleased to see me.

'I wasn't sure if you would telephone me. It can be difficult picking up the pieces of an old friendship.'

Both of us knew why we were there, and it wasn't to renew any friendship. I really only knew Emile in the passing when I attended the Institute, but we observed the etiquette of good manners and spoke in respectful terms to each other. Emile began our exchange with a polite enquiry.

'How are you getting on with your book? Is it coming along? I don't know much about Monsieur Utrillo, apart, of course, that he was a famous painter. Is he an easy subject to write about?'

'Quite the contrary. Utrillo's lifestyle kept him from providing us with opportunities to study him. We have to patch so much together from the fragments of information we have about him.'

'This is like science is it not? Piecing together tiny scraps of knowledge and hoping we get the right answers.'

'Yes, something like that.'

I wasn't in the mood to argue with Emile, but nor did I want to leave safe conversation just yet. I asked him about his own work, which he was happy to talk about in some detail. Every so often he would pause and change direction. I took this to mean he was about to mention Thérèse or Claude but thought the better of it.

I told him that my late wife had encouraged me to try writing about art. She was convinced I could make a go of it. 'Your heart is not in science,' she would tell me. 'Go where your heart leads you.'

I told him I began by writing small appreciations of some artists that were out of vogue. Painters like Nicolas de Staël, Matthew Smith and Mikhail Vrubel. I tried the American market, which was more sympathetic to new writers. Then I got lucky. I was commissioned by Hudson & Yale to write the text to a retrospective on Palance Strenver and Harlo Maguire.

I didn't go into the detail I shared with Yvette. I told him these two great painters had spent twenty years working together before falling out. I said I spent three months in New York, visiting their studios, meeting them in clubs, bars and restaurants. Both artists had one stipulation: I could not meet them together. They hated each other.

I found myself telling him how the book was a success and that I started to receive other offers. I returned home confident that I could make a living from my writing. My wife was excited for me. Then about a week after I returned home my wife sat me down and told me she had just received confirmation that she had a terminal illness. I was devastated. It was the last thing in the world I expected and just when we were getting things together. I wanted to get a second opinion. Maybe they had made a mistake. I remember her laughing as she told me she had done all of the things I suggested; that she had plenty of time to discuss all the options.

She had kept it from me during my time in New York, as she didn't want to disturb me when my work was going so well. I discovered later that she had known about her illness before I left for America. I was angry with her for not telling me. I was angry with myself not being there. My guilt tortured me. She died within three months of my return.

'She was a very brave woman, John. You cannot reproach yourself for her death. It is obvious to me that she wanted you to succeed. She must have loved you very much. Thank you for telling me this.'

I hadn't meant to tell Emile any of this. Yet I realised I was glad I had spoken about it. I couldn't remember the last time I had spoken about Angela. Now I was sharing my grief with a near stranger.

'And now you are back in Paris, in a new life as a writer. Yet the past has a habit of catching up with us, does it not? Paris must hold so many memories for you. I admire your courage in coming back, if only for a year. I would have thought New York would be the place to be now, even London. And this part of Paris too!'

I sensed that Emile was putting me in a corner. Every time he spoke I felt he was insinuating an act of treason on my part. I guessed he was leading up to my affair with Thérèse. It usually did.

A group of young Americans came into the brasserie. They wanted to know where Ernest Hemingway sat. We watched them for a moment before resuming our conversation. They ordered double Jack Daniels all round and began toasting the great American novels of the twentieth century. Emile dismissed their presence with the merest of shrugs and a flick of the hand. He then spoke at length about the Institute and his plans for upgrading his department. Apparently the Institute had inherited a legacy from the late Duchess of Windsor's estate and he had managed to obtain sufficient funds to refurbish one of his laboratories as well as the redecoration and carpeting of his study.

I wondered if the entrance of the Americans had interrupted his thoughts. Maybe I had misjudged his intentions as he began to speak of Thérèse's husband and life at the Institute. He told me that while Claude Dumard was a charismatic and inspired academic, whom he respected greatly, he lacked organisational skills.

'Thérèse was the organiser in that marriage. It was she who always made sure he was ready. He was quite lost without her, but he would never admit to that. His pride would not tolerate such an acknowledgement of his own inadequacies. Our colleagues at the Institute, but especially me, would make most of his external arrangements and attend to any domestic needs that arose within the faculty. Even after you left Thérèse, he could not bring himself to take her back, no matter how disorganised he had become. He muddled on as best he could. Your affair with his wife left him in complete disarray.'

As usual Emile managed to twist our conversation in such a way as to leave me dealing with the unexpected and, worse than that, in a position where I had to defend myself.

'Emile, I didn't set out to disorganise Professor Dumard or leave him in a state of chaos. What happened, happened by chance. Can we change the subject, please?'

'Of course, forgive me. I didn't intend to suggest anything more than what was happening at the Institute now and when you left.'

We sat silently for a few minutes. I felt I had been heavy-handed and clumsy in cutting across Emile. I tried to back-track a little.

'Did Thérèse and Professor Dumard ever manage to sort anything out? I mean at work…that sort of thing.'

I was hoping that by broaching the subject myself, Emile would be more open with me and a little more direct in our remaining conversation. Having said that, I wasn't prepared for what followed.

'No, John. They never managed to find any equilibrium. Claude grew to hate Thérèse. There was nothing she could have said that would have helped their situation. Of course, when he found out she was pregnant with your child he could not even bear to hear her name mentioned in his company. He really went downhill after that. It was not long after that he was diagnosed with the cancer that killed him. He suffered greatly.'

'She was pregnant?'

'Yes, of course. Did you not know? I always assumed she would have told you. Did you really not know?'

'No, never. I never knew.' I was shocked. I couldn't believe what I had just heard. Was he making this up? I felt my head begin to lighten and dizziness descend. I could feel my stomach begin to wrench. I felt sick. This was the last thing I wanted to hear. I was lost for words.

'I am sorry, John; it never occurred to me that you didn't know she was pregnant. I would not have mentioned it as I did if I had known you were never told. I assumed she would have called or have written to you explaining her position. I expected you to return, but when you didn't I again assumed you'd agreed to the termination. Claude was adamant that she have a termination. Thérèse was very, very distressed at the time, but in the end she did as Claude bid.'

'She got rid of the child. She had an abortion?'

'Yes, but not too many people know this. Claude wanted it to be kept quiet. Being cuckolded was bad enough, but for his wife to bear another man's child… This was too much, even for a Frenchman of Claude's bearing.'

Emile then began to speak as if I wasn't there. He sounded so matter of fact. He began to speak of Claude and how his lack of preparation began to affect his work. He had become disaffected, distracted by the merest whim. The Directorate was at a loss how to deal with the situation. Both Claude and Thérèse were highly regarded figures. It was not easy. Claude demanded respect; Thérèse was loved. Now both were pitied. Emile went on to explain that the Director decided that Claude should be given a new role within the Institute, one with less responsibility but still prestigious in status. Claude immediately saw through this ruse and felt he was being betrayed all over again. He began to absent himself from the Institute. Finally it was decided that Claude should take a sabbatical for a year while his position was reviewed. It was not long after he was told of this decision that his illness began. 'We all knew it was serious. Within six months he was dead.'

I was immune to Emile's ramblings about Claude. My mind was in a state of agitation.

'I never knew she was pregnant, Emile. I never knew she had a termination. She sent a couple of letters when we first broke up, but I stopped reading the others when they arrived. I just left them unopened. By that time I had made up my mind to stay in Scotland and thought it best that she stay with what she knew best. I wanted to put our affair behind me, to move on. I feel terrible. She must have thought me a callous brute'

'Claude certainly thought so.'

'Can you forget about Claude?' I shouted. 'He was partly

to blame for the affair starting in the first place.'

A few people close to our table turned their heads towards us. I was angry at Emile's insensitivity, but I was angrier with myself for not opening those letters. I could see I had embarrassed Emile. I had embarrassed myself.

'I think I should go now, John. I can see that you have other things on your mind. I am sorry I have upset you.'

With this he got up and took his leave. I was happy to see him go. One of the American girls at the bar grabbed hold of him and tried to dance with him as he passed. By now they were quite merry. Emile jostled free and made for the door. I could see he was annoyed at the incident. I was pleased he was upset.

11

A day at Chantilly

A man is given the choice between loving women and understanding them.
Ninon de Lencos

My research on Maurice Utrillo was going well and had kept me busy for the most part of my time in Paris. I wandered around Montmartre most days and some nights, taking photographs and scribbling notes as I visited the streets where he lived and worked. This was especially good for me now as my meeting with Emile had distressed me and I needed to keep my mind focused.

The Saint-Vincent Cemetery was a frequent stopping place. Occasionally I would go there and picnic near where Utrillo and his wife Lucie Valore are buried. My journeys went from rue du Poteau, where Utrillo was born, to place Saint-Pierre and rue Labat, where the infant schools are situated that the young Maurice attended. Each day brought a new adventure. I walked to and from my destinations, absorbing whatever atmosphere lay before me, trying to capture a little of the environment still left that Utrillo would have known.

Paris in the sunshine is an intoxicating city to be in. Its leafy streets and terraces have an ambience all of their own. Even at 125 metres above sea level, the streets of Montmartre, on a sunny day, are a dream to be in. I continued to wander in and around the 18 arrondissement, stopping to locate where a café or bar used to be that Utrillo frequented.

Then to my own surprise, one day I found myself in a part

of the city that had no bearing on any part of Utrillo's life. Here were middle class suburban houses with large gardens and laced curtained windows. It took a few minutes for me to realise that I had come to a part of the city where Thérèse and I used to walk freely, hand in hand, without concern. As I wandered along the leafy avenues, retracing our footsteps of more than a decade ago, thoughts of Thérèse began to haunt me. I found the small bench where we used to sit and make plans for our future. These were the forlorn dreams of lovers forever caught in their present. I sat down with a sense of despair hanging over me like an east-coast haar.

Past images came to mind like a montage of archive film that had been locked away in some dark psychological attic. The early images of a man and woman laughing together soon faded to be replaced by flickering flashes of argument, self-doubt, sullenness and solitude. A sense of guilt grew within me as I remembered one of the last few adventures that Thérèse and I shared.

We met that day at the Gare du Nord. The morning sun riddled the train-station in rays of corrugated sunshine. We sat near the main entrance, enjoying the warmth of the sun on our backs as we people-watched while waiting for the train to arrive that would take us to Chantilly. Nearby, an old woman, addled with wine and wearing two or three layers of coats, sang and danced along the concourse to the other waiting commuters.

The woman sang the songs of Edith Piaf with a hoarse and guttural voice. If she ever had a singing voice, it must have been a long time before her present predicament had taken its toll. The majority of the crowd ignored her, turning away as she approached them, her hand held out for a few centimes and the occasional franc. She reacted angrily to the rejection and began to scream at unsuspecting passers-by as they made their way across her path to their respective platforms.

Two gendarmes, who had been observing the old woman's antics from the main entrance, now moved across the foyer to remove her from the station. She left, struggling indignantly, cursing wildly at an unappreciative crowd. The people around us shook their heads in disgust as she was dragged away. Thérèse and I said nothing.

The journey to Chantilly was fairly pleasant and reasonably quick. It wasn't until we were past the outskirts of the city that we struck up a conversation. The little incident with the old woman at the station had troubled us both. We kept our own counsel until green fields became the norm. Then Thérèse spoke, her voice filled with sarcasm.

'Isn't it wonderful how we look down on people who have had the misfortune to find themselves down on their luck? It's as if we are saying we will always be all right and that nothing can happen to us. We will always be out of reach of the gutter. But, as for those who sink beneath our so-called 'decent' way of life, they have brought about their own misfortune. Did those people in the station think that old woman was always like that? Something happened to her that left her weak and miserable. That 'something' could happen to any of us. And are we that strong to resist any crisis? No, we are not …the fools!'

'Are you happy, now that you have got that of your chest?' I said this with a smile, hoping I could lighten the air a little.

For some time now Thérèse had been expressing her feelings quite strongly. It wasn't that I didn't agree with her when she spoke like this; on the contrary, I shared her opinions on most matters. But it was how she let little things of late get to her.

Thérèse hadn't finished.

'Oh, we are just as bad. We didn't lift a hand to help her. Sometimes I hate myself. I really do. What have I become? Is to be middle-class a crime? Do we leave any values we once had behind us when we achieve a little success, a little money and position? Am I so insensitive to the needs of others, or am I just scared that I might see myself like that one day?'

This wasn't an argument for winning or losing, nor for flippancy. I took a sympathetic approach and answered.

'Maybe we need to see sad situations like that with the old woman to remind ourselves of where our values should be. But we can't blame ourselves for everyone else's hardship, and we need to remind ourselves that we all contribute in different ways. We can't all be at the coalface.'

This seemed to suffice. For the rest of the journey Thérèse looked out of the window at the passing scenery and kept any thoughts she had to herself.

The town of Chantilly lies 48 kilometres north of Paris. It boasts the magnificent Chateau de Chantilly, which was featured in the films The Longest Day, and the Bond movie, A View to Kill, and has one of the premier racecourses in France. We had come to see Raphaël's Les Trois Grâces that hung in the chateau's Musée Condé. Our mood lightened as we walked from the station towards the chateau. Soon Thérèse was laughing and enjoying her role as guide and mentor.

We joined one of the official tours when we reached the chateau. The official guide was greatly put out by Thérèse's constant asides as she kept me informed of her version of what the guide was explaining. At one time I thought he was going to ask us to leave. One story he told that caught my imagination was that, when Louis XIV visited in 1671, his maître d'hôtel committed suicide when he feared the fish would be served late.

Raphaël's painting; Les Trois Grâces – based on the famous marble removed from Greece by Thomas Bruce, the 7th Earl of Elgin – is breathtaking in its beauty. We wondered why one of the Gráces did not wear a necklace like her two companions. Thérèse was of the opinion that Raphaël had forgotten to paint it in and pretended to take the apples the women were holding, thereby, according to legend, becoming immortal. As we stood in front of Raphaël's masterpiece the sheer artistry of the composition humbled our perception and understanding of art. I could have wept as I felt myself being lifted up and drawn into the painting.

Thérèse did.

Outside, we wandered past the parterres and moat-lakes before taking the path that led back to the town and station and ran along the edge of the great forest. As luck would have it we had the path to ourselves. Our mood became more sombre the closer we came to the town. I was lost somewhere in my own thoughts when Thérèse turned to me and said.

'Let's make love in the forest. No one will see us. Come on, it will be fun.'

She was making her way through the fern and bracken towards the trees when the realisation of what she had said penetrated my thoughts. I looked along both directions of the path before following her into darkness of the forest.

'For goodness sake, Thérèse. We can't do it here. Someone's bound to come along at any minute.'

She had taken off her skirt by the time I reached her.

'Please, Thérèse. Not here. Put your skirt back on.' I picked up her skirt and offered it to her.

'What's wrong with you? All of a sudden you don't like making love. How times change! You couldn't wait to get me on my back six months ago. Or, was it only sex back then? Is that it, John? Are we turning into an old married couple who has rules about when they do things? You've changed, John. You've lost your spontaneity.'

'Just put on your skirt. You're acting like a silly teenager. You're always trying to shock me. Let's do this or let's do that, and always wanting to have sex at ridiculous times.'

'And what's wrong with that?' Thérèse spat back at me. 'It's not a crime, is it? You know, John, you're just becoming a…a…prude, a Presbyterian prude!'

She climbed back into her skirt and tidied herself. I walked ahead reaching the path before her. There was no one to be seen. I walked slowly so she could catch up with me, without me having to wait or say something. Somehow she never seemed to reach me. Every time I turned round she was always studying a leaf or a piece of bark.

12

Dubonnet and lemonade

It is only in adventure that some people succeed in knowing themselves – in finding themselves.
André Gide

My meeting with Emile Renouf in La Coupole had affected me more than I first realised and I now recognised that I wanted to see Thérèse again, that I needed to see her. It had become clear to me over the last few days that my coming to Paris – and to Sèvres-Lecourbe in particular – was about much more than my research into the life and work of the painter, Maurice Utrillo. Whether my sub-conscious had steered me here, knowing there was unfinished business with Thérèse, or whether it was my fortune to be here, irrespective of any need on my part, and to deal with the consequences caused by my return, I could not say. All I knew was that somehow I had to make contact with Thérèse and take it from there.

My earlier attempts to find out where she was living had so far proved futile. Then it was curiosity more than need. There was no Thérèse Dumard in the telephone directory and the Institute had advised me that the number they had on their register was discontinued; not that they would give out the number if it had been valid to any casual caller, not even for a distant cousin such as I pretended to be. I had checked the French equivalent of the electoral register for the 7th arrondissement. There was no mention of her there. She could be living anywhere in Paris.

I needed something solid to go on but couldn't bring myself to ask Emile Renouf. I knew he would be expecting me to ask him at some point and would be looking forward to enjoying my discomfort. I was convinced he was playing with me; he had that way with him. There was nothing I could put my finger on that would prove my point; it was just a feeling, but a strong one. I decided I would engage a private investigator. At least this would free me from any obligation to Emile, real or imagined.

To my surprise I found that I had quite a choice of private investigators in the neighbourhood to pick from. I chose the firm of Seurel, Giraudat & Delouche, who had offices at the east-end of rue de Sèvres. I had other business to attend to at that end of de Sèvres, so this suited me fine.

When I got there I was ushered in to a small but tidy office where a rather nondescript man joined me. He struck me as a man in his late forties, medium height, medium build and so on. It crossed my mind that he was ideal for the demands of his chosen profession; an invisible man.

He introduced himself as Vil Delouche, one of the partners of the firm. He explained a little about his own experience and the areas of expertise of the company. I was impressed. Much of their work was now conducted by computer. The touch of a button on a keyboard did most of the search. He and his partners didn't get out as much as they used to.

I told him an edited version of my situation. He was confident that he would have all Mme Dumard's up-to-date details in 48 hours. His secretary would contact me in due course to arrange an appointment to exchange information. He preferred to do this face-to-face. He was old fashioned about this sort of thing. He then ushered me out into the corridor and directed me to the firm's accounts office. I turned to thank him. Monsieur Vil Delouche had vanished.

Once outside, I crossed the street, pleased that I was a little closer to finding Thérèse. On the other side, a little further along, I entered one of my favourite gentlemen's tailors in Paris – Arnys. Just being in this shop lifts one's morale. There is no finer establishment to browse within in the whole of the city. Every home should be like this. Its elegance is second to none. I wanted to buy a gift, maybe a tie or a handkerchief. These items were in my price range.

I made my way to the exquisite curved stairway that leads to the first floor, the black railings of the stair contrasting beautifully against the white and cream décor of the shop. I stood at the base of the stairs, appreciating the balance between architecture and colour, when, much to my amazement, coming down the stairs, laden with packages, was Yvette.

I don't know who was the more surprised and for what reason. Neither of us probably expected to find the other in a shop of such reputation. And if so, good manners forbade either of us from saying so. After our initial surprise, we agreed to meet in fifteen minutes at a bar on the corner with boulevard Raspail.

Ten minutes later, as agreed, I was seated at an alcove table in the little bar Yvette had chosen not far from Le Récamier restaurant. The proprietor looked not unlike Georges Brassens. This made me smile, as I had long been a fan of the jazz legend and his incorrigible accomplice, Moustache. The proprietor was tapping his fingers on the bar to the rhythms of Petite Fleur, one of my favourite pieces by another jazz legend, Sidney Bechet.

Yvette came in a few minutes later minus her packages. She ordered a Dubonnet and lemonade mixer before sitting down. Almost immediately, a waiter appeared with Yvette's drink before I had time to say anything to her.

'A votre santé' she said raising her glass before taking a large swallow. I had ordered a café noir five minutes earlier and lifted the little cup as high as I dared.

'Cheers.'

Yvette noticed my slight discomfort and smiled radiantly.

'So, tell me, John. Did you buy something nice from Arnys?'

'Yes, a tie for my English brother-in-law, Charles. A Charvet silk tie.'

'You must like this brother-in-law called Charles! Charvet ties are expensive! Do you have only one sister?'

Once again I found myself doing most of the talking. I told Yvette about my family, leaving out the skeletons that every family has. Yvette had that way with her that some people have, who can say nothing themselves but get you to tell them your life story. Emile Renouf was able to do that too, but without the charm. We ordered more drinks. This time I had my now usual large malt whisky. Yvette stayed with Dubonnet.

'Tell me a little about yourself Yvette. I've told you much about myself and know so little about you. What do you do at the hospital? Administration?'

'No, John. I am a doctor, a doctor of paediatrics.'

'But you're not listed anywhere on the hospital's list of medical staff.'

'Ah, you've been spying on me, monsieur! Serves you right for not finding me! I use my maiden name for my profession. Many women do.'

'You're married?' I hadn't expected this.

'I am – or was — for six years. I suppose I am still

married. Bear with me for a moment, John. You see, my husband lives in Africa. I should explain. He was in Africa working for Médecins Sans Frontièrs in the Bas-Congo Province. Then two years ago I received news that my husband had died. I was shocked. They said he was killed in a road accident. I was told a truck he was travelling in overturned. No one else was injured, apparently, but Edouard – that's my husband's name – hit his head against some rocks and that was that. I was so angry at him for dying on me. It broke my heart. He had wanted to take a year out to do something more worthwhile than patch up 'les mauvais' on a Saturday night. He wanted me to go with him, but I was studying for my final year in Paediatrics, so it seemed a good idea. I would get time to study and he would save the world. That was two years ago.'

'Yvette, I'm sorry. I had no idea…'

'Of course not. But that is in the past. This is the present. You wanted to know more about me, and I thought I would start by telling you that story. Anyway, that is what it was: a story, a piece of misinformation. Edouard didn't die in any road accident. It was another young French doctor working at the hospital who was killed in the accident, and somehow the French Consul got the story wrong. What is ironic is that this incident brought to light Edouard's deceit. When I first heard the news that he had been killed, I phoned the hospital he was working at to see if they could help me make some arrangements while I got ready to fly out to the Congo. The hospital administrator told me there must have been a terrible mistake, as Edouard was alive and well. I tried phoning his rooms but got no answer. I phoned back to the hospital to see if they had another contact number, which they had.

'I was so happy at this news that I dialled the number the

hospital had given me where Edouard could be reached only for some woman to answer. When I asked to speak to Dr Jourdain – that's Edouard's surname – I heard her say 'Darling, it's for you.' I burst into tears. When he came to the phone he had no idea it was me he was going to speak to. When he realised it was me on the other end of the line, he blurted out something about it being a joke his colleagues played on him. But it turned out he was living with a nurse that he'd met over there – or so I thought. Later I heard that they went to the Congo together. It doesn't matter now what version is the truth. He had left me and that is that. I'm over it. Let's have another drink – PASCAL! – The same again, if you please!'

Pascal brought over the drinks with a plate of canapés. He nodded to Yvette as he put the drinks down.

'Docteur—'

'—Merci, Pascal.'

I realised that the staff in the bar knew Yvette and she knew them. Now, I had stepped into a little bit of her world and wondered where it would lead me. Before I could say anything Yvette began talking again.

'I grew up in a town just outside Paris. My mother was a nurse in a nearby hospital. My father ran a small business, reconditioning automobile alternators. He had a workshop at the back of our house where my brother Gaston and I would help after school. It was our job to clean the alternators then dismantle them, separating the rotor from the stator. We would then check the contact brushes and, if they were too small, we threw them in the bin. My father had a small lathe where he would skim down the surface of the bakelite contact plates with their copper rings. We loved helping him. We thought we were engineers!

'After I finished school I came into Paris to attend the

Sorbonne, where I studied 20th century French philosophy. At that time I wanted to be an intellectual like Simone de Beavoir or Hélène Cixous. Their lives sounded so sexy. After my graduation I went to teachers training college, then taught Epistemology and Ethics at a private school for girls on the outskirts of Fontainebleau. But my heart wasn't in it. A girl can have too much of Jacques Derrida, Georges Bataille, or Michel de Certeau, you know! So I left.

'My mother encouraged me to train as a nurse. She said I was more suited to doing things than talking about them. She was right. After my training I got a job at the American Hospital in Neuilly. Then one day a new doctor appeared on my ward. It was Edouard. We fell in love. We married. He said I had the brains and ability to be a doctor. I wasn't so sure, but he encouraged me to study paediatrics. I did. Then he did the things he did. That's it. Have I missed anything out Pascal?'

I hadn't realised that the waiter was standing behind me, listening to what Yvette was telling me.

'Nothing major. You could have mentioned Philip Marquet. But then again... maybe not.'

'Pascal! You traitor!'

'Sorry, Yvette. But you did ask.'

'Excuse me,' I said, 'but am I the only person here who doesn't know what's going on?'

'Sorry, John, forgive me. Pascal and I grew up together. His father and my father were friends. We lost touch when I went to university. Then one day I came in here with some friends and there was Pascal. I come in here as often as I can. Pascal keeps in touch with some people from our hometown. He gives me all its news. But don't listen to him about Philip Marquet. He was a school sweetheart of mine when I was about nine or ten.'

'Didn't you say your parents left your hometown?'

'Yes, but they moved a few years ago, to the town Bessines, near Limoges, when an old aunt of my mother left her a rather grand house and enough money for my father to retire. Did I not tell you that the last time we met?'

Once again I tried to remember how I knew of this town Yvette had mentioned. I made a mental note to check my papers when I got back to my apartment. By now Pascal had drifted back to his station behind the bar. I leaned forward and whispered.

'Yvette, this is all so difficult for me. I've wanted to see you for weeks and had planned all the things I was going to say to you when we met again And now, this! Don't misunderstand me. I am pleased that you have told me so much about yourself. Believe me, I have wanted to get to know you better since that night we walked to the hospital together. I had made up my mind that I was going to ask you out properly. I wanted to stop all this flightiness and arrange a proper time together . . .'

She cut across me.

'Of course we can go out together; it's what I want too! I just needed time to sort a few things out and maybe play a little-hard-to-get. Isn't that what the British women do?'

I let her question pass. I wasn't interested in what British women did or didn't do. I was only interested in what Yvette would do. And now that I knew, I was trembling inside.

13

A dog barks when it is afraid

We do not judge the people we love.
Jean-Paul Sartre

My visits to Pierrefitte took me out of myself. It was good to get out of the city and leave my moods and mindings back in my apartment. A visit to Dr Bricard always lifted my spirits. He had told me so much. I felt I was beginning to get to grips with Maurice Utrillo. On this occasion we sat indoors. This was my preferred habitat. The garden was fine, but I much preferred the atmosphere of the study. I could smell the history.

I had started recording our talks. It became apparent from our earlier meetings that I was forgetting some of the stories I was being told. So we agreed that I would tape them. My recording of what was said that day was clear of any passing vehicles or noisy children. Listening to the tapes of Jean-Paul's voice was a pleasure. His accent was light, but most of all he had a timbre to his voice that made listening to him a compelling experience.

As an artist Maurice Utrillo had no need for women. He never painted a nude in his lifetime. As a man, he expressed little need for women in his life other than his mother and grandmother who tended to his domestic needs. This worried his mother from time to time. He adored her and likened her to a saint. Yet this was far from the reality. He compared all other women to his venerated mother and found most of them repellent. Yet it may be possible that his mother's behaviour with men, her promiscuity and the hurt this may have caused him would, in his confused state of mind, have been transferred to other women in general. He may have thought women as betrayers of trust due to his own mother's neglect when he was a child.

He showed little interest in sex too. This is not surprising given his stated views on women. His first sexual encounter occurred in 1911 when he was twenty-eight. He records that his reaction to this experience was one of shame. However, infrequent casual liaisons did follow, which he claimed were mostly with local prostitutes. There would have been an abundant supply on the butte at that time. How often he partook of their services is not known, but I doubt if it was too often.

We must remember that Utrillo lived where extremes meet. His reality was a jungle of contradictions and conflicts. Lucidity was an infrequent visitor to the mind of this painter. His reservoir of serenity was used up in the act of painting. All else hinged on the door to madness. In essence Utrillo was a child in a man's body. He wanted love but was offered sex, or so he thought. So, for him, women were both friend and enemy. Believe it or not, but Utrillo was capable of receiving love. Three stories exist that suggest this was possible.

He is said to have had an affair with an American divorcee who smoked Turkish cigarettes and cooked him Italian sausage. Apparently they would lie together on her Bokhara rugs listening to her recordings of Sibelius. We do not know this woman's name and I somehow doubt the veracity of this story.

But there is another, even more remarkable love story that is certainly worth the telling. This concerned a woman Utrillo met in a bar one evening while he sat alone drinking his wine. Her name was Trien van der Veen, and she was a deaf mute. She was the wife of a steel worker in a car factory who was also a deaf mute. When Utrillo offered to buy her a drink she indicated to him to write what he was saying on a pad. Later that evening they went back to her flat, where he allegedly pushed her on to the bed and made love to her. He left an hour later, madly in love.

Trien ran a small Flemish bakery on the rue du Poteau, the street where Utrillo was born. He was a frequent visitor to the bakery. He would sneak in the back door of the bakery and enjoy coming up behind her as she rolled dough on the table, putting his arms around her, his hands fondling her large breasts and pulling her buttocks towards him. They would spend many afternoons making love in her flat, which was upstairs from the bakery. Their affair lasted about a year until Trien's husband decided they were to move to Brussels to be near the convent school which their teenage daughter attended. Trien was devastated. She enjoyed her afternoon frolics with the mad painter. Utrillo was equally put out by what was to happen. They were never to see each other again.

Lastly, it has been suggested that Utrillo was in love with Marie Vizier, twenty years his senior and the buxom, blonde landlady of the cabaret, A la Belle Gabrielle. Marie's establishment was across the street from Maurice's lodgings in the bistro Casse-Croûte. Utrillo himself probably gave cause for this belief when he wrote on a painting depicting Marie Vizier standing in the doorway of her cabaret, 'Across the way I spent the happiest days of my life.' And to emphasise the point he drew an arrow pointing to Marie. Yet, while showing great kindness to Utrillo, Marie also beat him mercilessly.

Such romantic occasions in Utrillo's life were rare. As a rule he distrusted women or, as I have said earlier, was frightened of them. His mother tried to encourage her son to meet women. Sometimes she would arrange for girls to visit the studio in the hope that a mutual attraction would be struck. Most of her efforts ended in disaster, with Maurice either ignoring the girls or causing a scene.

One girl, who his mother brought into the household, that did appeal to Maurice was Suzanne's model and occasional maid. This was a girl remembered only as 'Gaby the Brunette.' She was a big, fleshy, good-natured woman who treated Maurice well. They became very fond of each other and Maurice seemed to trust her. Whether their friendship became anything more than platonic is a matter of conjecture. Sadly, it was not to last. Suzanne contrived to make a marriage between them, but shortly before the day of the wedding Gaby vanished. She was never heard of again and no-one tried to find out what happened to her.

Let us not forget that Utrillo's early history with women was never passive. As a boy he would run away from them. As a young man he exhibited frightening behaviour towards them. He would insult them as they passed him, using offensive language and making obscene gestures to them. As the women fled he would chase after them waving his fists. Maurice never caught any of the women he chased and the women of Montmartre soon learned how to deal with the crazy painter. Yet his behaviour was worrying if no less enigmatic. He only insulted and chased after working-class women; never a woman of middle-class. The only exception to this bizarre rule was his attacks on pregnant women. He tried, but always failed, to kick them in the stomach. Even they, however heavily pregnant, could outrun Utrillo.

It is thought that Utrillo's apparent hatred of women prevented him from having any physical contact with them and that, therefore, his violent public pursuit of women was purely symbolic. Again we have a contradiction. We know he could love a woman other than his mother and grandmother; so why the pretence of violence? Again, the answer probably lies deep in the relationship he had with his mother. His life revolved around her. He adored her, but at times she brought him to anger, especially when he was a boy.

As a young boy growing up in Montmartre, the young Maurice would've been acutely aware of the sexual liberalism that surrounded him; nor would he have been unaware of his own mother's sexual proclivities. Suzanne Valadon took many lovers, often from the world of art; most famously, Toulouse-Lautrec, Pierre Puvis de Chavannes and Auguste Renoir. The composer of the melancholic Gymnopédies, Erik Satie, was also her lover. (Did you know that Satie's mother was Scottish?) Some said, cruelly – and forgive my coarseness – that more men had passed between her legs than through the Arc de Triomph.

Suzanne was a survivor of the sordid streets she grew up in. She was probably no more promiscuous than many of the girls and women who lived in and around Montmartre at that time. Her attitude to sex was unequivocal. She once said: 'If I wanted a man, I made no bones about it. I was usually the one who undressed first.'

This is borne out in the story of Suzanne's seduction of André Utter, a young artist who was painting one day on rue Cortot. Suzanne caught sight of him from her studio window and asked him to come up. When he arrived he found Suzanne naked. When he left a little later he was a much more knowledgeable man.

Whether Suzanne's prédilections affected her son's attitude towards women in general – and we can only surmise that they did – the fact remains that Utrillo found women difficult to come to terms with. His later paintings depict women as figures of ridicule. He said of them, 'As for women, I give them more prominence, but I hardly follow fashion. Their big buttocks and hips must make you laugh. I see them all as mother hens. Mother paints her women with big buttocks, and I must have been influenced by her.'

Maurice was well aware of his mother's amorous liaisons. No doubt as a young boy he was jealous of the affection and time she gave to her lovers. Even the daily attention and care given to him by his maternal grandmother, Madeleine, seems to have mattered little to him. It was a mother's love that he craved

As an adult, Maurice witnessed a period of relative stability in relation to his mother's love life. Suzanne had met the banker, Paul Mousis, and lived with him for 11 years. Sadly, the life of a banker's wife did not suit Suzanne and she became restless. One day Maurice brought home André Utter, a friend, and three years his junior, Suzanne immediately took him as her lover. This was the same André Utter that Suzanne had seduced some time earlier.

This situation must have caused Maurice some embarrassment and no doubt fuelled an already burning fire. But somehow he accepted this situation and got on with his painting. Suzanne left Paul Mousis in 1911 and set up home with Utter, Madeleine and Maurice. This remained the family group until Madeleine died in 1915. A year earlier Suzanne and André Utter had married.

It was only when Suzanne reached old age that she once again considered the need for Maurice to have a wife. She recognised she could no longer look after him and that there would be a time soon when she wouldn't be around to keep him out of trouble. With this in mind she once again set about finding Maurice a wife. This was a near impossible task. No woman in her right mind would take on such a burden, as Maurice would no doubt be. Yet fate was to intervene in the shape of Lucie Valore, the widow of the banker Robert Edouard Pauwels, and a woman with delusions of grandeur. She considered herself a great actress who had missed her opportunities through no fault of her own. Valore was her 'stage' name. She was born Francoise Alexandrine Jeanne Lucie Veau, and grew up near the cathedral of Angoulème. She married a young sculptor, Joseph Bernaud, in 1901 and moved to Paris. Later, in 1915 she married M. Pauwels, whom she had met while touring in Belgium.

Utrillo married Lucie Pauwels at the Mairie of the 16th arrondissement on April 18th 1935. He was in his mid-fifties and semi-comatose. With her marriage to Maurice, Lucie was financially secure. His paintings sold for thousands of francs. He was fêted as a great artist. She bought a home for them at Le Vésinet in the department of Seine at Oise, some eighteen kilometres from Paris. Maurice had moved from one cage to another.

Lucie took up painting and considered herself a great artist. She insisted dealers buy a painting of hers if they wished to purchase a 'Utrillo'. Most could do little else but agree. Such pomposity enraged Suzanne Valadon, but Maurice was oblivious to his wife's actions. Lucie thought herself a woman whose value was not properly appreciated. Never one to understate her position, she boldly announced her importance to the art world, saying,' I found him in the gutter and saved him for France.'

The marriage was never consummated.

14

Not all news is good

No snowflake in an avalanche ever feels responsible.
Jean-Paul Sartre

The phone rang. It was the private eye, Vil Delouche's secretary with a time for what she called my 'appraisal appointment'. I jotted down the details and hung up. At last I would have something to go on. The thought that quite soon I could see Thérèse again excited me. I had much to say to her. It wasn't going to be easy; I had much to apologise for. In my defence, I hadn't been aware of the details of what was happening to her at that time. If it wasn't for Emile Renouf I might never have found out what happened to her. I wanted to put things right between us, if I possibly could.

I waited outside Vil Delouche's office for what seemed an eternity. The secretary I had spoken to on the phone earlier sat me on a leather bench in the middle of a long corridor. I didn't remember the corridor being so long or so busy. It seemed every second person in Paris had reason to be there. A lot were women, middle aged women. I made a few assumptions on the nature of their visit, most of which centred one way or other on errant husbands. Eventually the door opened and I was ushered in.

'My apologies! An urgent telephone call came through, which I had to take. It was a little more complicated than I expected. Such is the nature of the business I am in. Still, you are not here to hear my woes. You will want to know how I got on concerning Dr Dumard?'

I said nothing, but smiled at this inanity.

'Of course you do. Well, I have good news for you. We have found your friend. It wasn't that difficult. She had reverted to her maiden name, as many women do in these circumstances. Here it is. Ah, yes: Velpau-Mauriac. I have it written down for you. And another thing m'sieur: she no longer calls herself 'Doctor', just plain 'Madame'. She lives in an apartment in Issy-les Molineaux, just over the Périphérique on the D181. Everything is written down here in this file.'

He passed the file over. I opened it hesitantly, not knowing what to expect. Inside were two yellow sheets of what looked like a questionnaire. Behind the sheets was a print with six photographs on it. I gave it a cursory glance. I was aware the private eye was watching my every movement. I flicked back to the information sheets. I was impressed. Every detail you could think of was here. Monsieur Delouche must have read my mind.

'It is not so difficult, m'sieur. We French pride ourselves on our bureaucratic thoroughness. We like to keep note of many things, and with computers it is even simpler. The trick is knowing where to look.

'So it would appear, Monsieur Delouche. But I can't help thinking you obtained some of this information from outwith your government department contacts.'

'True, I still had to do a little leg work, visit a few places and ask a few questions. The Institute where Dr Dumard formerly worked was very helpful. They are used to enquiries of this nature. We French understand the need for cooperation.'

I sensed the interview was over. He was smiling.

'Well, if there is nothing else, Monsieur Gil-Martin, I will bid you good-day and wish you well.'

111

'There is one more thing, if you don't mind. When you contacted the Institute did you speak to anyone in particular?'

'I wouldn't normally reveal my sources, but in this instance I see no reason not to. Let me see, I have my notes here. Yes, I did speak to one of the staff who remembered the Doctor during her time at the Institute – a Professor, I think. Yes, here it is – Professor Emile Renouf.'

15

The opera singers

Better to be alone than in poor company.
Pierre Gringore

I left Vil Delouche's office with mixed feelings. I had the information I needed that would let me decide how I would make contact with Thérèse. But my privacy was compromised. It wouldn't take Emile Renouf long to work out who was behind the questions if Vil Delouche had been anything less that discreet. It was as if I was being haunted by Emile Renouf. I tried to put this latter thought out of my mind.

I could see the small bar where I last met Yvette. I made my way toward it, hoping that on the off chance I might bump into her. It was near enough time for lunch anyway. The bar was reasonably busy with a mixture of customers. Yvette was nowhere to be seen. I checked the bar to see if Pascal was working. There was no sign of him either. I ordered a sandwich and coffee and found an empty table that was through an archway that I hadn't noticed during my last visit. It was less busy and less bright than the main bar area. I was surprised to find a partially hidden upright piano in the far corner from my table. A row of stacked chairs partially obscured it. Had I glanced at the walls around me I would have been less surprised, as an assortment of photographs, mainly of opera divas, adorned each wall. I read the names on the wall above my table. I knew some but others unknown to me – Gemma Bosini, Emma Calvé, Rosna Buckman, Geraldine

Farrar, Ninon Vallin, Nellie Melba, Toti Dal Monte, Göta Ljungberg, Renata Tebaldi, Cathy Berberian, Maria Callas, Kathleen Ferrier, Birgit Nilsson, Elizabeth Schwarzkopf, Victoria de los Ángeles, Joan Sutherland, Montserrat Caballé and, of course, Régine Crespin. The list and faces went on and on.

I was tempted to go over and run my fingers over the open keys of the piano but decided against it. I hadn't played for a while. Instead I took out the envelope that Vil Delouche had given me and started to read. Vil had done his homework. Everything I needed to know about Thérèse's whereabouts over the last few years was here and some things I didn't need to know. I felt as if I was betraying her trust, spying on her. I told myself it was for the best. She'd understand.

The waiter brought my coffee and sandwich over to me. It was Pascal. I didn't know if it pleased me that it was he or not. He pulled out a chair and sat down.

'I didn't expect to see you so soon. Will you be becoming a regular to our little establishment, now that you are friends with Yvette?'

I didn't like his tone.

'Nice to see you too, Pascal.'

He smiled.

'Forgive me. I get a little over protective sometimes. Yvette has been a friend for a long time. She is still a bit vulnerable from her husband's deceit. I worry she'll get hurt so soon after all she has been through. It is a weakness of mine. Do you want to talk?'

'I'm not sure we have anything to talk about. You're an old friend and I'm a new one. Maybe we should just leave it like that. I only came in here because I had business nearby and I felt hungry. I didn't come looking for Yvette. We have our own private arrangements in place. Now, if you don't mind, I'd like some privacy to have my lunch, thank you.'

He said nothing, but got up from the chair and vanished through the archway. I was angry with myself for letting him get to me. Still, he should not have tried to pull rank on me in the way that he did. Anyway, now he knew where we stood with each other. I believe most men know what is expected of them when a woman is involved. Few men I know trust a man who claims to be a woman's friend. Most suspect that there is a jealousy somewhere behind their pretence of friendship; an unrequited love, an eternal hope that, when all else fails, they will be there, able and willing to pick up the pieces. Pascal struck me as that type. His so-called 'over protectiveness' did not impress me. It might fool Yvette, but it did little for me.

I was no longer hungry. I wrapped the sandwich in a serviette and stuffed it in my pocket. It would do for later. I swallowed the coffee and left through the archway. I put my money on the bar counter. There was no sign of Pascal.

2nd Movement

Nocturne #19 in e minor
Frederich Chopin

16

Confessions from the other side

The logic of the heart is absurd.
Julie de Lespinasse

Curiosity was getting the better of me. I had Thérèse's address in Issy-les Molineaux and had an itch to go there and see for myself where she was living. I had no idea what this part of Paris was like, other than what I saw on television when the Tour de France cycled past on its way to the Champs Élysées, and the prospect of investigating what lay on the other side of the Périphérique also intrigued me. Yet I knew I felt more than just curiosity. I felt guilt.

When Thérèse and I split up all those years ago it had a lot to do with my inability to deal with the situation we had created. Consequence was not high on my priority list. Making love regularly to a beautiful woman was all that I cared about, and Thérèse fulfilled all my wildest sex dreams. Little else mattered, and I enjoyed the status of illicit lover.

The taxi journey to the south of the Périphérique turned out to be like an assault on enemy lines. The cab, randomly chosen near Montparnasse station, set off in robust fashion with the driver displaying a fair amount of assertiveness towards his fellow motorists and pedestrians alike. Not being a regular user of taxis, I had no idea if this experience was a common one. Within a few streets from the station I could sense the suppressed violence emanating from the front of the taxi. My knowledge of the French language didn't permit me an insight into the vocabulary used by my driver. No one was immune to his wrath. I began to dread corners and traffic lights. I avoided eye contact with anyone looking my way. The drive down the N6 offered no respite from what was now open warfare. I was convinced the taxi was being driven by a sociopath. I told myself I would die in this taxi.

We slewed off the N6 in a manner reminiscent of a yachtsman leaning over the side of his yacht to counter capsizing from the other side. Then the taxi rocked sideways for a moment or two before steadying itself like a bull about to charge a wounded matador. What went before the N6 began to manifest itself again – the cursing, the gestures, the venom. When he finally pulled the taxi over to the curb and stopped, I had no idea where I was. Every bone in my body felt as though it was disconnected. I quickly handed over a fistful of notes and backed out of the cab and away.

'Merci! Merci!' he shouted. 'Have a fine day.'

I waved benevolently, glad to be alive and back on solid ground.

Any disorientation I felt lasted only for a few moments. A quick check with a nearby street sign told me I was exactly where I didn't want to be; that is, outside the apartment block where Thérèse lived. The taxi driver had been told at the outset to drop me off at the corner of the street, so I could collect my thoughts, as I had no idea what I was going to do next. Now I was standing in front of the entrance to Thérèse's home, and instinct told me that this was not to be the only mishap that was going to happen this day.

The block of flats was a little run down. The garden area at the front hadn't been tended to in a long time and the exterior paintwork was in need of refreshment, but the surrounding office buildings and apartments stood out well against the overall townscape. I decided that the best thing I could do was to go straight to Thérèse's apartment and deal with matters head-on. Any other course of action would result in my procrastination and eventual avoidance. Luckily for me there was no door entry system at the front entrance. I pushed my way in, praying I wouldn't meet anyone. Somehow I felt like a spy, an intruder. The hallway was bare and uncarpeted. My footfall sounded like a loud hand-clap. I instinctively began to walk on the balls of my feet, softening the sounds of my progress. I had two sets of stairs to climb.

The sign on the door read simply, 'T Velpau-Mauriac. There was no bell. I took a deep breath and knocked hard on the door three or four times. I could feel the tension in my stomach. I was about to knock again when I heard Thérèse's voice call out.

'Hang on, I'm coming.'

The door opened quickly and Thérèse stood before me. She didn't recognise me at first, then a gradual realisation spread across her face. Her look of inquisitiveness turned to anger. Her face reddened.

'You bastard! How dare you turn up here? How dare you?'

'Thérèse, I'm sorry, I wanted to…'

The door slammed shut. I stood for a moment in the echoing silence, not quite sure what to do next. She had every right to slam the door in my face. It was a natural reaction, given the circumstances. Yet, I had come here to see if I could make some amends for my past mistakes. I tried again.

'Thérèse. If you're standing behind the door, then you can hear me. Please listen. I didn't come here today to hurt you or to dredge up past pains. I want to apologise. If you open the door, I can at least do that to your face.' I held my breath for a second or two, letting my words permeate on the other side of the door, hoping she was still there. Then, cautiously, the door opened.

'Come in,' was all she said.

She led me along a short lobby and into a small lounge with the barest of furnishings: a sofa, TV and a couple of chairs by the window. I tried not to show my surprise. Even in the most difficult of circumstances, I expected a woman of Therese's making to maintain a little style, to keep a measure of comfort in her home. The room was adequately functional, but nothing more than that. The walls were bare, no art work or photographs adorned any space, no matter how small. She had been stripped of everything except her self-respect. Now I had turned up and was capable of stripping away even that. It became clear that I was not to be extended anything more than the necessary courtesy.

'Say what you came to say; then leave, please.'

I searched for any signs that might belie her coldness to me. All I could see was hostility tempered in anger.

'I'm not sure if you knew I was in Paris. I came over to do some research on a French painter. It's what I do now.' I shook my head – now wasn't the time to explain the details – and it was more than possible that Emile Renouf had told her of our meeting. 'When I moved into my flat in Sèvres-Lecourbe I was conscious of my proximity with the past. I would be a liar if I told you I never gave you any thought. Yes, I wondered more than once what I would say if I met you in the street. Then I met Emile Renouf and he told me what happened to you after I left…I'm sorry, I truly am. I didn't know any of it.'

'How can you say that, you liar? My letters explained everything!'

'I never opened them.'

Thérèse winced at my cruel words. I spoke quickly, trying to explain as much as I could before she could make sense of it all.

'I moved out of my parent's home a few weeks after my return to Glasgow. I told them to keep any mail from France and I would pick them up later. But I didn't. I wanted to put the pain of what happened with us behind me. It was a stupid thing to do. I know that now. I'm not proud of what I did. I was immature and acted within my scope of experience. Our affair was a fun romance that got too serious. I wasn't ready for that. And besides: we were different people with different lives, different backgrounds. I wanted to leave what happened in France, in France. Then things began to happen for me, and when the letters stopped I...moved on... I'm sorry. I'm really sorry.'

'I heard you the first time. You've made your apology. Would you please leave now?'

'But the things that happened to you after... Don't you want to talk about them? The pregnancy... Claude... the divorce...'

'None of these matters concerns you. It is none of your business. Go now. Please leave and don't come back.'

She stood up and walked to the door. She was right. There was more to say, but now was not the time to say it.

17

Wounded, but not beaten

As long as you know men are like children, you know everything.
Coco Chanel

A few days later, in the morning, I heard Chopin's Nocturne #19 in E minor on the radio and had a strong urge to play the piece myself. This was a work I knew well and had learned it by heart many years ago. It was one of my favourite Chopin pieces. My desire to play the piece meant that I had to go to Yvette's bar on the corner of boulevard Raspail to use its piano. This is a good omen, I thought. Yvette is sure to be there over lunch. I grabbed a jacket and left.

I hadn't visited the bar since that day when Pascal and I had spoken privately. The bar itself held no attraction for me. I'd been in too many bars like it all over Britain to think it cute and ethnic. Still, it was Yvette's preferred drinking establishment and that made all the difference.

I hoped Pascal would be off-shift, as I had no desire to see him so soon. His sneering manner annoyed me. The lame excuse he used, that he was protecting his school chum, didn't hold water as far as I was concerned. The guy had feelings for Yvette but wasn't man enough to do something about it. He was a loser, the perennial second best, always loitering with intent, scratching for a few love-crumbs. It struck me that he was the type that hung around attractive women in the false belief that if he was last man standing he would, by default, win the hand of the fair maiden.

Maybe I'm overstating the case, but I had met his type before, always hanging around on the edges of company hoping for a disaster; a social leech clinging on to any blood supply that was vulnerable and susceptible to empty promises and flattery. I considered the guy a creep.

Thankfully another barman served me, an older man with an uncanny resemblance to Yves Montand. That's two look-a-likes in one small bar in Paris, I told myself; whatever next, I thought. He poured an excellent large malt whisky. I picked up my glass and moved towards the back room where the piano was situated. There was no sign of Yvette.

I ran through a couple of practice pieces to warm the fingers before attempting the nocturne. I hit a few duff notes and started over again. It had been too long since I last played.

'You need a bit more practice, John.'

Pascal stood by the doorway. He had that look on his face. I wanted to slam shut the piano and slap that grin off his face.

'Yes, it's been a while since I've played this piece. I'm a bit rusty. Do you play an instrument, Pascal?' I stared hard at him, challenging him. I knew he didn't.

'No, John. I don't. I never seemed to have the time. I was always too busy helping my mother and father with their business. Music was a luxury we left to those with idle hands.'

His sanctimonious attitude stung me. He was trivialising music by trying to trivialise me. I retorted:

'It's more a matter of values than necessity; an appreciation of higher needs and the stimulation of man's desire to develop his skills at a deeper level, at a higher intellectual plain if you like. Some of Europe's greatest composers and performers came from humble beginnings. It's more about recognising where you want to be than where you're at, if you take my meaning.'

I started to play again, confident that I had scored a telling point. He would think twice before mounting another attack. This time I was note perfect. He stood silent and still in the doorway until I had finished.

'That was a lot better; really good. Has Yvette heard you play like this?'

'No, we spend our time doing other things. And, anyway, this is the only piano that's available to me. I don't have one in my apartment.'

'That is a pity. You can play so well. It's a shame she probably won't get the chance to hear you play your party pieces.'

'And why will Yvette not get the chance to hear me play? Are you getting rid of the piano?'

'No, John. We are keeping the piano. It's just that Edouard, Yvette's husband, has returned from Africa and is looking for reconciliation with his wife. Yvette says he is very remorseful and is genuinely sorry for what he did to her. I thought she was going to break down when she told me. She is thinking it over, I believe. C'est la vie, eh? Another whisky, John?'

18

The revelation of François Salerou

In all things, we can be judged only by our peers.
Honoré de Balzac

The train journey to Pierrefitte to visit Dr Bricard was a particularly enjoyable one. I and the other passengers in the compartment were entertained by a young boy explaining to his little sister how baby rabbits are made. The young girl was mesmerised by the descriptions offered by her older and oh-so-wiser brother. Meanwhile the heavily pregnant mother of the children could be found either with her head buried in a wedding magazine or staring out the window, her gaze fixed solidly on the middle distance; an attitude that made the situation all the more humorous. It was only when the little girl turned and said, 'Mummy...?' did the woman react by pushing both children hurriedly into the next compartment.

My walk from the station was equally as pleasant as the train journey. Faces I recognised from my previous visits smiled and bid me good day as I strolled along rue du Général Moulin. Their politeness made me feel less of a stranger and more a part of their everyday life in this part of the town. A few lesser known faces also bid me well as we passed each other. I supposed my friendship with the good doctor and my frequent visits to his home had given me some degree of recognition in the vicinity. Having said that, I have always enjoyed the formality of the French. Their manners are, at best, impeccable.

When I reached the doctor's villa I had a sense of

something amiss. I had to laugh when I realised that what was missing was the old Citroën DS from the driveway. Whatever next? I thought. Has he actually gone and sold it. I had assumed it was a permanent part of the garden furniture. I couldn't wait to hear what happened to it.

'Monsieur, Monsieur, can I have a word please.' I looked over to the back of the garden and saw François Salerou, one of the doctor's neighbours, who I had been introduced to during an earlier visit. He had stopped cutting his hedge when he saw me.

'Good day, Monsieur Salerou. How are you?' I waved in acknowledgement and walked towards him. 'I see the automobile has gone at last. I doubt you won't be too upset at that.' He nodded repeatedly and quickly as if he wanted to say something else.

'Monsieur Gil-Martin. Please excuse me if I am saying something you already know.'

'No, please say what it is that's on your mind,' I replied.

'You've heard about the doctor, about what happened. She would have phoned you, no doubt, and explained to you...'

'No, heard what? Who was to phone me?'

Monsieur Salerou looked apologetic.

'What is it, man?' His anxiety made me feel nervous and a bit desperate. 'Who would've phoned me? What's happened to Doctor Bricard? What has happened? Tell me, Monsieur Salerou. I don't know.'

'Jean-Paul is dead. He died a week ago. He's already buried. I thought when I didn't see you at the funeral she might not have told you. I told Madame Salerou that very thing. His friend would have come to the funeral; I bet he doesn't know yet. She had the car towed away two days ago. The house is locked up. She says she is going to refurbish the house and move in.'

'Who is saying all this?'

'His daughter, Marie-Clémentine. She was his only child. She's a full-grown woman now, of course, but never came by that often. Poor Jean-Paul, she was a handful!'

I was stunned. Dr Bricard was dead! I had only spoken to him the weekend before last when I was making the arrangement to visit this very day. I couldn't take it in. I shook my head in disbelief.

'How did he die, François? What happened? Was it an accident?'

No, no, he died peacefully sitting in his chair here in the garden, next to his beloved lemon tree. His heart just gave out. It was Madame Salerou who noticed he had slept longer than he normally did. He was in the habit of having a nap after lunch. She called on him but he didn't answer. Then she called on me and I went over the fence just here, where we are standing right now. I knew he had gone before I reached him. He was sitting so peacefully. He had a little smile on his lips. He was one of the kindest men I knew. A true gentleman. I will miss him sorely.'

I felt a little calmer at the news that he had slipped away peacefully. François invited me to join him in his home where, he said, he could explain everything better and raise a glass or two of good cognac to the doctor's memory.

Monsieur Salerou told me everything he knew about Dr Bricard and his daughter, Marie-Clémentine. My first surprise was that the doctor's daughter was the same woman in the Musée du Vieux Montmartre who had put me in touch with Jean-Paul in the first place. Maybe I should have guessed there was a connection, but it didn't happen.

According to François, she brought no end of trouble to Jean-Paul when she was a teenager. The gendarmes were always knocking on his door about some complaint or other, or bringing her home when she got into trouble. No one could understand how Jean-Paul, as a noted psychologist, could not bring his daughter under control.

The gendarmes were always sympathetic to the situation and never took her to the commissariat. This made her all the angrier. Then one day she left to stay with an aunt, the sister of Jean-Paul's late wife, Adélaïde. The aunt lived in Brest and was married to a naval man. When Marie-Clémentine was next seen in Pierrefitte-Sur-Seine she was a sullen, morose women in her early twenties, with nothing good to say about anyone. Whatever had happened with her aunt may have brought her into line, but her personality had not improved. She rarely spoke to anyone in town and ignored Jean-Paul for most of the time.

Not long after she returned she got married. No one had ever seen her with a boy at her side but, sure enough, she had met the boy locally – a postman – and made Jean-Paul agree to the marriage, which took place some weeks later in Paris. The young couple moved into rooms just off the rue de Caulaincourt. In some respects Jean-Paul was relieved that she had found some happiness in her life, but he had hoped their relationship would have been different when she returned from Brest. It wasn't. He blamed himself and would say to his friends that he had failed Marie-Clémentine and Adélaïde. That's when he began to drink. Everyone noticed. It was so unlike him – he was an expert on alcohol, after all! At first he'd sit in the garden with a glass of wine; then a bottle would appear on the little wooden table; then another bottle would be brought out before he fell asleep in that old chair of his.

Sometimes he slept through a rainfall. No one ever said anything, but he knew everyone knew.

The only time he ever saw his daughter was when she was short of money. Her visits were always short. She wouldn't stay for dinner—always had somewhere else to go. It broke his heart, but what can a father do?

Then she left her husband. They had hardly been married a year before she turned up in Pierrefitte looking for a place to stay. According to Jean-Paul, his son-in-law had been hitting her. What was a girl to do when she was married to a man like that? No one in the town believed this story, as the boy had never been known to lift his hands to anyone ever before and, besides, he had an easy going nature by all accounts and, even if he had hit her, he must have been sorely tempted.

François had the generosity of spirit to admit that he may have coloured his account due to his distaste of Marie-Clémentine Bricard. It was an understandable confession on his part. He had stood witness to his dear friend and neighbour suffering the trials and tribulations of parenthood. He had been guilty of loyalty to someone he admired and respected. He had no family of his own.

There was little to add from this point on. François saw little of Marie-Clémentine over the intervening years, and Jean-Paul spoke little of her. Of the occasions that François ran into Marie-Clémentine on her rare visits to her father, he considered her behaviour arrogant and distant; a woman to be avoided at all costs.

François gave me directions to the local cemetery. I promised him that I would look in the next time I was in town. I thanked him and left a sadder man. I took a taxi to the cemetery and asked the driver to wait. I found Jean-Paul's grave and placed a small wreath that I purchased at the cemetery gates on his grave. There was no headstone yet. I promised myself that I would come back in a few weeks' time and pay my respects properly and see what his daughter had arranged as a fitting tribute to her father.

19

Pigalle revisited

In love, the chase is better than the catch.
Étienne Pasquier

The Musée du Vieux Montmartre at 12 rue Cortot is not too far uphill from where the Lapin Agile Cabaret sits on what is said to be the most visited street corner in Paris. The entrance to the museum is through a pavilion archway. Utrillo had a studio in the upper floor of the pavilion in 1906. His mother, Suzanne Valadon, Auguste Renoir and Raoul Dufy also used the pavilion as a studio.

Marie-Clémentine Bricard wasn't on duty in the museum when I visited shortly after my visit to Pierrefitte. Another woman, much smaller and friendlier, with a bouncing name-badge of 'Nanette', explained that she was still on bereavement leave. This surprised me. I didn't imagine the bold, cold Marie-Clémentine as the sad, grieving daughter; and, with her father buried, there didn't seem much point in her not returning to work.

The smiling Nanette told me, after a little confusion on my part, that Madam Bricard was known by her married name of Tréhot. I couldn't recall if François had told me this, but I thanked Nanette anyway and, after a little persuasion, the friendly little woman gave me Marie-Clémentine Tréhot's telephone number, on the proviso that I didn't say it was she who had given it to me. This I gladly promised.

I was determined to meet Jean-Paul's daughter and made

my way to the nearest bar to call her. She answered almost immediately. I explained who I was (she remembered) and that I was hoping to meet her to convey my condolences and discuss the work I was doing with her father. To my surprise, once again, she agreed and told me to meet her in a bar that sat at the foot of the steps from rue Drevet that opened onto the rue Des Trois Freres. I had a rough idea where it was and, after another café noir, set off to find it. Thankfully it was downhill from the butte.

I've drunk in many bars all over the world, but few smaller than that of the choice of Marie-Clémentine Tréhot. It was small; really tiny. Three people standing drinking made it seem busy. Two men my size filled it to capacity. The only other bar that I can recall being so small was a little gem just off Glasgow Cross: you had to go outside the bar every time the barman needed to go down the trap door to the cellar.

I managed to sit myself on a chair facing the door looking out on to the curve on the street ahead of me. I was a few minutes early. The street was busy enough for late afternoon. I must have watched a few hundred people of all persuasions pass by before I spotted Jean-Paul's daughter approaching the bar. The woman can walk, I told myself. She knew it too, and more than a few men's heads turned as she cut her swathe through them.

She recognised me instantly and started talking the moment she stepped over the threshold.

'Get me a glass of dry white wine, please. Not the puerile stuff on the shelf. Gaston keeps better stuff in the back room. Tell him it's for me.' She sat in the seat opposite me and lit two cigarettes.

'Certainly, Madame Tréhot. Or can I call you Marie-Clémentine?' I had turned away from her. She didn't reply. As

I approached the bar the barman winked then nodded to me in acknowledgement before stepping into the back room. He had clearly heard the instruction. A few moments later he returned to our table with two glasses of wine.

'Madame, Monsieur, voila, merci.

'Call me Marie, Mr Gil-Martin. It's been a long time since I used the name my parent's christened me with.'

'Of course, Marie. I apologise, and please, call me John. Let's not stand on ceremony. After all, we have much to discuss.'

'Monsieur Gil-Martin, you may have much to discuss, but I do not. I agreed to meet you because you knew my father. I respect that and I was interested to find out what kind of man you are. I do not know any men from your country, so I am intrigued a little bit. Let us get to know each other before we discuss what it is you want to discuss. My father died last week. I do not pretend to be grieved by his passing. There are things you do not know about my family. To you, he was a kind old man who regaled you with stories about a great painter that everyone's now forgotten; of times when la butte was the place to be. But I did not see him like that. I knew something different. So you see, Jean...pardon... John, I am not of a mind to discuss Jean-Paul Bricard before I know more about the man who wants to know.'

She never once took a breath. I'd swear on it. Yet, I had drunk my wine and smoked my cigarette by the time she finished. She called to the barman, Gaston, 'More wine, please.' and offered me another Gaulois.

I declined the cigarette and eased myself back into my seat. 'I accept your conditions, Madame. Let's drink to a meeting of minds.'

'That remains to be seen, monsieur.' She lifted her glass.

'Enchanté, John. To us...'

Our conversation stayed on safe ground for the remainder of our drink, then Marie suggested we go to a bar she knew where we could talk in private. I accepted readily. I was enjoying this assignation. It was all part of my research. What harm could it do?

We wandered into streets I had never visited before, streets that bore the signs of distress, human distress. All around me were the remnants of rot. This was social stagnation, the likes of which I had never seen before. The scenes reminded me of a description by George Orwell in *Down and out in Paris and London*, where he said he lived on a 'very narrow street – a ravine of tall, leprous houses, lurching towards one another in queer attitudes, as though they had all been frozen in the act of collapse.'

Halfway down an alleyway, filled on one side with putrid garbage, we came to a bar that – had you not known it was there – you would never have found. It bore no evidence on its exterior that it was a public bar; no neon light, no advertisement for wine or spirits and no name of any licensee. It probably didn't exist in any formal or legal basis; just a crusted door on a dilapidated building, long forgotten by the authorities. Inside it defied belief. Its only redeeming features were that it was dark and stale. Everything else about it belonged in those parts of your mind that you try and suppress.

The walls held no decoration or ornamentation. The plaster had long since been removed, no doubt by endless fights and neglect. A curtain – or what remained of it – provided the merest veneer of privacy possible between the bar's toilet and the 'saloon'. Only darkness could protect the modest.

Marie sat down in a booth in the furthest corner. I passed through a thick cloud of smoke to join her.

'I've surprised you, John. I don't think you were expecting this when I suggested we move to somewhere more private.'

'Can I take your word for it that we are safe in this hellhole? I've never seen so many of the damned in one place before.'

'Not many outsiders know of its existence. You won't even find it in your British *Rough Guide to Paris*. It is quite unique, even for Pigalle.'

As my eyes continued to adjust to the darkness I began to pick out a little of what I feared might be around me. In small but cavernous booths sat some of life's forgotten: disfigured faces pocked and scarred, bodies twisted and lame; human debris – or what remained of it – blown in from the gutters and sewers from across the city.

The barman brought two drinks to the table and sat them down without a word. Marie nodded her head towards him.

'What is this?' I said, lifting a glass for closer inspection.

'Absinthe,' was all that Marie said before putting her glass to her lips. I followed suit.

'I brought you here for a reason, John. The people that you see around us are what my father spent his life trying to understand. In here are men and women who live to drink, just like the Utrillo and Modigliani that you so adore and hero-worship. My father was obsessed with every aspect of people like this and their miserable lives. His obsession destroyed our family and what did he achieve? A reputation? A medal? His name in scientific journals? Yes, all of these things. But at a price... You think of my father as a gentle old man, full of grace and generosity. Not to me he wasn't; nor to my mother. To me he was a cruel and unkind father who drove my mother to suicide. Did our good neighbours tell you that? Of course not! He browbeat my mother every day. Nothing she could do was right. He made a fool of her in company, treated her like a servant. She cried every night when he was out. I grew up hating him, hating his every breath. I promised myself I would shed no tears for him, no matter the reason. So, you see, his death is just an end; that's all – an end. I will not make it into anything more than that. He deserved no more. None of this did you know, but now you do. You don't have to take my word for it. Go back to Pierrefitte and ask around. You'll find out I am telling you the truth.'

The cackle of a woman's laugh brought a moment's distraction from Marie's story. I looked over to where the laughter came from and could make out a man and woman in close embrace, the man's hand rummaging about under the woman's skirts – the man frustrated by the layers of rotting material; the woman finding the episode a great amusement. Marie and I both sat quietly for a few moments.

'I am giving the bulk of my father's research papers to the hospital where he worked. You can have his papers on Utrillo in the meantime. There's not really that much; just a couple of boxes. What you saw in his study had been strewn around for years. He kept all his important papers locked away. I don't want any part of his work. His research on Utrillo didn't come to much in the end. He couldn't get the answers he needed. Utrillo was too far-gone too early in his life for any proper research, and that harridan of a wife of his kept my father at arm's length.'

'Your father told me he only met Utrillo a few times. Are you saying he worked on Utrillo in a professional capacity, as a psychologist?'

'Of course he did. My father was visiting psychologist to a

number of sanatoriums around Paris that couldn't afford permanent staff. He met Utrillo when he was a young doctor and Utrillo an old man. He saw him on and off for about ten years, right up to when the old guy died. My father was about twenty-five when he first met the artist. My mother would tell me how my father would curse Utrillo because he could not get any insight from him, and he would curse the old guy's wife as an old whore on the make. This used to make my mother laugh… at my father's discomfort, I mean. It's all in his papers. You'll see I am telling the truth'

Marie waved over to the bar for another two drinks. We were rewarded with another two glasses of absinthe. 'It's all Gaston keeps,' Marie told me. 'He finds there is little call for any other spirit and no one drinks beer or wine in here. So, voila – ordering is easy.'

'His name is 'Gaston' too? You called the last barman Gaston, as well. Is this your name for all the barkeepers in Paris?'

'Of course not! They are cousins. I got to know of this place from the other Gaston. He didn't recommend it, of course; he just mentioned one day that his cousin had a bar down here, and I came in out of curiosity. I couldn't find it at first. But I saw two women leaving from this building quite drunk; so I pushed open the front door and found myself in here. It was fascinating. It took me a few minutes to realise the room was filled with people, all staring at me. I was going to be put out by Gaston, as this was not a safe place for a proper lady, until I told him I knew his cousin well and, besides, I was no lady.'

I was glad of the diversion. I didn't know what to think about what Marie had said about her father. There was too much conflicting detail. And did it matter anyway? I told myself. He had helped me so much and I appreciated it. Nothing I was going to say now was going to change my experience or anything else for that matter, so why bother. Let sleeping dogs lie was my decision.

Marie now said we should leave and go to another place she knew of. I was grateful for this suggestion, as my attention kept on being drawn to the man and woman in the booth across from us. I could work out that the man's hand had now reached where he was trying to get to earlier; and, although I could not see clearly what he was doing, it was evident enough by the woman's moans. Besides, I could feel the effects of the absinthe on top of the wine I had drunk earlier. It was time for some fresh air.

Marie led me back into the world I understood best – or, at least, the fringes of it – as we resurfaced into streets filled with people going about their daily business. I was still thinking of the poor sods back at the bar as we walked in silence. I had no comprehension of the circumstances that take men and women into the levels of depravity I had just witnessed. I realised that any insight I had was merely a glimpse, a flicker of knowledge gained from reading such work as Camus's *La Chute*. I could not imagine that the life the character Jean-Baptiste Clamence found himself in was in any way comparable to the scenes I had just left. I made a mental note to myself to re-read the novel. I wanted to re-examine the process Camus provides us with in Clamence's fall from grace.

20

Marie full of grace

The desire of the man is for the woman, but the desire of the woman is for the desire of the man.
Jean-Paul Sartre

I was glad to be sitting in the foyer of a small but smart hotel just off the boulevard de Rochechouart. I had ordered a large single malt to clean the palate of the taste that lingered from our previous drinks. Marie had gone to speak with someone she knew who worked in the hotel and left me to arrange the drinks. I was beginning to form a different opinion of Marie than the one I had in mind when I spoke with her father's neighbour, François Salerou.

The Marie I was getting to know was a strong-minded and independent woman who was subordinate to no one. Her conversations were always conducted on an equal basis and not littered with the insecurities, or the need for re-assurance, that some women and men inhabit their talk with. I recognised that, to some people, Marie would appear quite masculine in her attitude and approach. Maybe this was how M. Salerou viewed the actions of the young Marie. It was of little or no concern now; merely a source of reference.

Marie returned and picked up her glass of wine. 'Let's go,' she said, turning towards the stairs. Let's go where? I thought, trying to rise and follow her. I caught up with her at the foot of the staircase.

'Where exactly are we going to?' I asked her, as I rested

my arm on the balustrade.

'Where do you think? I've got us a room on the first floor. My friend has sneaked us in for the evening. We have to be out before the night shift manager comes in. He, apparently, doesn't approve of short visits, if you take my meaning. But I'm sure we will be ready by then, don't you?'

I hadn't expected this manoeuvre on Marie's part. It never occurred to me that our meeting would lead to anything more intimate than a handshake. I enjoyed her directness and respected how she presented herself. Her manner and language could be intimidating at times, but it still did not cross my mind that her forwardness would carry into how she manipulated her love life. Suddenly I was aware that at no time was I in control of any of the events that had happened during the last few hours. And even now I was being led in a sphere of sexual negotiation that is normally associated with men. I was being presented with a fait accompli, by a woman who knew what she wanted and how to get it. I raised my glass to her and began to climb the stairs.

Once inside the room we wasted no time in getting naked. We threw ourselves carelessly onto the bed, uninhibited by our recent introduction and, true to the nature and character I had recently discovered, Marie was an assertive lover who was comfortable with all aspects of lovemaking. I also found, to my pleasure during those hours together, that she liked to take the initiative and once or twice introduced me to womanly contact that up till then I had only fantasised about.

As I lay warm in the comfort of satisfaction, Marie turned towards me and, with her elbow supporting her, rested her head on her hand.

'I've enjoyed our time together. It has been fun. You should get the boxes on Utrillo in a couple of days' time. I'll arrange their delivery tomorrow. I hope they're of value to you. And when you've finished with them, would you pass them on to the hospital's research department, to go with the rest of the papers they're getting? Now, I have to get going myself. I'm glad we met. It was good, but let's leave it here. You know what I mean?'

With that Marie was up and dressed and waving goodbye as if it was the most natural thing to do. I lay on the bed, shaking my head and wondering what had happened to me. I was more than bemused. What an incredible woman, I thought, before bursting with laughter. Game, Set and Match to Marie-Clémentine Tréhot.

21

A surprise in the park

Hope is a risk that must be run.
Georges Bernanos

Marie was as good as her word; two days later the two boxes of papers arrived by special delivery. I thought of phoning her to give my thanks but changed my mind. I knew she knew I'd be pleased with her father's papers. And, anyway: she had made her position quite clear when we parted, that she didn't want any residual contact. I poured a coffee instead and opened the boxes. Marie has included a hand-written note detailing where I should send the papers once I had finished with them. I was impressed with her trust. She was taking a gamble.

I spent the rest of the morning going through exercise books, letters, assessment forms, all sorts of medical records, draft speeches, scribbled notes and scraps of paper with ideas and doodles scrawled across the pages. Jean-Paul had kept everything. What he didn't do was keep his papers in any sort of order. I realised I would have a job on my hands just dating the material, before trying to categorise any of it.

While I recognised I had taken on a labour of love, I was exhilarated to have possession of first-hand material between Jean-Paul and Utrillo, or doctor and patient, legally or otherwise. I decided to take myself to the park. My spirits were up and the weather was fine. I would buy a little food on the way from Grandma Moses – my name for an old matriarch who owned a greengrocer shop on the way. The old woman always gave me a few extras 'to keep me healthy,' she said – and anyway, 'big men always need more!' This was said with a girlish smile.

At the park I found my usual bench and unwrapped my assortment of fruit and vegetables. I had no idea what Grandma Moses had given me. Her accent was beyond my ken and no doubt mine was a stranger to her. But we laughed a lot and always parted with a cuddle. She didn't disappoint me.

I broke some bread I had bought earlier and took from my pocket a small plastic container filled with a tasty Merlot I particularly liked from M Bourdan's shop on rue Lecourbe. It was my intention to spend an hour or two reading some of the stories of old Montmartre by Sidonie-Gabrielle Colette, one of my favourite writers and a good source for providing sketches of the streets Utrillo walked on.

Remarkably, this incredibly talented and sensual woman lived her life almost in parallel to the years Maurice Utrillo lived. Colette died a year earlier than Utrillo in 1954. Granted, they knew of each other; but there is no evidence that they ever met. What Colette would have made of this bizarre genius is anyone's guess. I dismissed the thought.

None of the regulars were in the park. I was disappointed. I had hoped to see, at least, the 'dealer' in his regular place, for no other reason than I considered him the most intriguing of my 'park' companions.

My choice of reading material was the rather uninspired-named literary sketch entitled, 'Montmartre Cemetery and Flora and Fauna in Paris' – a piece Colette attributes to November 1913. Never underestimate Colette: she is a writer of genius, especially when you least expect it.

The wine tasted fine, even from a plastic bottle. The bread

was divine and, as usual, my Colette was a source of wisdom, sensibility and understanding. Even with the loss of my usual park compatriots, this was a good day. From my reading I made a mental note to visit the Bois de Boulogne at some future date. Colette's observations of a young girl's revelation had made me laugh. I, too, was on occasion just as short-sighted.

The park was nearly empty when I looked up and surveyed its solid prospect within the confines of some of the most attractive apartments in Paris. This was a good place to be, even if most of its users were only passing through on their way to and from a day's work. My own home city is known as 'The dear green place', due to its preponderance of public parks. I usually try and visit at least one park when I am in a city or large town. A park tells you a lot about a place. Every park in the city of Glasgow is a joy and a source of wonderment. The mighty Glasgow Rangers Football Club was started by four young men having a picnic-lunch in the magnificent Kelvingrove Park in the heart of the city.

I was just about to start reading a small book of essays by Léon-Paul Fargue — another contemporary of Utrillo — whose poems and essays I admit to finding that morning in one of the good Doctor's boxes of papers, when I was distracted by the quietest of voices reaching into my sub-consciousness.

'John. Hello, John. Can I talk with you for a moment?'

Never have I been so taken aback by anyone than I was at that moment in time. I turned quickly. Thérèse was standing in the shadow of a plane tree just a few feet from where I was sitting.

'I'm sorry to disturb you, John, but I needed to speak with you. I guessed you would come here sometime. You always liked this place. Remember? You brought me here once and told me it was your special place. I've been watching out for

146

you every day since you came to my apartment. Please don't be angry with me. I need to talk with you. You were right. We have things to say and I shouldn't have cut you off the way I did that day. Will you listen?'

I was still in a state of shock when she stopped talking. She was the last person I was expecting to meet. I took a breath.

'Thérèse, of course I will talk to you. You startled me just now. Come and sit down.' I took another breath.

'Thank-you. I wanted to explain to you that I felt very bad with myself after you left my flat. If what you said that day was true, then you are not entirely at fault with what happened. But I still think you are a chauvinist pig for not writing back to me. Did you think I was going to act like a hysterical girl? Did you think I was going to arrive on your doorstep, calling you names? Who knows, maybe I would have. I don't know what I would have done. It all seems so long ago now. Yes, I was angry with you back then. But I was angry with myself too. Claude was making my life a misery. He played the part of the victim so well, telling anyone who would listen how I had betrayed him. I didn't know what to do. Everything in my life began to crumble and I couldn't even hit you.'

A slight smile flickered across Thérèse's face. It was a smile of resignation, a smile that said she was tired of carrying her burden through the years. She wanted peace.

'I'm sorry too, Thérèse. What I did was unforgivable. It was immature; the pathetic actions of a man running away from any responsibility, real or imagined. I went into a sort of denial at that time. Our fractious ending rankled with me. I cursed you a lot. I suppose I thought that by not writing back I was teaching you some kind of lesson. I had no idea that you were pregnant.'

'Let's not go there today, John. Maybe we can discuss that

147

another time. It is silly: we have said so little, but I am feeling tired already. I should go now. Maybe we can have another talk sometime. Goodbye, John. Thank-you for listening.'

At that Thérèse rose from the bench. I didn't want her to go right that minute.

'Stay a while yet Thérèse. We could go for something to eat – or a coffee if you like. We have so much to say to each other. Your coming here today is such an opportunity. Let's not waste the chance.'

'Another time, John, but not now. I wasn't sure if coming here was a mistake. I had so much wanted to talk to you about all that happened between us, but it doesn't seem that important now. Forgive me. Today has drained me. Your coming back to Paris has brought to the fore memories I had managed to lock away in the back of my mind. Yes, I am glad I came here today. I'm glad we spoke. But now I want to leave.'

'When do you want to meet? Where? Just say and I'll meet you there.'

'All right, John. Let's say next Saturday, on l'île des Cygnes. It's where we last spoke to each other, remember? Maybe we can pick up from there. You know the time. I'll see you then.' She turned away from me. I called out quickly, trying to keep the moment alive.

'Right. Saturday. I'll be there.'

I watched her until she passed the trees and out through the park gate. She still had that elegant way of walking that combined pride with the allure of a woman who knew men wanted her. I still wanted her and wondered if she, when she walked away, realised that.

22

The black crows' circle

As far as men go, it is not what they are that interests me, but what they can become.
Jean-Paul Sartre

I found this brief sketch among Jean-Paul's papers. It is a fragment of what I think was intended to be a speech or article on the effects of certain types of mental health problems experienced by artists. From my knowledge of Jean-Paul and what I had read on his thinking on this subject, I suspected it was an introduction to his theory that the impact of certain mental health conditions could create the artistic temperament and talent in an individual that would otherwise not have surfaced under normal living conditions.

Jean-Paul had a belief that certain types of mental illness – for example, Asperger's Syndrome, or a variation of it – impacting on that part of the brain that controlled creativity and social accomplishment, would result in one area responding by way of an increased development at the detriment of the other. In other words, the more talented one was, the less socially articulate one would be.

Jean-Paul believed that artists like Utrillo, van Gogh, and Jackson Pollack were social failures who were dependant on alcohol to achieve a social voice, whereas they produced works of genius in their respective fields of art. He thought this applied to others like the Canadian pianist, Glenn Gould, and the chess genius, Bobby Fischer. Whether Dr Bricard is right or wrong, the following transcript of a scribbled note on the back of a paper on the effects of autism is worthy of reproduction here.

Artists like Utrillo and van Gogh lived all their lives with substantial psychological problems. It is well recorded that Vincent van Gogh was an extremely difficult man to be with. His manic depression presented in violent and unpredictable mood swings. His tempers manifested in bouts of extreme anger, cantankerousness and contrariness. He could become passionate and withdrawn. A man out of control; a danger to himself and those around him.

Yet at the heart of this clever, clever artist was a desire for love and contentment. He depicted this longing in his later paintings — drab landscapes became filled with vivid colour signifying his desire for happiness, starry-night skies and lantern-strung streets filled paintings with elemental romance. As time moved on, his colours became even stronger, the outlines bolder. He began to use black paint to envelop and lift his foreground subjects from their background. This was a lonely man who expressed his ultimate dream of happiness in his paintings and possibly predicted his own tragic end in one of his final paintings.

Utrillo had no such aspirations, but his paintings reveal just as much about his state of mind as those of van Gogh's. For Utrillo the skies were often grey and overcast. Only rarely did he colour his sky blue. For the most part he painted walls. All types of walls. Walls on houses, factory walls, streets of walls, some converging, others not. Utrillo was a painter of dead-ends and culs-de-sac, a painter whose streets turn into blind corners. Here is a man whose turbulent life offered no hope of a future; a man trapped in a troubled mind with no view or interest of what was to come.

Utrillo feared people. He mistrusted their actions; they abused his weaknesses. And when he introduced figures to his paintings of once empty streets, they appear as grotesque caricatures. Men are shown as insignificant slight figures, women as fat, broad-beamed, ugly harridans. Yet, at his peak, secluded in his small studio, free of the people that tormented him, he captured a beauty, on canvas after canvas, of those back streets in Montmartre; a beauty and magnificence that no artist since has achieved to the same acclaim.

While this brief note could not establish one way or another if artists like Utrillo had a mild form of autism – and, in my view, this is not the case with Utrillo or Van Gogh – there is now a great deal of evidence available that some men and women of great creative skills do indeed have a form of autism; usually Asperger's Syndrome. Unfortunately, it is not always easy to research such cases without the compliance of the individual, and getting this agreement is easier said than done.

23

A sense of loyalty

Now and again it's good to pause in our pursuit of happiness and just be happy.
Guillaume Apollinaire

Saturday wouldn't come quick enough. I couldn't get thoughts of Thérèse out of my mind. She had aged, certainly, and wore the countenance of a woman who had experienced hardship, but she still had the beauty and character of a once magnificent woman. I was struck by how much our last meeting had affected me. I tried to equate my feelings for Yvette against how I was reacting to Thérèse. There was no rational conclusion to my deliberations: my emotional self was in the ascendancy; logic was coming in a poor second in this particular mental battle.

I decided not to wrestle with such thoughts; nothing good would come from it. Both ladies were separate entities in my life and neither held a primary place in my calculations. I had work to do that was proceeding well and nearing completion with regard to a first draft of the book. Thérèse and Yvette would have to wait. After all, it wasn't as though there was a choice on offer with a deadline to meet. I was seeing Yvette; we were possibly a couple looking to see if we could be a pair. I was rankled at what Pascal had told me. I hadn't spoken to Yvette about this revelation. I had made the decision that I would wait till she contacted me; after all, we had only recently exchanged telephone numbers. I didn't even know where she lived! We had never got round to discussing it. Pascal had irritated me, and I admit I was taken aback by his news. I had half-expected Yvette to get in touch, but, typical of the woman, I had heard nothing from her.

Thérèse was a diversion from the past, albeit an attractive one that I needed to make amends with; no more, no less. And, anyway, I was making arrangements to fly to London in the next few weeks to meet with my editor and designer. They were keen to start their part in the book's process.

There was another important event on my immediate horizon that had to be dealt with before anything else. I had been invited to take part in a discussion on my prospective book in an arts programme on Radio France. I was to be part of a fifteen-minute debate on the relevance of the written biography in today's new age of mass communication. I had agreed to this solely to promote my forthcoming book, and to remind France of the genius of Utrillo.

Like the rest of Europe and North America, France had fallen into the trap of categorising Art into one school of thought or another. Painters of the calibre of LS Lowry in Britain and Utrillo in France were being sorely neglected because they didn't fit easily into a convenient academic stratification. Try buying a book on Maurice Utrillo in London, Edinburgh or Cardiff. It is mission impossible. You might be a tad more fortunate with Lowry.

The radio programme was my chance to take on the critics and academics at their own game. At no time in the history of Art did its significant contributors create their masterpieces to conform to current academic thinking. Impressionism was named after Monet had painted his 'Impression of a Sunset', not before it! To ignore an Art form simply because it doesn't fit neatly into one or more cosmetically and artificially named boxes speaks volumes about those who proclaim to have a profound understanding of the very subject. The coming computer age would free Art from the shackles of the big publishers and let those with eyes see for themselves. I was up for a fight!

I was still musing over these matters when the phone rang. It was Yvette.

'Speak of the devil,' I told her.

'Excuse me!'

'It's a saying we have back home when we are thinking or talking about someone and they appear – or, in your case, telephone.'

'I hope you were thinking good things.'

'Of course.'

'Are you sure? Pascal told me he let slip my husband was back in Paris.'

'Yes, he did. But it didn't sound like a slip to me. I thought he took great pleasure in telling me. I'm afraid Pascal and I will never be best friends.'

'He's jealous of you, John; and a little protective of me too.

'Let's not talk about him; it gets my back up. What's happening with you? I had hoped you would have got in touch with me earlier. to let me know about your husband's return. I didn't like hearing it from a waiter.'

'I'm sorry, John. It all happened so quickly, and I was working nights at the hospital. I intended to phone you; then Edouard wanted to meet me, and I thought it best to speak with him first and see what he wanted before I spoke to you. Believe me, I wasn't trying to shut you out. I was trying to do the right thing.'

Yvette had decided she would come with me to the radio station, so that we could go on to a little bar she knew not far from there to talk about her and Edouard. She wanted to explain how things stood, now that her husband was back in Paris. I was still angry that she hadn't told me about his arrival. She was angry that Pascal had spoken out of turn, as it was her intention to explain recent events rationally – in context – as she put it. We were both a bit upset.

We agreed to meet outside the imposing building that is home to Radio France on the riverside. Her presence at the radio station put me at a disadvantage. I found myself thinking about what I wanted to say to her, when I should have been concentrating on the imminent interview. I needn't have worried: as it turned out, the interview went well and Marcel Maloret, the programme's host, was sympathetic to my argument. He, too, felt that there was too much classification and stratification in the world of art literature, that many good artists didn't get the attention they deserved because they didn't fit in to a particular style of painting and that some lesser artists got too much attention only because they were part of an accepted school of painting.

I made my own position clear: writers had little to fear from new technologies. Instead, we should embrace its progress, as more and more people across the world would get the chance to see Art that wasn't pigeon-holed by bird-brained historians. Monsieur Maloret could have argued some of my points but chose not to. When I left the radio station, I was feeling pleased with myself: I had spoken to the French nation!

As we walked to the bar, Yvette pointed out a few mistakes I had made in translation and pronunciation. This deflated my puffed-up chest and I began to wonder if I had misrepresented myself on air. Yvette assured me I had not. My next thoughts suggested that her criticisms were a ploy to put me off-guard for what was going to be a difficult conversation ahead. I looked towards her, searching for a sign of her guilt, but she looked so innocent and beautiful in the evening light.

I tried to dismiss these notions as we entered the bar on the north side of rue de Ranelagh. I resisted asking her if she knew the barman and if he came from her village. Now was not the time to express petty jealousies. We sat at a corner table next to the window. Yvette was concerned that I would take news of Edouard's arrival as a threat to our new found relationship. As far as she was concerned, Edouard had failed her and would not be a part of her future. She had hoped to deal with this before explaining to me that he was back in France. Apparently, he had no intention of living in Paris and was re-locating to a private hospital in the French Riviera. His stay in Paris was a mere detail, to sort out some papers and to ask for a divorce. At this Yvette eyes began to water. I asked why she was crying. Surely this was good news for her. She owed him no favours after all that he had done to her.

'I know, I am being silly, but I'm sad too. I loved the man and thought I had a good marriage. I think a woman takes divorce differently from a man. I don't know. I'm just guessing. It's never happened to me before. I've got a lot of mixed feelings. Please forgive me. Everything is fine. Excuse me.'

Yvette dried her eyes and went to the rest room to tidy her make-up. When she returned, she was full of ideas and joked about my broadcast to the nation. I took from this change of mood that the subject of her resurrected husband was now closed. I let it pass and joined in her teasing of my interview. My chest puffed out again. All was well with my world.

24

In a once forgotten island

Nothing fixes a thing so intensely in the memory as the wish to forget it.
Michel de Montaigne

At the Grenelle bridge end of l'île des Cygnes stands the Statue of Liberty. She looks far out along the Seine, past the working barges and boats that haul coal and other minerals into the heart of the city, towards her more famous sister across the Atlantic in New York Harbour. She has turned her back on the island she calls home, with its narrow rows of trees and benches, since 1937. Before then, she had stood proudly facing east towards the Eiffel Tower since her inauguration in 1899.

I had all but forgotten the island's existence until Thérèse had mentioned it in the park. Now I was standing at the walkway at pont de Bir-Hakeim, ready to cross into the unknown. The bridge was originally named the pont de Passy (after the former commune of Passy). It was renamed in 1948 to commemorate the Battle of Bir Hakeim, fought by Free French forces against the Nazi Afrika Korps in 1942. As I made my way across, I wasn't feeling very heroic.

The island's only walkway is known as l'allée des Cygnes. It is 850 metres long and tunnels its way through heavy foliage. Starlings swoop down at you, head-height, like kamikaze pilots; then veer off at the last moment, much to everyone's relief. I found Thérèse sitting near the statue. She was flicking through a magazine as I approached. Thankfully, no one was sitting beside her. I sat down. At that moment I was filled with a rush of passion and wanted to grab hold of her. Instead I said how nice the morning was. She concurred and put the magazine down in the space between us.

'I wasn't sure you'd come, so I brought a magazine to read, just in case.'

'Did you think I would run out on you again? I can live with that. As you said in the park, it was here that we last spoke to each other before I left for Glasgow. You weren't best pleased with me that day and stormed off, but that was twelve years ago.'

'I'm sorry. John, I didn't mean my words to imply what you thought. I didn't mean anything by it. It was just a passing comment about a silly magazine. Let's start again.'

'I'm sorry too. I suppose we're both a bit tense this morning. If we get nothing else out of our meeting, let's at least leave as friends.'

'Let me start our conversation, John. I've given a lot of thought to what I want to say this morning. I've had a lot of time to think about it.'

Thérèse had turned towards me, facing me directly. I followed suit, holding her eye contact. Then our knees accidentally touched and both of us jumped a little to one side. Thérèse laughed first.

'Now we are behaving like silly teenagers on our first date.'

We re-adjusted ourselves into roughly the same position as before, but with a little added space between us. This time Thérèse didn't make eye contact but stared into the middle distance as she thought for the words she had rehearsed for this day.

'When you left to return to Scotland, it didn't occur to me that I wouldn't see you again for twelve years. I thought that, after a few weeks had passed, we would've both calmed down and realised how much we missed each other. I knew you weren't contactable by phone, so I wrote to you, telling you that I was wrong to try and keep you in Paris. When you didn't reply, I was angry with you. I was sure you were just trying to prove a point… you know… being a man. At the same time, I realised that I might be pregnant. I was fraught with worry. My gynaecologist confirmed my worst fears. I was pregnant, right enough. She was a good friend and realised from my reaction to the news that the baby wasn't Claude's, and was decent enough to suggest she could help – if my health deteriorated. I knew what she meant.'

Thérèse was reaching into herself to relate her story. I could see the pain on her face as she recounted each detail. Her eyes kept staring into the middle distance. At no time did she acknowledge my presence. It was as though she had no control over her words. She was almost robotic. Each word spoken followed the other in semi-rote fashion. She was unburdening herself of a great weight and could not stop mid-stream.

'I decided I had to go to Glasgow and find you. I wanted you to know about the baby – our baby – but I never got the chance. I wrote to you explaining what had happened and how I desperately wanted to talk to you. Foolishly, I did not conceal my letter but left it on my bedside table. When I returned home that evening, Claude was in a rage. He had my letter in his hand, waving it about, calling me names and screaming he would disgrace me. There was nothing I could say or do. Like a schoolgirl I just cried and cried as he went on and on with his threats.'

It was my inclination to put my arm around her as tears began to run down her face. A few passers-by looked in our direction before moving on.

'Claude was true to his word. He did everything that was humanly possible to hurt me. He said he was going to go to Glasgow and kill you. I begged him to leave you alone, that you didn't want to know me, that you had ignored my letters. This made him all the angrier. Anything I said or did just made him angry. He said he would ruin me. And he did. I promised I would do anything he wanted if he would leave you out of it. He was going to track down which hospital you worked in and do as much damage to you as possible. He claimed he knew a few microbiologists in Scotland.

'I had to move out of our home. He had arranged a small flat for me that was sparsely furnished. I found out later, to my embarrassment, that it was a love nest for someone he knew. My two children, who were both at boarding schoo,l wouldn't meet with me to hear my side of the story.

'I was distraught, but Claude was not finished with me yet. I quickly realised that certain people at the Institute knew of our... of my situation. I was interviewed by the Vice-Director, who advised me that, if it wasn't for Claude's good reputation and regard, he would dismiss me on the spot. I had breached my professional code and brought the Institute into disrepute. However, I was to confine myself to my office until such time as other duties could be found for me. I was told he was disgusted with me, that I had acted like a bitch in heat and had betrayed more than just my husband. Then he had the blind nerve to suggest that, if I laid low for a while and did his bidding, so to speak (at this he put his hand on my knee), he would see to it that I didn't lose all my privileges.

'I was trying to deal with everything at once. I was beside myself with worry. Claude had said he would ruin me and nearly did. While I was shunned by family, friends and colleagues alike, I still tried to maintain a dignity about me and told myself that life would get better. Then, one evening, I answered my door to Claude. He never asked how I was doing; nor did he sit down. He only had a few moments, so he had to be quick. He then presented me with his final ultimatum. I had to lose the baby.

'If only I could live that part over again, I would never have gone through with it. I was disorientated from all of my anchors in life. Nothing made sense any more. I went to see my gynaecologist and she arranged everything. It was all very discreet. It was the worst decision of my life. I'm sorry, John, but twelve years ago I had nothing and no one to reach out to. It seemed the right thing to do; the only thing to do. It would be one less problem to deal with. How I regret what I did! I had reduced myself to the point of nothingness. I was devoid of finer human feelings and expression. I had let myself become a victim and, like many other victims, I began to act accordingly. It was hardly discernible at first, but by the end of the year I was immersed in tragedies, not all of my own making.

'Looking back, I had reached my nadir but was completely unaware of it at the time. I drank more than was sensible; a lot more. I justified these actions by mitigation. I cursed you for being a coward. I cursed everyone. Other people had put me in this predicament. I thought I could cope in spite of them, but I wasn't ready for what happened on one particular evening. I had taken a bath and was curled up on the sofa in only my dressing gown and with a bottle of cheap cognac by my side. By this time my salary was severely reduced to reflect my new and pointless duties. It was late and I had reached that point when vision becomes slightly blurred with too much alcohol but one's mood dismisses the condition as an irrelevance anyway. Then I thought I heard the door to the flat being opened with a key but ignored it. I was feeling warm inside and all my demons seemed far away at that moment.

'It was only when the door to my living room opened and two men walked in that I realised what was happening. One of the men told me he was the owner of the flat. He was a friend of a friend of Claude and had been working in America and Germany for the best part of the year and hadn't realised I was still staying in the flat. I was still lying on the sofa at this point and tried to get up, but I was a little too drunk to manage it easily. We all laughed at my efforts. I made one more effort to swing my legs round and push up, without realising for a moment or two that I had caught one side of my dressing gown under my thigh. And when I pushed up, I exposed my top half to the men. I tried to cover myself up. But when I did this, the bottom half of the dressing gown opened up and I think they saw the rest of me.

'Nothing happened for a few minutes, as I remember it. They helped me sit up and one of them got another two glasses and poured out the remains of the cognac. They sat either side of me laughing and talking. I think I laughed too. Then one of the men, the owner of the flat I think, slipped his hand inside my dressing gown and massaged my breasts. I tried to stop him but felt another hand push down between my legs. I don't know what I thought at the time, but I do remember they both had sex with me. I don't remember much else that happened that evening, but when I woke the next day they were gone. The owner left a note telling me I had a week to get out of the flat.'

I sat in stunned silence. Mixed emotions surged through my veins. Anything I said would trivialise the events I had just heard for the first time. I wondered if Emile Renouf knew this detail. No doubt he did. I recognised my part in the tragedy, my contribution in a beautiful woman's downfall. Twelve years ago I had trivialised our relationship by my actions, considered it a learning experience and thought no more of it. Was Thérèse right when she called me a coward? Of course she was. I had used and abused her. I was no better than the two men who raped her.

We both sat quietly. No doubt Thérèse had her own thoughts as she remembered the past. I certainly did. I wanted to reach out to her, take her hand, tell her I cared. Instead, I stared out along the river, watching the barges unload coal and other materials. I could hear the bargemen's laughter in the distance. Did the men who raped Thérèse laugh? Was it just a bit of fun to them? I felt ashamed and at a loss for words. What could a man say at a time like this? What could I say? I was spared having to do anything by Thérèse. Something or someone had caught her eye.

'Do you see that man over on the walkway? I think he just took a photograph of us.' Thérèse was pointing towards a medium-built man walking away with his back to us.

'I'm sure I've seen that man before, but I can't think where.'

'Are you sure he was taking our picture? He could've been taking a photograph of the statue.'

'No, I'm sure it was us. He was acting furtively. That's what drew my attention to him. I wish I could remember where I've seen him before.'

As I watched the man hurry away I didn't have the same doubts as Thérèse. I knew where I had seen him before and, more so, knew his name. It was Vil Delouche.

25

A bolt from the blue

The more one judges, the less one loves.
Honore de Balzac

My work continued at an acceptable pace. I had thought when Dr Bricard died that I would struggle to retain the intimacy in my writing that he provided so much of on those peaceful afternoons in Pierrefitte. My work did not suffer, as many of the papers I found in the boxes Marie gave to me were written in a similar intimate style. Quite often, as I read a passage or two, I could hear the good doctor's voice filling the room as if he was reading aloud from over my shoulder. It was my intention to dedicate the book to his memory.

In all the time I have lived in this tiny apartment I could count on one hand the number of times my doorbell has rung; so I was quite surprised a few days later after seeing Thérèse when its grating noise broke my concentration. Unfortunately there is no intercom to allow me to find out who is calling on me before I open the downstairs door. I ambled down the stairway, annoyed at being disturbed and deliberately taking my time as a form of punishment for the guilty person intruding on my private time.

On reaching the front door, I called out 'Who is it?' To my surprise I heard the reply, 'It's me, Yvette. I need to see you.' I opened the door and Yvette brushed past, heading for the stairs. She looked upset and was clutching a large brown envelope in her hand. I passed her on the stairs and led her to the top floor. Neither of us spoke. She entered my apartment with a degree of hesitation. This was the first time she had been here. I hoped I had made the bed.

'Don't bother with any courtesies; I'm not in the mood. I've come straight here. Look at these and tell me what's going on.'

Yvette threw down the brown envelope she had been carrying. I leaned over to pick it up from the sofa. 'At least sit down, will you?' I was trying to remain calm. Floods of tears were running down Yvette's face.

'I'd rather stand, if you don't mind.' Her voice was trembling.

I opened the envelope and pulled out a photograph of Thérèse and me sitting on a bench. Three other photographs were similar, but the last one portrayed the pair of us as if we were kissing. I knew that whatever I said at this precise moment could ruin everything between Yvette and myself, so I said nothing initially. I put the photographs slowly and neatly back into the brown envelope, took a breath, and then said in a slow and deliberate manner: 'These photographs were taken by a private detective by the name of Vil Delouche. He took them last Saturday morning at l'île des Cygnes. The woman in the photographs is Dr Thérèse Dumard – or, as she prefers to call herself now, Thérèse Velpau-Mauriac. We were meeting to discuss a matter private to ourselves that occurred over a decade ago. You will find her personal details in the top drawer of the desk. Her telephone number is there too. By all means phone her and ask her any questions you like. I'm going to make myself a coffee.'

'Don't you dare move from that spot, John Gil-Martin. By the looks of those photographs, especially the last one, your private matter is still going on.'

'Yvette, there is nothing going on between Thérèse Dumard and me – nothing at all. I'm just disappointed that you felt the need to spy on me, and in such a sordid way too! The lady in those photographs would never stoop so low!'

'I didn't spy on you; Edouard did! He gave me the photographs. He said you and she were lovers.'

This time I did go to the kitchenette, but not for coffee. I lifted an already opened bottle of Burgundy and two glasses and went and sat down on the sofa. I put the two glasses down on the coffee table and poured equal measures of the red wine into each of them.

'Stand if you prefer Yvette, but you'll be more comfortable sitting on a chair, no matter what I tell you. And I for one prefer to hear my bad news sitting down. The choice is yours.'

Yvette sat down and took one of the glasses of wine. We were both quiet for a moment. Logic told me that she should start in the first instance to explain the how and why of the photographs. I knew Thérèse and I had been photographed by Vil Delouche, because he had been clumsy in his work, but I didn't know who had paid him. Emile Renouf had no motive, or none that I could think of. In my book that just left Pascal. We hadn't hit it off and we both admitted to not liking each other, so he was my front runner. Edouard was too new to the scenario; but, then again, he could have been checking out the terrain around Yvette before he came home, and Monsieur Delouche was, after all, in the phonebook. No, this was Pascal's work; I was sure of it. He had the motive, the opportunity and Edouard was the weapon he used. I spoke first.

'Yvette, I've made many a mistake in my life, but this is not one of them. What we have together is good, and I'm not that foolish to ruin it in this way. What I am going to say next is very important to me and I hope it is important to you as well.

I'm not having an affair with anyone at the moment; not with Thérèse Dumard or anyone else. I'm not even sure if we are a romance. But I will tell you this: I once was deeply in love with Thérèse Dumard. Yes, we were lovers; passionate lovers. But I acted like a fool and ruined much of her life. What you see in those photographs are two people, sitting down in an out-of-the-way-place, trying to put together pieces in a very cruel jigsaw. It's ironic, but when we parted last Saturday we shook hands. We didn't arrange to see each other again, but I hope we do. In the few weeks that I have known that women again my respect for her has soared. How she can be civil to me is a mystery. But I am grateful for it. I owe her so much. I doubt you would understand.'

'John, I am so sorry. I saw those photographs and Edouard said he knew for a fact that my 'lover-boy' was two-timing me. I just reacted. I've been so hurt in the past that I didn't know what to believe. I just grabbed the photographs and came here. I wanted to hit you.'

'Did you not stop to consider how your husband got these photographs so quickly? I don't suppose for a moment that my name appeared high on your agenda of all the matters you and he had to discuss since his return. If truth be told, Yvette, I would imagine I am a footnote in your recent history. No, Yvette; someone else supplied your estranged husband with these bullets to fire.' I pointed down to the brown envelope lying on the coffee table. 'Now who do you suppose that can be?' I oozed sarcasm, but I don't think Yvette read it like that.

'Oh, my God! It never occurred to me that Pascal would do this. We've been such good friends down through the years, and he never really got on with Edouard. But why would he do such a thing to me now? We are all friends. He has a girlfriend. Why would he want to hurt me – and you?'

'I can't answer all the questions that this little scenario presents to us. I'm just glad that no one – meaning us – has been hurt by his jealousy.'

'What do you mean jealousy? Pascal and I are like brother and sister. We don't think like that. We have never seen each other in that way.'

'You might not have seen it like that, but let me assure you your country 'brother' does not share your views. He's a man and he wants you, in the same way as I want you. The difference is he doesn't know how to get you!'

'And you do, John?'

I knew a challenge when it slapped me in the face. I lifted myself from the sofa and took her by the arms and lifted her to her feet.

'I do Yvette, and it is about time you knew it.'

I kissed her as passionately as my heart knows how. Her arms cradled my body intensely, her hands running over the contours of my back. With ease I gently arched my back, lifting her feet off the floor, and, while still holding her within my arms, I carried her towards my bedroom. Thankfully, I had made the bed.

26

A bird in the hand...

Women are always eagerly on the lookout for any emotion.
Stendhal

Making love to a beautiful French woman is one of the finest of life's experiences. They have a passion and elegance not often found in other women. The memory of my first night with Yvette will stay with me for the rest of my life. Sometime during the night, between laughter and loving, Yvette asked me not to seek out Pascal. It was her responsibility to deal with him. She argued that my involvement would only make matters worse. I was in no position to argue; nor had I the breath.

We agreed to meet later that day. She had a busy schedule in the afternoon at the hospital, but before that she would see Pascal. Her husband could wait.

That morning I received two phone calls. One from my editor in London, calling me over for a development meeting, the other was from Emile Renouf. The second I heard his voice my attitude changed. Back came the tensions I had momentarily lost in the arms of Yvette. He was inviting me to attend an Open Day at the institute. He thought I might enjoy seeing the changes he had helped create in 'the old place'. I was to think it over. He left the details and hung-up, as was his way. I was left looking into the telephone receiver.

It is not that often I buy a newspaper in any language, but for some obscure reason that morning I drifted out onto rue

Lecourbe for a paper and a café au lait. I had just eased myself onto my usual bar stool in the corner bar when my eye caught a piece about a shooting in the park in Square Saint Lambert. To my horror I read that a woman had walked up in broad daylight, with witnesses sitting all around the park, and shot dead local businessman, Rene Rousselier. Monsieur Rousselier, I was reliably informed, was a dealer in antiquities and well known in the Montparnasse district. The woman gave herself up to the police and allegedly said 'He had it coming'. At the bottom of the column there was a photograph of the murdered man. It was my 'dealer', the man I nodded to in the park and had seen at the station with the woman in a white coat and red scarf. The paper didn't give the name of the woman who had been arrested and charged with the murder. I had my suspicions.

'I bet it was the woman who always sat in the shadows who shot him.' I said out loud to no one in particular.

'What's that, Monsieur? Do you know the woman who killed Rene?' This was the barkeeper talking.

'No, Jacques. But there was a woman who used to sit on a bench at the far entrance to the park, next to the school. I never saw her face. She was always in the shadow of the large trees there. But I used to imagine her as some mysterious spy or exotic mistress waiting for her lover or next victim.'

Jacques leaned across the bar, his head almost touching mine and said quietly, 'A lot of people had reason to shoot Rene Rousselier, especially a few women around here. He was a brutal man who lent money, dealt in drugs and anything else he could make a franc with. He used the park to do some of his business. He was paranoid about the cops listening in to his 'business' calls. The next time you are in the park, let me know if your mysterious woman is sitting in her usual place?'

A little later I met Yvette at the gates of the hospital where I had left her that night we had first met. She had the air of a woman in love. I told her about my day and the killing of the 'dealer'. She was more interested in the fact that I had bought a newspaper, today of all days, when I don't normally buy one at all.

'We women have an intuition about such things. You were meant to buy a paper today.' I realised she was being serious, so I thought better than to argue with her.

'Did you speak to Pascal earlier? What did he have to say for himself?' I tried not to sound too eager for her reply, but it is hard to sound nonchalant when all you want to do is to knock someone into the middle of next week.

'Yes, I went round to his flat after I left you this morning. He admitted he had hired the detective. He said he did it for my own good, that he was worried for me after what Edouard had done to me. I told him it was none of his business whatsoever, and that I was angry with him for going behind my back and doing such a despicable thing as employing a spy-person to go about checking up on other people's lives. He could have done so much damage to people he didn't know anything about. He begged me to forgive him, but I told him it was not I that he should be begging forgiveness from, but you. He said he would never do that, so I told him it was that or our friendship. The choice was his.'

'What did he say to that?' I was hoping he would throw himself off Pont Neuf and be lost in the Seine forever. But all Yvette would say was that he was thinking about apologising.

Love women or loath them, but never forget they have a way of thinking about life that men will never understand. I looked at Yvette and saw that she was proud of how she had handled the situation. I loved her all the more for it!

We had supper in the Bistro de la Gare and talked of matters of no concern. As we were leaving, Yvette suggested we go to her apartment, as it was closer. At that moment I realised that I didn't know where she lived. It was only recently she had given me her phone number and, before that, I had to wait until she contacted me. Now we were walking arm in arm towards her home. A difficult day was ending on a high. The air was good to breath.

Yvette's apartment was a little bigger than my own, but not by much. It lay just off the boulevard near the traffic lights where we first met. She had managed to make the most of her space by introducing mirrors to great effect. But what surprised me most, and in pride of place above the false mantelpiece, hung a large painting. It was a Utrillo! I was beside myself with joy.

'Look Yvette. A Utrillo. An original Utrillo! '

'Yes, John, I know. I put it there.'

I felt foolish at my inanity. 'Tell me all about it. How did you come by it? It's brilliant! Why didn't you tell me you had a Utrillo in your living room? I'm flabbergasted!'

'I'll tell you all about it in a moment, but first sit down and pay me some attention. It's why I brought you here.'

I was far too taken with the painting on the wall to be interested in small talk, but went through the motions of showing interest and sat down where I could see both Yvette and the painting.

'You never said you had an original Utrillo hanging in your lounge. I don't understand. You know I am writing his history, yet you never mentioned it. Why not? This is a bit strange for me, Yvette… Don't you agree?'

'Certainly not! I knew you would see it one day, whatever happened, but I wanted to see if we were going to become friends first of all. I wanted you to find out this way. I told Pascal not to mention it. If we had not become friends, I would have invited you to come and view it. But as it turns out we did become friends, and now you've got the best of both worlds. You have me and you get to see the painting. What more could you ask for?'

I knew there was logic somewhere in what she said but I was having difficulty tracking it down. By now, Yvette was snuggling into me as we sat on the sofa. I put my arm around her.

'You know I'll have to examine the painting and verify its authenticity. And then I'll have to...'

She put a finger to my lips.

'But not tonight, John. You can start in the morning.'

27

News from the East

The capacity for passion is both cruel and divine.
Aurore Dupin

The discovery of Utrillo's painting of rue Francoeur diverted me from my planned research; and, if truth were told, so did Yvette. I wanted to make love with her at every moment of the day, and quite often we did. I had virtually moved in with her and struggled with her sense of duty when she took herself off to the hospital. I also realised, albeit frustratingly, that I had to return to my own apartment if I was to meet my deadlines.

Reluctantly I did so, calling in to Monsieur Bourdan's fruit shop on the way. He was pleased to see me and had been wondering where I had got to over the last week or so. I explained that research can lead one all over the place and that time was not always your own. He laughed; then winked, telling me that Madame Carńe must have missed me, as she had confided in him that we were 'looking out the same window', as it were. I hurriedly left with my apples.

I was hardly back in my apartment when the phone rang. I was expecting it to be Yvette and answered, 'Hi, Yvette. I made it home after all...', to which a woman's voice replied, 'Well, good for you! I was wondering where you had got to. Remember me? Fiona? Your editor? You were to call me and let me know when you were coming over.'

I had completely forgotten to make arrangements for my

trip to London. I had promised my editor and personal Torquemada, the inimitable Fiona Shaw, that I would come over for a progress meeting. A mere love distraction would not be a suitable excuse.

'Sorry, Fiona, but listen! I found an original Utrillo a week past and have been checking out some facts about it…'

'No doubt with this lady friend, Yvette.' Fiona cut across me.

'Well, that too.' I demurred. I gave her a brief, if not entirely accurate, story of how I discovered the unlisted Utrillo. Any excitement about the painting's discovery was one sided.

'Will I see you soon?'

'You can count on it.'

Fiona Shaw is one of the top editors in the publishing world with a first class reputation, but she can also be a hard taskmaster. She is a beautiful raven-haired woman from my own country, but rarely does she let that interfere with her ambition, and I knew by her tone that she wouldn't call again. I booked a flight to London.

There was one other thing I wanted to do before going to London, and that was to contact Thérèse and arrange another meeting. There were still some matters that I needed to know about, and the sooner the better. My only problem was that I could not find the file Vil Delouche had made for me. I was sure I had left it in the top drawer of the desk, but I must have put it somewhere else for safekeeping and couldn't remember where. This happens frequently to me. Then the phone rang again. It was Emile Renouf.

Whenever I speak to Emile I become hesitant, and today was no exception. I approached with caution telling him I was pleased to hear from him and that it had been a while since we last spoke together. If ever a weasel will be able to speak, it will sound like Emile Renouf. He told me all was well with him and – as he let slip – he was, in reality, now running the Institute by himself since the Director's latest illness. After all, who else could do it? So few had his experience. I agreed wholeheartedly and suggested it was good of him to step into the breach time and again, and that the board of Trustees was lucky to have him. Without a word of protest or embarrassment, he concurred with me absolutely. It was, as he said, only a matter of time until he would be asked to 'take over the reins' permanently. 'No one deserves it more,' I said, without an honest word in the sentence. I was appalled with my own lack of sincerity.

It wasn't like Emile to phone an ex-student and appraise him of his progress, so I was waiting for him to tell me the real reason for his phone call. After a few more mundane exchanges he told me he was phoning to remind me that the Institute was having an Open Day for school leavers to visit the faculties and learn more about the wide range of excellent opportunities available at the Institute. He still thought I would be an ideal person to be there, 'to man a stall' as he put it. 'You know – as an old boy.'

I could hear myself agree and see me noting the time and date as if I was having an out-of-body-experience. Then came the barb that was so common of the man. 'You never know who you'll you meet on the day. I've invited Thérèse too. At least you'll have someone to talk to.'

I had half expected this and gave a fatuous reply. But Emile wasn't finished with me yet.

'John, I was wondering also if you could remember a fellow student from your year: an awkward boy, from Poland I think. He had no French and poor English. I don't know how he got past our vetting committee. God only knows how

Thérèse... Dr Dumard ever managed to teach him anything. Still, you will know more about that than I do.'

'Do you mean Lafcadio?' I was becoming exasperated.

'Yes, that's the boy. I'm not surprised it ended badly for him. His girlfriend wasn't much better either, if I remember correctly. A typical arrogant German...'

'What do you mean, it ended badly for him? What happened to Lafcadio?'

'Apparently he was killed in a fight outside the National Library in Warsaw. Stabbed, I think. Well, that's what his girlfriend told me. How true this all is, is questionable.'

'Emile... Emile, how do you know this? Who is Lafcadio's girlfriend? Do you mean Frieda – Frieda Pechstein? Is that who told you? Why would she phone you? Forgive me, Emile, but you're the last person she'd tell. Goodness, poor Lafcadio! Do you have any other details?'

'Well, for a start, your friend Frieda lives in Paris and has done so for quite some time. She married a Frenchman – albeit from the St Denis area – and works in a laboratory for one of the large pharmaceutical conglomerates. She kept in touch through the alumni magazine. It was in the last edition that I read of the boy's death. Hang on, I have it here. Yes, here it is. Her married name is Fénéon. She doesn't give any details, so I don't know how I got to hear that it was murder. Someone must have told me. There is a phone number. Do you want it?'

I took down the number and hung up. I had had enough of Emile for one day. My head was birling, trying to take everything in at once. I poured myself a straight Glenlivet and gulped it down in one go. The fiery liquid went down smoothly enough but, as expected, came roaring back up my gullet and burned my throat in an act of vengeance for treating it with such scant regard. Needless to say it brought me to my senses.

To think my day had started so beautifully, and now this! I was more irritated at losing Thérèse's phone number than hearing of Lafcadio death. When I realised this, I felt ashamed of myself. Someone I knew had lost their life through no fault of their own. Or so I believed. Though I couldn't help thinking that of all who were in the 'Foreign Legion' that year at the Institute, Lafcadio was the one I would have bet on to come to a sticky end.

I spent the rest of the day getting my papers in order for my trip to London. I had amassed a considerable portfolio on the life and works of Maurice Utrillo from a great many sources, and was pleased with how I had brought together the diverse elements of his life. I had also sent periodic drafts to London by fax, so that the design team could start to piece together some proofs for the meeting that I had just booked flights for. With this done, I had one final search for Thérèse's file before locking up and heading back to Yvette's apartment. After what I had gone through, I wanted the love and lust of a wicked woman, and Yvette delighted in that very rôle.

28

The lady vanishes

Women distrust men too much in general, and too little in particular.
Philibert Commerson

When I got back to Yvette's apartment she wasn't there. I found a note on the coffee table, telling me she had to attend to a matter concerning some woman or other that she knew and that she did not know what time she would get back. Her absence annoyed me. I had so much to tell her and needed to explain my plans to visit London. I didn't want to have to write it all down, so I scribbled a note saying I would be back in three or four days and left it on the coffee table.

Before leaving I looked at the Utrillo hanging majestically above the mantelpiece. It had been painted during his 'White Period' and held all the features of his style at that time. You could almost smell the decay of falling plaster and rotten wood; yet the street scene had a poignancy that defied pity. As usual for that time, Utrillo left his painting void of people and brought his streets to a dead-end. I stood there, staring hard into the painting, trying to see what Utrillo saw that day in 1909. This would have been a busy street, bustling with people going about their daily business; yet Utrillo only saw the emptiness of it all. For him the beauty lay in the solitude and strength of the walls and roofs and railings. He could trust the immovable beauty of the man-made edifices. He could not trust the people who made them.

I drew over the door and headed back to my apartment. I

decided to walk, even though it was raining quite heavily. Paris shines in the rain unlike any other city I have visited, with the possible exception of Aberdeen with its glistening granite buildings along the environs of Union Street. As the rain eased I wondered where Yvette had got to. What could have been so important to take her off without speaking? There were times she could be so elusive and mysterious. She'll turn up in her own good time, I thought to myself; it's just her way.

As I approached boulevard Garibaldi the rain had almost stopped. The wheels of the Nation train thundered on the bridge overhead. I managed to cross the junction without too much difficulty and was about to walk the short distance to my flat when my eye was drawn to a billboard outside the newsagents that read:

MURDER IN PARK
TRIAL STARTS IN SIX WEEKS

I was surprised to read this. I had imagined the trial to be some time off, as is often the way of such things. I couldn't leave Paris as scheduled, now that I knew the trial was to start so soon. Not that I had a firm view when I would leave Paris. But I would have to fend very much for myself, as my year here had been funded by Reid & Seymour, my publishers, as an advancement on the book. I was intrigued to find out more about the shadowy life of Rene Rousselier, my friend from the park, and who was the mysterious woman that killed him. Was she the woman who always sat in the shadows? I had to know. I couldn't go to the park to see if she was sitting in her usual seat, as it had been sealed off by the police at the time of the murder and no-one had thought to open it again.

I hurried upstairs to my flat and poured myself a whisky.

I was catching an early flight to London the next day and had papers and photographs to get ready. Yvette's absence was nagging me. She knew I was leaving early, so why hadn't she been in touch. What could be so important?

The phone rang. It was Yvette, at last. 'Where are you?' I asked, a little too impatient.

'It doesn't matter, my love. I'm sorry I missed you this morning, but something came up that I had to deal with today. Please forgive me, but I also won't be able to get back into town till much later this evening. I'll make it up to you when you get back from London, I promise. I'll see you then. Take care and have a safe journey.'

She was gone. It was so her. A few words and then she vanishes. I didn't know whether to laugh or cry. Instead I poured myself another whisky and ran the bath.

29

A touch of genius

There are only two things that bring happiness: faith and love.
Charles Nodier

My time in London was brief but successful. My editor was pleased with the work I had produced, and I was pleased with the artwork that the designer had come up with for the book's cover. I was confident before I left Paris that the design would be of the first order, as the contract had been given to a friend of mine, Gillian Lamb, who had collaborated with me on a previous book (on the abstract expressionist, Hans Hofmann), with excellent results.

It was Gillian who met me at Heathrow and drove me into town. It had been four years since we last met and she was as beautiful as I remembered her and just as gracious. I was disappointed to discover she had recently remarried and was, by my reckoning, deep in the first flush of renewed love. Still, any time spent with Gillian was a treat, and I was pleased that she (and her husband) were letting me stay with them at their flat in Maida Vale for the duration of my visit.

As it turned out Gillian's husband was an okay-sort-of-guy who had read all of my books. He confided to me that this was initially at his wife's insistence, but he had come to enjoy them on their own merits. At least he was trying to be friendly.

Thankfully, Fiona Shaw was pleased with the 'Utrillo Project', as she called it. 'This book will get one over on Taschen and T&H,' she told us at our meeting in her Soho office. Fiona had a good instinct on what would sell well in the Art publishing world and considered Utrillo long overdue for a retrospective. Apparently, she considered Utrillo's life to have all the qualities of a good 'Van Gogh' story, and thought it would attract a large student interest.

With business over, we made our way to one of Soho's many drinking establishments for some light refreshment. We found a space in a corner of a busy bar and ordered three whiskies. The bar was full of people who looked vaguely familiar. The women began to identify some of the imbibers as writers and actors they recognised from 'days gone-by', as they put it. I was quite fascinated by this turn of events and began trying to put names to a few myself.

After a few minutes of playing this game, we were interrupted by a rather rotund man sitting to our left. He had had one too many by the looks of it, but I leaned over slightly to hear what it was he saying.

'You're Scotties, aren't you? Down in the big smoke for a holiday, are you?' His words were slurred and he was drunker than I gave him credit for.

'Just passing through,' I said, hoping this would appease him. There is always a danger when speaking to a drunk that he will invite himself into your conversation and settle in. I needn't have worried in this case. My rescue from what was possibly going to be monologue on the failures of the Scottish people (I could hear him mutter to himself, 'What do you call three Jocks in a pub...?') arrived in the shape of a silver haired man, who walked across to our seats and rebuked the drunk.

'That's enough from you, Terry. These people are friends of mine.' I could hear the drunk mumbling something back, but it wasn't distinguishable. He turned away from us.

'Thanks, we appreciate it,' I said quite quietly.

'No problem. I recognised Miss Shaw from a few previous visits she has made here, and I know of her work in the publishing world.'

This took Fiona by surprise. She was all smiles.

'Well, thank you very much for rescuing us,' she said, 'But I'm afraid I can't return the compliment. Are you in the publishing business too?'

'Oh, well... Yes, I suppose. But only on the fringes – nothing big. I do a bit of writing now and again... Anyway, let me buy you a drink to make up for my friend's rudeness.'

We protested to no avail, and three whiskies and a large vodka were brought to the table. No money was exchanged. I considered for a moment that he must either be the owner of the bar, or be important enough to have a tab, which is no mean feat anywhere, let alone London. To me, he didn't look like the landlord type; so I considered him to have some kind of importance in the area. Either way, he was a man to respect. The drunk didn't argue with him, and I wasn't about to either.

He was talking to the ladies. 'I have this theory that a country is to be respected if its people have had the good sense to invent an alcoholic drink, and Scotland produced one of the finest in the world. Though I don't drink it myself – I much prefer the white spirit from Russia. But cheers anyway!'

'Slàinte'!' We said this in unison, much to our own amusement. I told him I liked his theory and added that climate appears to be a factor, too, in determining the strength and flavour of a country's drink. 'Cold winds blow hard', I volunteered tentatively, hoping not to offend. He agreed entirely. I was impressed by our benefactor; he was of good stock, as my father would say. The ladies thought him charming.

We left a little later than we had planned. We were in high

spirits as we made our way back to Fiona's office. Jeff (he only introduced himself by his first name) had entertained us with stories of London, and Soho in particular. It was an afternoon none of us would forget in a long, time.

Back at the office, it was agreed by the two raven-haired conspirators that I could continue to spend my last few weeks in Paris to tidy up any loose ends I still had to conclude on Utrillo. I was pleased with this decision. I had unfinished business back in Paris, and was keen to return.

3rd Movement

Metamorphosis # 5
Philip Glass

30

The beginning of the end

Every man is guilty of every good he didn't do.
Voltaire

I returned to French soil after some visits to London's best galleries and a few days' rest. The visit had been both pleasant and productive. Most of my time now would be spent with Yvette, her painting by Utrillo and taking in the murder trial. I would also try and see Thérèse too. I wanted to see her. I needed to see her. Believe it or not, I still had feelings for her; not sympathy for what happened to her, but that potent mixture of lust and love. It was a strange brew of mixed emotions and physical attraction. It made me feel a little disloyal to Yvette.

I had tried to call Yvette during my stay in London but only succeeded in getting her answering machine. I was disappointed but not annoyed. She would be busy and neither of us owned a mobile phone. Yvette had made me promise that I would keep the existence of Utrillo's Rue Francoeur a secret to the wider public. I was unhappy to do this, as news of the painting was an ideal marketing and publicity coup for my book. Fiona Shaw thought so too. In fact Fiona's last words to me were to get some kind of deal on that painting.

Yvette's absence began to trouble me for no apparent reason. There was nothing I knew of that would keep her away so long. It did cross my mind that, when we first met, she was missing for two weeks; but that turned out to be a family holiday. I decided to busy myself and wait for her contact.

I didn't have long to wait. The very next morning the phone rang. It was Yvette. She was full of apologies for not being here when I got back from London. She had every intention of surprising me at the airport and whisking me off somewhere romantic, but some personal business had cropped up which she had to deal with. She sounded so deliciously apologetic on the phone that I found myself telling her that I was sorry for being impatient with her lack of contact. We agreed I was to go round to her apartment straight away, as we had so much to catch up on. I would have sprouted wings and flown there if I could have.

Yvette met me at her door, wearing a smile and little else. Any doubts I may have had about seeing her again were quickly despatched as she led me by the hand to her bedroom. There, she treated me to hours of lovemaking most men can only fantasise about.

Later, as we lay together, spent from our desires, we spoke of what had happened to each of us during our time apart. Yvette insisted I tell her all about London and if any English women had made a pass at me. I told her all about my business meetings and how my colleagues were very happy with my work, but thought we were missing a wonderful opportunity by not capitalising on the discovery of a Utrillo when my book was published. I also assured her that no lady had shown the slightest interest in me during my visit to England.

'Huh, Englishwomen,' cried Yvette with a pleasing disdain. 'They appreciate nothing. More fool them.'

'Would you have preferred it had they shown an interest in me'? I asked.

'Maybe just a little… Then, maybe not.'

We both laughed as we teased each other about our days apart.

I made some coffee and returned to bed. I wanted to know a little about what she had done during the past week. How was her work? Was Pascal still a pain in the neck? Did she meet any interesting people? Yvette was silent for a moment and looked at me as though she was a child about to confess some misdemeanour. I sensed her unease and told her that, if the matter she had to deal with during my absence was none of my business she didn't have to tell me. We could talk of something else. What she said next was both unexpected and somewhat alarming.

'I've been to see your Thérèse Dumard. I'm sorry, John. I should have told you straight away, but I didn't want to spoil our reunion. Please don't be angry with me. I just needed to know if this woman was going to come between us. I'm not normally the jealous type, but after what Edouard did to me I wanted to be sure it wasn't going to happen again.'

She said her words quickly and precisely. I wasn't angry, but I was shocked to hear her say she had been to see Thérèse. Then confusion set in. I began to throw questions at Yvette. How did you find her? Did she contact you? How did you get her address? What did you talk about? What right did you have to do this? Haven't I explained my part in her life?

Yvette put her fingers to my lips. 'Please, John. Let me explain what happened and why I did what I did. In no way was I trying to check up on you or anything like that. Well, not really. I do trust you, but I just needed to be sure. I hadn't planned to do it. I suppose it just happened because I saw some papers lying on the table on your flat with her name on them. I was curious, as a woman in love can be sometimes. You were that busy, getting yourself sorted to go to London, I didn't

191

think you would miss them. I only took them to read. I had no plans to meet her. But, John, I am so glad I did, for what she told me filled me with sadness and – to be honest – not a little happiness for our sake.'

I said nothing. I had nothing to say at that moment. All my questions were still in the air. I waited, still lying down, but with my eyes fixed firmly on Yvette's. Before she spoke, she leaned forward, punched her pillow, then sat upright in bed. Her nakedness, even now, attracted me and, for an absurd moment, I wanted to ravish her as hard and furiously as I could; so much so, that I had to shift my position in bed for fear of her noticing my arousal.

What followed was a little bizarre. Yvette began to relate her meeting with Thérèse in such a way as if Thérèse was telling the story herself. This reminded me of the way Dr Bricard would speak of Utrillo. It was as if they closed their eyes and made the story come to life in its own way. This was Thérèse's story...

31

Thérèse's story

One is very weak when one is in love
Madame de Lafayette

Like all true stories, my story has two beginnings. There is the one where I meet my young lover for the very first time and begin, by my own hand, as it were, a set of circumstances that I could not control, and which led me to where I am now. And then there is the other beginning, the one that made everything that happened to me at that time possible, and it is there that I must begin. Yet, to be truthful, I do not know exactly when or where my story begins. Like so many of the episodes in our lives, we are slow to recognise the exact moment when change begins. And so it was with Claude and me.

Our life together was not so different from that of our friends. We were successful in many ways. Claude had a senior academic post with the Pasteur Institute. We had a beautiful home that overlooked the Luxembourg Gardens. We kept another, a summerhouse, near Ambois in the Loire valley; though if truth were told, Claude used this more than I did. We had two beautiful children: Clara and Marc. Both have now left home and found success in their own ways. Marc is a Doctor in Lyon and Clara teaches in a secondary school in Rennes. Claude and I were very proud of them. So, in many ways we were fortunate, and by most people's considerations we should have been content with everything we had, and in many ways we were.

Yet sometimes the truth comes to you from an unexpected source. There and then, you realise that something is amiss – a condition that has been in front of you for no little time and you did not see it; then something is said or done unexpectedly, and for the first time you see clearly that which you did not see before. This was the situation that happened to me.

I had arranged to meet a friend for lunch. She was a good friend of long standing, and we both enjoyed our lunches together as we rarely met at other times. We both knew why this was so – Claude did not like my friend. He thought her a frivolous woman, a woman of no substance. This, of course, was not true. Colette was anything but frivolous, but we both knew Claude would not accept her or her husband, a salesman, into our intimate circle of friends. Colette did not care. She thought Claude a pompous ass and would laugh about his high and mighty ways. I laughed too.

It was Colette who opened my eyes that day as we lunched in Chez Gramond. She was complaining that her husband, Georges, was spending too much time away on business and that when he did come home he was too tired to spend time together with her. I laughed at this and told her many married women would be glad of this; for some this would be an ideal marriage. Colette laughed hesitantly, then said that Georges had suggested he sleep in their spare bedroom so he would not disturb her. Georges told her he would put his clothes in the spare bedroom too. It was the best arrangement under the circumstances.

Colette didn't know what to think. Georges rarely came near her. He showed no interest in lovemaking. Not that he had shown any recent inclination when they had shared a bed, she told me. What did I think? Was he having an affair? Was their marriage now to be platonic? Should she confront him? Was she expected to remain celibate? Should she take a lover? Colette went on like this for five minutes or so.

It was as I was driving back from my luncheon with Colette that I realised my life – and, in particular, my marriage to Claude – had taken a similar path. Claude had shown little interest in me after

Clara was born. He became more wrapped up in his work, accepting speaking commitments at various universities, as well as leading in quite important research at the Institute. He argued that it was for all our benefit that he worked so hard, and time would show this to be true.

In many ways Claude was right. His work did bring us material gain. We moved from small apartments to larger ones, until Claude purchased our home in rue Guynemer. This was the right type of home for a professional couple, he said. We sent the children to private school and Claude indulged my passion for works of art.

It was the first year when the children were both at school that Claude suggested he move out of our bedroom and into one of the other rooms. It would be more convenient for both of us, especially during the week, when he had so many commitments. We could double up – as he put it – at weekends, when he would be at home. I didn't see any harm in it, so I agreed. The space would be good for Claude.

It was not long after this that Claude bought the summer house. He argued we needed a place in the country so we could relax as a family, but not too far from Paris in case he had to return promptly. The Loire valley was ideal, he told me. I was delighted. The children were excited. We could be a complete family.

What occurred was different from what I imagined. More often than not, the children and I went to the summer house and Claude stayed in Paris working on some project or other. Or the opposite happened – Claude would use the summer house as a base while giving associate lectures in universities in that region. The children and I would stay at home so as not to disturb Claude's preparations.

When I thought about it, I supposed that my marriage was similar to many other couples who led busy lives. The lack of intimacy did cross my mind from time to time, but I had become accustomed to infrequency in the physical side of marriage due to Claude's life style.

When we did make love, it was always a little disappointing. We had lost our grand passion for each other and accepted that this was what happened in a relationship. Apparently, the first sixty months is the premium time for sexual activity in any relationship. Claude and I had well and truly passed that time.

It crossed my mind on a few occasions that Claude might be having an affair. Colette had said that men always do things for a purpose that is different from what they say. If she was right, then Claude had an ulterior motive that I was not aware of. I could only guess what it was. Colette said that men see their wives differently from other women, that wives become 'mothers' whereas other women don't, irrespective of whether they have children of their own. Men still see them as sexual prey, an attractive commodity, while their wives evolved into their own mothers. I thought Colette read too much.

(It later transpired that Colette had misjudged her own husband's actions. Georges' motives had been honourable. He had been under pressure at work and was working longer hours to try and keep up with his younger colleagues. He didn't want to tell Colette in case she'd worry. He tried to hide his reduced libido by moving into the spare bedroom. The man was mentally and physically exhausted. When Colette got to the truth of the matter, she must have regretted taking a lover.)

Claude wasn't best pleased when I told him I wanted to return to work, and preferably in lecturing. He preferred the status quo. His chauvinism could be annoying at times, but I would always get my way in the end. When he capitulated, it was as if he had balanced out the merits of my needs against his sense of loss in some process or other. If it didn't affect his needs and ambitions too much, then he would concede and withdraw his objections. I applied to the Institute for a post in microbe research and was given the job much to Claude's chagrin.

I hadn't been at the Institute long before I realised that Claude spent some considerable time with his assistant, Dr Emile Renouf. Any time I dropped by his office (he was chair of microbiology), Dr Renouf was always there. I must admit it became an irritation. I began to feel that Emile Renouf was a barrier between my husband and me. Claude dismissed this, of course, and told me I was being ridiculous, and that he and Emile were working on a number of projects that meant they had to spend important time together. He said I was acting like a wife, not a colleague.

Not long after I took up my post, I was put in charge of the 'Foreign Legion', the non-French post-graduate students. I didn't mind at first, as it allowed me to use my knowledge of languages – I speak five European languages – and practice makes perfect. The work itself was a little repetitive and very limited. I found myself going over the same material each year and, in an attempt to stave off boredom, I experimented with my teaching practice to see if my students responded differently.

It was during the year that I attempted, for the first time, to emulate Pythagoras' method of disembodied teaching that John Gil-Martin came into my life. He was a student from Scotland, which was unusual, as most of our 'Legionnaires' from the UK came from England and Northern Ireland. He was one of the very few Scottish people I had met, and I found that he, like many of his fellow countrymen, had a reticence to speak at length. He spoke in short sentences and said no more than he had to. It was as if words were rationed and only so many could be used in any day. This was a great shame for me, as I loved his accent and tried to get him to speak as much as possible.

Colette told me over lunch one day that a man's voice was his sexual resonance and that, if a woman was attracted to a man's voice, she would be fulfilled sexually. This, apparently, was why film stars like Marlon Brando and Yves Montand were so sexy: they had great voices. I didn't make the connection but, then again, I didn't always make a connection with Colette's logic. For me, John Gil-Martin had a lovely accent and he was pleasant to look at. He was tall, too. My Claude was not.

At first I did not consider that I was attracted to this young man from Scotland; nor, for that matter, had I considered the possibility that I was attracted to any man. It was another student who took me aside one day and pointed out 'the error of my ways', as she put it. Her name was Frieda Pechstein, a rather pretty young woman from Dusseldorf with a very sharp scientific mind. Her accusation bemused me, but not before I had dismissed her notion as a fantasy of her girlish imagination.

I told Colette. She said I was in love but didn't want to admit it. She said that a woman's subconscious mind always recognises our biological needs before the brain interprets it as lust or love or a bit of both. Apparently I was in an early stage in the process. I laughed at this and told her she was being silly. She gave me one of the looks that she liked to give when she was saying, 'I'm telling you girl, you're in for a surprise.' I left wondering if she could possibly be correct in her assumption. I did like the boy. I couldn't deny it. He had an interesting way with him, which made me smile. But to be in love – this was folly!

Colette wouldn't let up. She phoned me every other day, wanting to know if anything had happened yet. 'Of course not,' I would reply, only to hear her chastise me for an act of cowardliness in the face of potential happiness. Eventually I gave in and told her I would invite John for dinner on an evening Claude was staying at the summer house. It would be a civilised evening of light conversation and music; nothing else. I felt nervous at the very thought of it. Colette was ecstatic

It rained the day I chose to ask John to come to dinner at my home. In fact it rained so hard that I didn't think any of the students *would turn up for classes. I cursed myself for choosing that particular day, but there was no alternative. John would be in class that day, we had no class the following day, and I wanted the timing of my invitation to appear natural and carefree.*

When I arrived at the small anteroom I use as a store when I am lecturing, there were about half a dozen students already there looking for towels to dry themselves. They were soaked through. John Gil-Martin was one of them. Seeing him made me begin to feel excited and not a little nervous. I had to dry myself as well, as I too had been caught in the downpour as I ran between buildings. In a few minutes, there was only John and I left in the anteroom. I could smell him standing close to me, almost touching. The heat and scent of his body, mingled with the damp odour of his wet clothes, was a powerful intoxicant. I wanted to hold him then and there. Colette was right, damn her! I needed this man badly.

With as much control as I could muster, I suggested to him we go for a coffee to warm us up. Thankfully, he agreed. When we got to the refectory I didn't know what to say to him. My confidence left me. I felt I was just saying things to fill the void between us. He sat there looking so confident. I cursed him for being so cool and collected. If only he knew how I was feeling. And then I said it. I asked him to come to my house for dinner. I might as well have asked him to have sex with me there and then. I felt like a whore on the street. I was shaking with fear. He would see through my ruse. What else could he take from it, a married woman inviting a man to her home for dinner? I would have laughed if I hadn't felt so stupid. He just sat there for a moment before asking – no, probing – if there were other guests invited. I had to get out of there – the refectory. I was suffocating in excitement and fear.

I didn't see him again until the night he came for dinner. He hadn't attended any classes, as I checked. He never mentioned why and I didn't ask. That evening was one of the most exhilarating of my life. Everything he did was so cultured. He played the piano beautifully. I was in heaven. He was so patient with me. I felt loved for the first time in my life.

We took every chance we could to meet after that night. I was falling in love and I knew it. I felt no guilt for what I was doing. Claude had never really loved me, and I felt I had earned my chance at love. We just had to be careful. And we were. Well – we thought we were.

For about six months, we were the ideal couple. We took ourselves off to places where we would not be recognised and pretended to be married. I knew then what my marriage to Claude should have been like, but never was. Then something changed in John. He became irritable at the least thing. At first I thought it was because he was nearing the time when he was expected to return to Scotland. We had never discussed in any great detail what we were going to do. I assumed we would work something out that would keep us together in some way. Anytime I broached the subject, John would say we had plenty of time to discuss our future and that we should enjoy the moment. But I knew something was wrong.

The end came as abruptly as we started. We argued, and he was gone. It was as simple as that. Before I could draw breath he was back in Glasgow. I should have realised what was going to happen. Our relationship was too much for him. There were too many complications. I suppose he wanted out before he had to confront my feelings or needs.

32

A sense of guilt

It is better to be hated for what you are than to be loved for what you are not.
André Gide

When I heard this part of Thérèse's story I felt ashamed of myself. I had acted like a stupid boy who could not face up to any responsibility. The feelings of guilt I had felt on my arrival back in Glasgow now haunted me once again. I felt sick to the stomach. I got up and poured myself a Scotch. Yvette seemed to be watching my every action as I returned to bed and quietly sipped my drink.

'Was there anything else she said that I should know about. I mean...the baby and what happened after that...?'

Yvette ignored my question and replied with questions of her own. 'Why did you run away, John? Didn't you still love her?' Yvette spoke in almost a whisper. I watched her get up from the bed and slip a robe across her shoulders, then walk over to the window. She seemed to stare out at nothing in particular. She turned back to face me.

'Could you not have written back to her? Was that too much to ask? She had given all of herself to you and you just walked away. Have I got that right?'

I could hear the hurt in her voice. What had occurred between Thérèse and me appeared to be a matter of the highest importance to Yvette. I knew I was being judged on what I had done, rightly or wrongly, and on anything I would say in my defence. In her mind, she had every right to know what kind of man she was involved with, and I suppose I wouldn't have blamed her if she had asked me to leave there and then.

Yvette sat on the edge of the bed and pulled her robe tight across her waist. She reached out for my glass and took a drink of the straight Scotch. She said nothing. It was my turn to speak. I offered no defence. How could I? There was none to be had.

'I ran because I was scared and wanted back where I felt safe. Yes, I still loved her, but thought that I was doing the right thing by us both. We had no future together. She was married, had a good job. She was going nowhere – well, not for me. She was a made woman. And yes, I often wanted to write back to her. But every time I sat down to do so, I couldn't think of what to say, It all sounded so unreal, a kind of lie. For me it was over. It needed to be over for both our sakes. We were different people, from different worlds. Logic told me it would never work. No matter what we did, one would start to resent the other. We would have ended up bitter, with even more debris than we already had. I honestly thought she would start to forget our affair and put it down to some kind of expendable experience. I prayed she would stop writing.

'My mother gave me hell over those letters. She wasn't very proud of me. Every time a letter arrived, she would phone my flat and give me a lecture on decency. I never told her any details about Thérèse. I mean, she never knew she was my tutor or was married. Anyway, she kept the letters in a shoebox for me. A little later, I met Angela and I soon forgot Thérèse. Once Angela came on the scene, my mother never mentioned the letters again. I assumed they'd stopped coming.

Yvette finished my drink then began to dress. I had no idea what she was thinking. I decided the best policy was to say no more. If I have learned anything about women, it is never to second-guess them. They have an innate sense of justice that transcends male logic and common law, and is not to be trifled with. I began to dress. Whether I would enter Yvette's bedroom after today was beyond my jurisdiction. We returned to the lounge. Utrillo's painting caught my eye. There was so much at stake here, and not just whether I had a love life or not.

Yvette made some coffee and poured two cups. I felt the need to say more in my defence, but kept tight-lipped. We were on a proverbial precipice, and I didn't want to be the one who tipped us over the edge. I sat waiting for the next instalment. Thankfully, Yvette spoke.

'There's more, John – a lot more. What you did or didn't do was bad enough. You acted like a juvenile running away from the first serious decision you ever had to make. Some men are like that. But what Thérèse told me, about after you left her, was nothing short of a tragedy. I can't help thinking, John, if you had acted differently, what followed may not have ended the way it did.'

Apparently I was guilty of all charges in Yvette's eyes. It was in some ways the old adage that ignorance of the law is no defence. I was guilty by association. I had set a chain of events in motion that, irrespective of my knowledge of their existence, would not have happened if I had acted responsibly in the first place. In Yvette's mind, offering a plea of alibi was not going to be an acceptable defence.

33

Thérèse's story continued

All the reasonings of men are not worth one sentiment of women.
Voltaire

Thérèse's story haunted me for the next few days. I didn't hear or see Yvette during this time and was glad of it. There is only so much of a bad thing a man can take, and I knew there was more evidence to come; evidence that, in Yvette's eyes, would find me guilty of all charges. Did Yvette know about Thérèse being raped by the two men? Did women confide in other women the horrors of such events in their life and, in Yvette's case, a virtual stranger to Thérèse, who turns up at her door out-of-the-blue? I hoped not.

The fact that Yvette had gone to see Thérèse behind my back, as it were, irritated me. That she would take a private document from my desk, and use the information it contained for her own purposes, upset me just as much. Yet I was the one being held to account. To Yvette the end justified the means. That her actions were deceitful was an irrelevance. The greater crime was mine.

My work on Utrillo suffered from the events of the last few days. I had hoped to authenticate Yvette's painting by Utrillo. This can be quite a complicated procedure that requires evidence of the painting's provenance, receipts of ownership, records intimating the existence of the painting and other documentation that will satisfy the appropriate bodies. Instead of doing any of this, I found myself spending afternoons in the corner bar, following the TV coverage of the last stages of the Tour de France.

The Tour is the greatest bicycle race in the world, but it is not without its curiosities and failings. Its history is riddled with events that make it unique in world cycling. According to a recent article in the newspaper, L'Equipe, the Tour de France rarely passes without incident. Just a few years ago some members of ETA (the Basque separatist movement) bombed followers' cars overnight. A year before that, the riders refused to race for 40 minutes because one of the riders, Urs Zimmerman, was penalised for driving from one stage finish to the start of the next instead of flying. That same year, the PDM team went home early after all of its riders fell ill, one by one, within 48 hours. The year previous to this, the organisers learned of a blockade by farmers in the Limoges area and diverted the race before it got there.

The race has been affected by strikes taking place. In 1988 the race went on strike in a protest concerning a drugs test on rider Pedro Degado, and in 1987 photographers working on the Tour went on strike, saying cars carrying the Tour's guests were getting in their way. A few years before that, a walk out of some striking steel workers halted the team time trial. The same article reported that, in 1978, the field rode slowly all day and then walked across the line at Valence d'Agen, in protest at having to get up early to ride more than one stage in a day. Even the journalists covering the race have been on strike, after being accused of watching the race 'with tired eyes'. This was a response to criticism by the journalists that the race was dull. I have never considered journalists to be so sensitive; but, again, this is the Tour de France, where anything can happen and often does. Bizarre events are not new to the race. In the 1950 tour, two Italian teams left the race after one of the riders thought a spectator had threatened him with a knife. If that wasn't enough for one year, the paper said that later in the race, because of unusually hot weather, many of the field got off their bikes and ran into the Mediterranean at Ste-Maxime. Some riders were said to have ridden into the sea without dismounting. All the riders involved were penalised by the judges.

Jacques, the barman, was a keen follower of the Tour and was a fan of Miguel Indurain, who had won the previous five tours. This was not to be Indurain's year, as he became ill during one of the stages and was penalised for taking drinks illegally. This had infuriated Jacques, as he felt the organisers had been too harsh on his favourite rider especially – according to Jacques, the race was riddled with riders who were taking the drug, erythropoietin (EPO). The tour was eventually won by the balding Danish rider, Bjarne Riis.

A day or two later Yvette got in touch. She wanted to continue our talk about what happened to Thérèse. She had more to tell me. My heart sank. There was no way I was going to come out of this episode in my life with any dignity or self-respect. I was in a no-win situation, no matter what was going to happen. It crossed my mind that maybe Yvette had gone to meet Thérèse for a second time. I hoped not. Once was bad enough, but to go behind my back for a second was an act of betrayal. I was filled with a sense of paranoia that the sisterhood was acting against me.

We agreed to meet on neutral ground. A café on the corner of the boulevard Montparnasse, diagonally facing the department store Galeries Lafayette was to be our meeting place. It was a café I knew well, and had passed the occasional hour just people watching from its curved windows that looked out on to the busy intersection. Yvette felt that this venue would be better for both of us: no domestic distractions.

We found a table in a quiet space near the back of the café. No doubt the waiters thought it odd, as most other customers were sitting outside in the glorious sunshine. Yvette appeared to be in good humour. She had been shopping. I was feeling defensive, waiting for the attack to begin. I hadn't long to wait. After a few pleasantries were exchanged, Yvette said we should continue our discussion from the week before. I was relieved to hear that she had not gone back to visit Thérèse. What she had to tell me was a continuation from her first meeting. Once again she began to relate the story as told by Thérèse. I could hear Thérèse's voice clearly as if it were she who was sitting across from me. This was Thérèse's story…

When I told Colette what had happened, she went into a rage. She said she would find John wherever he was and castrate him. She is a good friend and meant well. I told her the problem was at the other end of his body, as it was in so many men. I tried to laugh, but this didn't appease her. She still wanted to make garters of him, if you know what I mean. She was beside herself, and to took a while – and a large vodka and lime – to calm her down.

I met with Colette every week at different cafes and bistros so we could talk things through. She was my only true friend during all of this time and helped me enormously. When I realised I was pregnant I didn't know what to do. Colette, as usual, had a practical solution.

'You can't have it. You have to terminate this baby before it is too late. Having this baby will leave you vulnerable to both these so-called men in your life. Be smart and do the right thing.'

In the end that's what happened, but certainly not for those reasons. I felt abandoned. I was grieving for a lost love, and my husband was making my life a misery since finding out about everything. Claude was so vengeful. It never occurred to me in all the years we were married that he had such a mean streak in him. I'd never heard him raise his voice until he confronted me with the letter I was sending to John. He raged at me for humiliating him, making him a laughing stock to all and sundry. He promised he would ruin me. I would regret the day I was born. He was right.

Not long after this two things happened that added to my burden. I was forced to move from my lovely home to a flat that Claude knew about, and my young daughter, Clara, phoned me to tell me she never wanted to speak to me again. Claude had told her what had happened. She was so upset. I tried to explain, but she let me know in no uncertain terms that my betrayal of her father was unforgivable. She said I was no more than a common slut.

I dreaded what my son was going to say, but he never phoned. I rang his school, thinking this was the right thing to do, but his house parent told me he was too upset with me to speak to me. She also asked me not to phone back; that Marc would phone me when he was ready. He never phoned. Claude had set the children against me. They were at a vulnerable age and would view their parent's fallout in black and white terms, and I was the guilty party.

My work was my escape – or so I thought. Emile Renouf acted as some kind of go-between. He was always around, asking questions. Strangely, he never once condemned me. He was always the gent. Yet I knew he was Claude's friend and that anything I said would go straight back to Claude.

The Institute made it clear I was now surplus to requirements. I was told that, if my actions ever found their way to the media, we would all be ruined. As it was, I had to share my duties with a new member of staff, who would report to Emile on a weekly basis. My walls were crowding in. I took a week's leave and terminated my *pregnancy.*

That summer was wasted on me. Every week brought me to a new low. Poor Claude didn't escape either. For every act he perpetrated against me, he somehow managed to find himself mired into a descending circle of his own. The Institute treated him badly, and marginalised him. He was forced to take a sabbatical; and then, if that wasn't enough, he was diagnosed with a terminal cancer. I truly felt for him. Not that he wanted any solace from me. I was told to stay away. Emile kept me posted. This was the only time I ever saw Emile distressed. He seemed genuinely to care for Claude. Once or twice I thought he was going to blame me for Claude's cancer, but he managed to restrain himself. He was always that kind of man.

After Claude died, the Institute couldn't wait to get rid of me. I kept some dignity for a few months, then left by my own accord. Emile got Claude's chair. It was, in some way, a consolation prize. I took a job in a technical college, teaching chemistry to apprentice engineers. It wasn't a great job, but it kept me sane and the salary was more than I had expected.

Around this time I experienced another first for me. I was attacked and badly beaten by two men. Thankfully, I recovered quickly and told the college I had fallen off a friend's motorbike. After that incident I began to get my life back into some sort of order. I had already changed my name back to my maiden name. This gave me some anonymity. Emile still kept in touch. I had given him my address and telephone number, just in case he had to contact me. I couldn't think of any circumstances that would warrant a call from him, but I felt I couldn't sever all my links with my past. He played the role of the magnanimous professor. I was to call on him if and when I needed assistance with anything.

So, here I am, living on the other side of the Périphérique, no friends or family to speak of; even Colette doesn't see me that often. I no longer mix in her circle so I can't blame her. I've tried on numerous occasions to contact my children, but they still resent me and blame me for their father's death. Neither wants anything to do with me, especially Marc; so I just wait and pray that a day will come when they can forgive me. Now, all these years later, my past returns to confront me, to resurrect old emotions and not a few new ones. It is like dealing with everything all over again.

I met with John. At first I was angry with him, but then I realised he wasn't aware of many of the things that had happened to me after he left. What I can't forgive is that he never even opened the letters I sent him. It was as if he wanted to wash his hands of me, forever. This still hurts.

He came to my flat in Issy-les Molineaux. I opened the door and there he was. I was shocked to say the least. I didn't want to see him. I had told myself many times that, if I ever saw him again, I would kill him. Now here he was, on my doorstep. I slammed the door in his face. I stood behind the door in a panic. I was shaking all over. What was I to do? Then he spoke to me, through the door, so to speak. He seemed genuinely sorry for what he'd done. I was confused. I let him in.

I could see in his face that he had been taken aback, as it were, with my living conditions. He tried not to show it, but I could tell he felt pity for me. This made me angry and I asked him to leave. I can't remember what he said. My mind was in a state of agitation; my emotions were dictating my actions. It was only after he left and I had managed to calm myself that I told myself I had acted badly. I decided I would try to see him again. I wanted the chance to tell him what had happened to me, to put some accountability his way. But it was more than just a scorned woman's revenge. There was something deep inside me that told me I needed to see him again, even after everything that had happened. If truth be told, I wanted to see him again.

Yvette spoke first. She was out of Thérèse's character, her own voice now penetrating the space between us.

'She still loves you. I could tell that from her voice. A woman knows such things. You were her hope for a better life, but all you gave her was despair. The poor woman! I pity her.'

So there it was. Guilty as charged. Neither of us spoke for a few moments after this. At least Yvette didn't know about the rape. That would have been too much for her to bear. I hadn't realised that Thérèse had been badly hurt in the attack. It didn't occur to me that the attack was more than she said at the time.

The next few minutes were awkward. Did Yvette expect me to respond to this latest instalment of Thérèse's story? What was I supposed to say? I was still sore that Yvette had gone behind my back to get information. I decided not to comment on what had been said preferring to take the 'discussion' forward.

'Would you prefer it if we stopped seeing each other from now on? I'm sure Pascal and your ex would like that. Is that what you want too?'

I could see that Yvette had been taken aback by the directness of my question. She had lost the upper hand in our dialogue. She was no longer in control of the negotiations, if that's what this was. Now she was being forced to decide one way or another. Her choice was simple: leave the past where it belonged or move on.

'Is that what you prefer?' Yvette leaned in close again. 'Would you rather end our relationship now? I can understand if you do. None of this is easy for either of us. You think I have gone behind your back, that I am spying on you. Yes, I wanted to know who this Thérèse Dumard woman was – or is. It is bad enough having one man cheat on you, without worrying if another is doing the same. Maybe I shouldn't have gone behind your back, but I wanted to know what I was dealing with. And, yes – I think she still loves you. So if you want to leave things as they are, I'll understand. And by the way: I couldn't care less what Pascal or my ex thinks. This is none of their business.'

I came back at her quickly.

'Am I to assume from what you have said that you want to continue seeing me. If so, then I am happy to continue seeing you. Can we leave the past behind us and move on? Let's not discuss this any further today. We both need a rest from it.'

Yvette agreed. I think she realised that to debate the issue in detail would destroy what feelings we had for each other. We both made excuses of places to be and left the café without further talk.

34

Preludes and nightcaps

At any street corner the feeling of absurdity can strike any man in the face.
Albert Camus

I left my meeting with Yvette in a solemn mood. We hadn't discussed the latter part of Thérèse's story in any detail. Yvette knew that Thérèse had told me this part of her story, so she let it lie. When she said that Thérèse wanted to see me again, I thought I detected some kind of resignation in her voice. It was if she had expected it. I made no comment about it; nor did I tell her that Thérèse told me the men in her story had raped her. I knew Thérèse would have told Yvette if she wanted it to be known. It wasn't my place to mention such matters. And anyway: it would only have added to my list of crimes.

I was surprised that Thérèse told Yvette that she had wanted to see me again, and not just to satisfy any residual feelings of revenge. Was she really expressing a desire to be with me again, or was this my male ego getting in the way of the facts? Did Yvette explain to Thérèse that she and I were lovers? I hadn't thought to ask Yvette how she introduced herself when they met.

I walked back to my flat. The buildings around me distracted me away from thoughts of Thérèse and Yvette. I wondered how many artists and musicians had lived in the apartments above me. When Modigliani left Montmartre it was a street nearby here that he moved to. Utrillo would come here on visits. The south of the river would have been like a foreign country to him, so seldom did he venture out from his northern hill.

It began to drizzle as I reached the intersection below the Sèvres-Lecourbe metro line. I was closer to the corner café than I was to my flat, so I headed there instead. It would add to my distraction. The café was quite quiet – the lull between storms – the early evening crowd would soon be here, grabbing a quick aperitif before venturing home. I sat at the bar, hoping for conversation. The usual bartender, Jacques, was off-shift. Still, I was not to be disappointed. The young bartender behind the bar was in jovial mood.

I discovered that he had just become a father for the first time and that he and his divine angel – as he referred to his wife – had been delivered of the most beautiful baby boy. Now, he told me, every day was a blessing. As much as I was pleased for him and his angel, I had hoped for another kind of conversation – one that I could contribute to. My chance came a few moments later, when a burly character with an Audenesque face came in and sat at the stool next to mine. He didn't acknowledge me, but ordered a coffee and spoke directly to the smitten barman.

'I see they are bringing the trial forward. No bad thing either. Better to get these things over and done with as soon as possible. Anyway, its cut and dried. She'll get done for it, poor cow.'

It took me a minute or two before I realised he was talking about the murder of Rene Rousselier, my 'dealer friend' from the park. I had completely forgotten about the trial.

'Excuse me, when does the trial start?'

He took out a newspaper from his jacket pocket and threw it on the bar counter.

'It's all in there. Keep it.'

I ruffled through a couple of pages before coming to the piece on the pending trial. There was a mug shot of Rene Rousselier, but only a very blurred photograph of the accused. I couldn't make out if the woman in the photograph was my mystery lady from the shadows in the park or some other woman; possibly the woman I saw him with leaving Montparnasse station. The article claimed that the deceased was a well-known figure in the criminal underworld and that the accused, a Magdalene Dupré, was the wife of one of the dead man's associates, who had been murdered a year earlier in a gangland hit. I mentally took a note of the details and left the newspaper on the bar. The murder was being seen as a revenge killing. The trial would be interesting.

When I returned to my flat there was a message from London, asking what developments I had made with the Utrillo painting. If truth be told, the answer was none. Yvette would not allow the painting to be proofed; nor would she let me take it from her apartment. She argued that she knew it was an original work because Utrillo's mother had given it to Yvette's great aunt in 1917, and that the two women were related. This was news to me. I was intrigued. Was Yvette a relative of Utrillo? Why hadn't she told me this? I wanted to find out more, but Yvette was reticent about revealing any more of her family history. Nor would Yvette let me arrange for a photograph to be taken. She was very forceful about this. I had let it go when I first spoke to her about it, but I knew I would have to go back to her whether professionally or otherwise.

The next day I received my invitation to attend the special Open Day at the Pasteur Institute. Emile Renouf had scribbled on the card that he hoped to see me there. I sensed that Thérèse would also have received one – Emile would have made sure of that. I had never trusted Emile, and still didn't. He had that way about him, where everything he said seemed to have a sinister meaning but was always said in the most pleasant way.

I decided not to decide whether I attended or not. There was too much happening all around me at this time to play silly games with the little professor. There were things I had to fix, or at least try and make good. My work was all but finished, so I had no real reason to stay behind in Paris. I could cut my losses and run. Fiona and Gillian back in London had a new commission for me – a documentary on the Irish artists, Milo Marsh, Luke Sweteman and Narcissus Netterville. Channel 4 had agreed to make the film but wanted a known historian to front it, and had agreed provisionally to my participation.

There is always a time in life when it is important to do the right thing, and I felt this was mine. I had to clarify where I stood with Yvette and deal with my feelings of guilt about how I treated Thérèse. I had come to terms with the fact that I still had strong feelings for Thérèse, but whether these feelings were about love or sympathy I couldn't be sure. I kept telling myself – never go back. What's in the past should stay there. Yet I found myself thinking more and more about her as a woman – a living, loving woman – a woman to be loved – a woman to be made love to – by me.

To make matters worse, I wasn't sure any more about my feelings for Yvette. The fact that she had gone behind my back to find Thérèse irked me. Did she have any grounds to do this? We weren't exactly committed to each other, and her recent behaviour towards me struck me as self-serving. Maybe I was too. It crossed my mind that events were becoming a little too toxic for our romance to survive. Even so, it was better I stayed in Paris for the time being. I would know the outcome of my questions soon enough.

35

The love of isms

Believe those who are seeking the truth. Doubt those who find it.
André Gide

I decided to let the London office negotiate with Yvette for any pictorial rights on her Utrillo painting. I recognised that I was too involved emotionally to undertake the task. It was better for all concerned if a more objective person led any transaction. It crossed my mind that it was for the overall good if a woman did the business in this circumstance, a woman like Fiona Shaw, my editor and publisher. Both women had similar qualities. Each had a strong and purposeful character, with an inherent sense of fair play. They could sort it out much better than I ever could.

I began to clear my desk of any residual papers concerning Utrillo. There was nothing else to add to what I had sent to London. If they had any issues, they would get back to me soon enough. A writer never truly knows when a piece of work is finished. In my case, I can fiddle around for weeks, adding and subtracting words and sentences here and there. In the end the writer is word-blind; the printed page a jumble of meaningless words and phrases. Thus the importance of a good editor, and I had one of the best.

One task I agreed to do for my publishers was to write an article about L.S. Lowry for the forthcoming book the company was publishing in the next few months. I decided I would write a piece that highlighted the similarities between Utrillo and L.S. Lowry. This way I could plug my book, which was going to be published under the title, *Utrillo: The man who loved walls*.

I began by arguing that their respective art establishments had marginalised both artists. The subject of their work was now seen as regional to an establishment that was preoccupied with international schools of thought; what some critics describe as 'a love if isms'.

The article went on to say that Lowry and Utrillo painted the environments in which they lived. They depicted its culture with the eye of an outsider looking in. Both artists were inherently lonely men. Many of their canvasses express a bleak outlook. For Lowry, the crowded streets in many of his paintings did not represent a sense of belonging but, rather, a position of exclusion. As for Utrillo, he rarely bothered to put people in his paintings, and when he did, they were often grotesque or insignificant figures. Both men used a substantial amount of white in their work. Skies were invariably overcast. Buildings were architecturally formidable and textured. It was even said of L.S. Lowry that his paintings represented the Apocalypse of Grime.

Another aspect of their lives that played a significant part to both men was their love for their mothers. Both artists were devastated when their mother's died. Lowry never married; Utrillo, only in later life. That both painters are now considered minor artists is a critical misjudgement on the part of twentieth century art critique.

It didn't take me long to finish the article. Much of what I had written I had rehearsed a hundred times before in discussions with friends and foes alike. I also wanted to emphasise how the art establishment in England was class-conscious and had a tendency to neglect any artist who didn't fit nicely into its middle class criteria. In many cases, it was usually left to an artist's home town to promote their work and memory; especially if they came from outside London and the Home Counties.

I was confident that, if I had overstepped the mark in any of my political comments, Fiona Shaw would see to it that my remarks were neutralised, so that they did not alienate anyone in her networking world.

36

Dancing with pigeons

Every existing thing is born without reason, prolongs itself out of weakness, and dies by chance.
Jean-Paul Sartre

There are few places more beautiful than Paris when the sun is setting, and none more beautiful in Paris than the Luxembourg Gardens at sunset. It was here that Isadora Duncan danced in the hours before dawn and where the destitute Hemmingway hunted pigeons to stave off starvation. It was here I had arranged to meet my former fellow student, Frieda Pechstein.

I had contacted Frieda some time earlier to see if she would be happy to meet up with me again. Emile Renouf had given me her contact details, no doubt hoping I would do this very thing. He would have his reasons, and I had mine. Frieda was a good friend to me during our post-grad year at the Institute. I was looking forward to seeing her again.

As I strolled along the many paths, with the gentle rays of the setting sun flickering through the overhanging branches, my thoughts turned to those days when we both attended the Pasteur Institute as part of the so called 'Foreign Legion'. Our time at the institute had been intense; yet most of my memories were of fond moments where laughter filled the air. As a disparate bunch of students, we managed to bond well and, if my memory serves, we all managed to complete the studies and gain our post graduate diplomas – even Lafcadio, who always seemed to struggle due to his language difficulties, but was always helped by the woman I was about to meet.

We had agreed to meet at one of the statues at the boating pond. When I got there, a woman was standing with her back to me, watching a man navigate a radio-controlled yacht with bright red sails across the basin. I wasn't sure if the woman was Frieda and didn't want to call out her name in case she was the man's wife. As I approached her, the woman suddenly turned round. She was beautiful. It wasn't until I was nearly upon her that I realised it was indeed Frieda. She was smiling.

'Is it really you? Do my eyes deceive me? Is it really John Gil-martin that walks towards me?'

'Have I changed that much?' I replied feebly.

'Au contraire, Monsieur. You are as handsome now as I remember you. The years have been kind! How I envy you men your youthfulness! I, on the other hand, have aged pitifully; but you are still the man I remember from all those years back.

'How can you say such things, Frieda? You look stunning.'

'You are too kind. I am what I am. Anyway, enough of these pleasantries. How are you, John?' We exchanged kisses. 'Shall we sit down?'

She had lost most of her German accent. If I closed my eyes, I would swear I was talking to a French woman, from Paris too. We sat at the far side of the pond, just catching the last few streams of golden-light before the sun settled behind the trees and buildings beyond the park.

'We have much to catch up on and so little time to do it. I was very surprised when Emile Renouf contacted me and told me you were working in Paris... and a writer too! I always thought you would end up a famous scientist living in America. How wrong can a woman be?'

'Life has its twists and turns,' I said, not wanting to explain all that had happened over the years.

'And a philosopher too!' Frieda exclaimed with a broad grin on her face. We both laughed.

As the gardens began to empty, Frieda filled me in on all that Emile Renouf had told her, which was quite substantial. She knew what had happened to Thérèse and my part in her subsequent fall from grace. She made no judgement and kept her conversation matter-of-fact. Then she told me about her own life after she left the Institute, and how she met her husband. Apparently they struggled in the early years of their marriage, and survived mostly on her earnings from her laboratory job until the first baby had come along. Thereafter, she said, it was downhill all the way. At no time did Frieda castigate her husband for his lack of earnings. She had married for better or worse. They had another baby, which didn't ease their financial worries, but she was happy she had her children, who were a blessing to her, even more so now that her husband had died.

Frieda didn't explain what had caused her husband's death; nor did I enquire. I believe it is best to leave such matters to others. They will tell you if they want to. Neither did she say where her children were and how they had coped with their father's death. By my reckoning, they would only be aged around ten and eight. I suppose I didn't need to ask.

Throughout her marriage, Frieda had kept in touch with Lafcadio, our friend from Poland. She had even managed to visit him on a couple of occasions. Her visits had not been enjoyable. Poor Lafcadio didn't have his troubles to seek. Even with a good education, he couldn't seem to get away from his impoverished past. If something was going to go wrong, it was going to go wrong for Lafcadio.

I listened quietly as Frieda listed everything that had happened to Lafcadio since he left the Institute. He hadn't returned to Krakow after he left Paris, but chose to try and find his sister who lived in Warsaw. He thought living and working in Warsaw would be the making of him. Sadly, this was not to be the case. He found his sister living in a squalid housing scheme on the outskirts of the city. She had been abandoned by her husband and was bringing up three children on state benefits. At first Lafcadio tried to help in any way he could, taking the younger children to school or helping to keep the small flat clean. He would babysit a couple of days a week at night, while his sister went to her part-time job. The kids didn't like him and made his stay there difficult.

The biggest problem he faced was that he couldn't find work. All his applications were returned with a polite rejection. It seemed that, even with his qualifications, he was not the right sort of material for work in the field of microbiology. Eventually he got a job as a deliveryman driving a small van around the city. His journeys took him to many parts of the city he had never been before. Then, during one of his trips, he spotted his sister and a man going into a particularly seedy hotel near a freight station on the eastern part of the city. He was surprised to see her as far out of the city as this. She had no business out here that he knew of. He tried to get her attention, but she either didn't see him or chose to ignore him. He waited outside the hotel for his sister to emerge. A seed of a suspicion was growing in his mind. He waited to see if his suspicion was right.

When his sister emerged from the hotel alone, he dragged her into the van, demanding to know what was going on. Was she selling herself? She laughed in his face. 'What do you think?' she spat back at him. 'How do you think I manage to pay the bills? Not on the money you bring in, that's for sure? This way I survive!'

From that day on Lafcadio said nothing to his sister about her part-time job. Soon after the incident, he found a place of his own in an even seedier and more squalid housing project. This was where he stayed until the day he died. He never found better work, but spent his time doing odd jobs in between his delivery round. Like many others in his position, he drank too much and spent whatever earnings he had left after paying his rent on take-aways, videos and vodka.

Lafcadio was knifed to death outside the National Library in Warsaw, in what was described by police as a drug related incident. Frieda disputed this version of events. It was her theory that Lafcadio had just got into an argument with a gang of boys out looking for trouble. She insisted that Lafcadio did not take or deal in drugs; not after his sister had died from an overdose a year after he left her. Whatever his cause of death, no one had been arrested, nor were the police actively looking for someone.

The Garden was now quite dark and the air had chilled. The man with the red-sailed yacht had long since departed. This was now the time when a different type of Parisian enjoyed the Garden's facilities. Frieda and I agreed that we would meet again at the Institute's Open Day, which was only a week away. We shook hands; then Frieda kissed me gently on both cheeks. We smiled. I wondered if she was thinking what I was thinking. 'If only...' Then I remembered something Frieda had said earlier about Emile Renouf contacting her. It had irked me earlier; then I became engrossed in her story.

'Before you go, Frieda. Did you say to me that Emile contacted you? It's just that he told me he read about Lafcadio's death in the alumni magazine.'

'Yes, he phoned me one day, quite out-of-the-blue. He said you were in town, working on some arty thing, and were coming to the Open Day – as was Thérèse. He thought it would make for an interesting day. He then told me a little about what had happened between you and her after we all left the Institute. I have to admit, I was a little hurt at what had happened. If you remember, I held a torch for you myself back then. I told him about Lafcadio's death. It must have been him that put the announcement in the magazine. I didn't.'

We parted company, both no doubt musing the inner mind and machinations of Professor Emile Renouf. Why would he lie? What advantage did it give him? What pleasure could he take from any of this? I tried to shut him out of my mind and think of the news I had learned from Frieda, sad though it was. Frieda had left the Garden by the main gate, which led to the boulevard St. Michel. I turned around to walk across the Gardens. It was best we went our separate ways.

On the other side of the pond, I found myself drifting toward the gate that led to where Thérèse once lived. I began to reminisce about our early romance, when we were both silly with passion. Soon I was approaching the area near the gate where we would sometimes make love, hidden by the trees and bushes, thinking ourselves two young teenagers with nowhere else to go.

My thoughts on times past were brought to a sudden end by the emergence of three men from the shrubbery on my right. I knew instantly that they meant harm – they had the look of men intent on violence – and tried to outrun them to the gate. I only managed five or six metres when the nearest one hit me such a blow that I immediately fell to the ground. I cursed my bad luck and tried to shield myself from their kicks. My last conscious thought was a prayer that they wouldn't kill me.

37

A red mist in the morning

Dare to be yourself.
André Gide

I awoke in a hospital bed with no immediate recollection of how I had got there. Every part of me was aching, and I was heavily bandaged on both arms. Slowly, I began to remember the few brief moments that led up to the attack – nothing more. I wasn't even sure how much time had passed since the attack. A nurse came to my bedside, acknowledged that I was awake, then left. I was too sore to think. A doctor appeared with the same nurse as before. He was talking to me, but I was finding it difficult to understand him. My head hurt and I felt disorientated. Then they both left. I began to drift into sleep. Answers would come later.

The next time I awoke, I felt a little better. If they had given me painkillers, then they were doing their job, though to try to turn still proved painful. A little later another doctor came by.

'It would seem that someone doesn't like you, by the looks of the beating you took last evening. Luckily for you, some passers-by raised the alarm and your attackers fled before they could do more serious damage. The police were here earlier to interview you about what happened. You were unconscious at the time. They said they will be back later. I suggest you get as much rest as you can and let your body heal. There is nothing broken, but plenty of cuts and bruises. We've run a few tests and, if they come back clear, then you can probably go home tomorrow. We prefer to keep you here today, more as a precaution than anything else. Is there anyone we can contact on your behalf? A wife, maybe? You'll need a bit of help for the first few days at home.'

'No, doctor, there is no wife. But I can arrange some support. I will be fine. Don't worry, I'll take it easy.' I didn't want to phone Yvette, partly because I didn't want to worry her, especially only for one day. But if someone did set those thugs on me, I was sure it would have something to do with Yvette. I couldn't imagine that it was a random attack.

Within half an hour, the police turned up asking all sorts of questions. What was I doing in the Gardens? Did I know my assailants? Did I have enemies? Could I think of a motive for the attack? They were sure the attack was planned and that my attackers knew I would leave the Gardens by that gate. Robbery was not the motive, as nothing had been taken. After some more tedious questions, and a promise they would speak to me later, they parted with a final comment.

'Someone has it in for you, monsieur, and you and I both need to know who that person is. Au revoir.'

Like any great city, Paris has its undesirables. I had seen some of these unsavoury characters the day I spent with Dr Bricard's daughter, Marie. The French film industry built its reputation making films of the city's low life. My first tentative thoughts were that I was just unlucky. I was in the wrong place at the wrong time. I should not have been walking in a park at that time of night. Tourists are well advised to be careful of the city's parks after dark, especially the Bois de Boulogne where all sorts of nocturnal activities take place that are best left unseen by decent people. That anyone would want to have me beaten up or, maybe even killed, seemed absurd. As I lay still, my thoughts began to dwell on what the possibilities and probabilities of someone wanting to hurt me were. I couldn't imagine that Thérèse would be behind some wild revenge attack; not now, so long after our break-up, when we seemed to have put much of what had happened in the past behind us. Nor would any of her children be behind anything as remote as an attack on my person – I was a mere detail in their lives. No: if there was a perpetrator, he or she came from my recent history. That ruled out Emile, not that he would ever countenance anything so barbaric. There was only one name I could think of that fitted the bill, and that name was...Pascal!

It had to be him. It was he who was behind the photographs given to Yvette, of Thérèse and me when we met on l'île des Cygnes. He admitted he had done it to get at me. This was the sort of thing he would do, coward that he was. There was no other answer. Pascal was the culprit.

The following morning I was impatient to be discharged. I had spent most of the night thinking about the events in the park, trying to remember if my assailants had said something that might give me a clue about the attack and who was behind it. My mind was a blank. All I was able to do was visualise the moments up to the attack. I couldn't even describe my attackers. When the police returned, I was even less helpful than before. The more my faculties returned, the less I could tell them. I certainly wasn't going to give up Pascal's name, no matter how much I loathed the man. If it was him who arranged the attack – and I was sure it was him – I would deal with it my own way. The police left with nothing more than what they already knew. We agreed I would get in touch if I remembered anything that might help them find my attackers.

Eventually a doctor came and said I was fit enough to go home. The tests were clear. I was to rest as much as possible over the next few days and, if I felt unwell for any reason, I was to come back to the hospital immediately. I dressed as quickly as I could under the circumstances and departed. I took the first taxi I could find, having declined the services of an ambulance. I wanted to get back to my apartment as fast as I could. I could lick my wounds there and, with a change of clothes, make ready to confront my nemesis.

When I got back to my flat, I washed myself thoroughly, avoiding the bandages where possible. My face was covered in black-and-blue bruises, and my ribs still hurt as hell. Fresh clothes made me feel a little better, and a quick malt whisky before leaving sharpened my senses for what I was going to do. I locked up and hailed a passing taxi to take me to the bar where Pascal waited drinks. I wasn't sure what I would say to him or if he would even be there. All I knew was that I would challenge him to deny he had set up the attack on me. What I would do after that remained to be seen.

The journey was painful in the extreme, but no more so than the journey from the hospital. As luck would have it, Pascal was standing behind the bar as I entered. He looked shocked to see me and exclaimed, 'What's happened to you? You look terrible. Have you had an accident?'

'As if you don't know, you piece of scum. You can't fight your own battles and need to get someone else to do it for you.'

'What are you talking about? You're mad! Are you saying someone did this to you and you blame me for it? You're off your head! I don't like you, can't stand you, but not enough to get someone else to do my dirty work. I would rather have done it myself. That way, I would have got the pleasure from it.'

I felt my temper rise and lunged across the bar, grabbing Pascal by the front of his apron and pulling him towards me.

The pain from my injuries sent a searing heat through my body, but I kept hold of him tightly, dragging him closer to me. Bottles and glasses sitting on the counter spilled over and fell to the floor. The sound of the breaking glass brought the older barman who worked there rushing through from the back room where the piano was situated. He grabbed hold of me, pulling my arms down on to the counter, exacerbating my pain to the point that I could no longer hold on to Pascal. I lurched back in agony, then, curled into myself, crossing my arms around my chest, tried to regain an even breath.

The old barman sat me on a seat in the corner, letting me recover from my pains. He even brought over a whisky and told me to sip it slowly. I did as I was told. The whisky did its job and I began to ease. I was still in pain, but at least I could straighten myself up. As I looked around the bar at the few people who had witnessed my act of folly, nodding my head apologetically, I realised someone was missing. Pascal was nowhere to be seen.

I asked the barman for another drink and paid for both. He insisted the first drink was free; for medicinal purposes. I thanked him and told him I would pay for any damage, and took my drink through to the room with the piano. He mumbled something about no damage being done, other than a couple of broken glasses – a daily occurrence – and for me to relax – the excitement was over.

I pulled out the piano stool and sat down carefully, then began playing. I probably should have left the bar. If Pascal didn't have anything to do with my assault, he was probably on the way to the police station to report my attack on him. What if the same two policemen turned up at the bar, the scene of the crime, and here was I, guilty as charged? There again, he may have run off because he was as guilty as sin. My fingers, sore as they were, began playing Philip Glass's Metamorphosis #5.

38

One confession too many

There is only one happiness in life, to love and be loved.
George Sand

I was on my fifth or sixth large whisky, my playing becoming slower and slower with each whisky, when Yvette came into the bar with Pascal a few steps behind her. I ignored them and continued playing. Yvette looked angry. Pascal retreated to safety behind the bar's counter, reinforcing my view that the man was a coward. I looked up at Yvette and smiled. I tried to give the appearance that none of what she had no doubt heard from Pascal was of my doing, and I was just passing some time enjoying the piano and having a drink. Yvette stood by the piano for a few moments, then said: 'Let me take you home, John. My car's outside. You're in no condition to sit here and drink. Pick up your jacket and let's go.' She sounded annoyed. I stayed put.

'I didn't know you had a car. You've never mentioned a car before. Did you just buy one?' I could hear the slight slur in my voice as I questioned Yvette. She looked indignant.

'I've always had a car, John. It's just that I very rarely need to use it. Please don't be awkward. Come to the car with me and don't say anything to Pascal. It wasn't him who set those men on you. So please, don't do anything silly and please stop playing that piano. It sounds terrible, like a dirge. Let's just go.'

'Just like that!' I said, trying to snap my fingers with little success. 'And don't frighten little Pascal. Well, if it wasn't the little rat, who got me beaten up by those gorillas? Who was it, then?'

'Just get in the car, John. I'll explain everything when we get to your apartment.'

'Goodbye, piano. Goodbye.' I closed the lid, picked up my jacket and brushed past Yvette on my way to the door. I staggered a little at first, then found my balance. I wanted to say something rude to Pascal but couldn't think of anything clever that would do the trick. Instead I just thanked the old barman who had been kind to me and walked out of the door.

Yvette's car was a small Citroën – the smallest one manufactured, by the look of it – and had never been washed. Well, not recently.

'What colour is the car?' I asked sarcastically, before getting into one of the tightest spaces I had ever sat in, every movement causing pain.

'I told you. I don't use it very often. It collects the dust of the passing traffic. Anyway, it's blue, as you well know.'

Every time I tried to ask Yvette a question about the attack, she would tell me to wait till we got to my apartment. I tried to sit quietly, but every time Yvette braked a surge of pain would make me call out. Yvette would then apologise. But it would happen again and again until we got back to the flat. She gave one final apology as she got out of the car and came round to help me do likewise.

I felt quite light-headed as we walked the few metres to the front door. I was keen for a coffee and a little sleep. Yvette was good enough to make a coffee and help me settle on the sofa once we got inside. I could see that she was troubled and trying to pick her moment before explaining her part in my downfall. I sipped my coffee and made myself comfortable. Yvette sat across from me. I was sobering up fast.

'A lot has happened in the last few weeks, John. Not all of it good. In fact, very little of it good. However, it has made me think long and hard about what is happening in my life just now, and how you are central to most of it.'

I wanted to post a marker by saying the attack two nights ago wasn't my fault and that my argument with Pascal was justified. However, I sensed that Yvette didn't want interruptions at this point, and held back from making any comment.

'When I first met you, I was very taken by you. You are a very desirable man, and I quickly fell in love with you. I needed someone to love and you came into my life just at the right time. I remember the day when Monsieur Bourdan, the fruit merchant, first told me there was a man living nearby who was writing a book about Utrillo. I was so thrilled that someone, who wasn't French, was writing a book about Utrillo. He said I would know you when I saw you. He described you perfectly.

'What you need to remember is that I am a relative of the man you are writing about – Maurice Utrillo – albeit a very distant relative. I still have family other than my parents in Bessiness-sur-Gartempe, where Maurice's family came from, that I visit from time to time. When Madeleine, Maurice's grandmother, brought her young four year old daughter, Marie-Clémentine, to Paris in 1869, they stayed with my great-great aunt near the Bastille. She was Madeleine's aunt. When Maurice became famous, his mother gave one of his paintings to my great aunt as a gift. She wanted to thank my family for their support down through the years. That painting hangs on my living room wall. It's the one you covet so much – Rue Francoeur.'

Now I remembered why I knew the name of Bessiness-sur-Gartempe. Utrillo's grandmother came from the town. I cursed myself for not remembering this, and now I was being told by my girlfriend that she was a distant cousin of the subject of my book. Yvette's revelation slowly sifted into my brain.

'Wow!' I said. 'You kept that quiet. I'm surprised you told me.' I couldn't hold back my sarcasm. 'It seems I am the last person you tell anything to. Is this your normal modus operandi?'

Yvette ignored me and poured more coffee. I still didn't know who had set me up two nights ago, but I was intrigued with her story. I knew that the Valadon's had found refuge in the Bastille area when they first came to Paris, but no-one – to my knowledge – knew who with. What concerned me more was that I was beginning to think I was hearing a confession by Yvette. I wasn't sure where her monologue would take us, or leave us for that matter. I felt a little uneasy. We were going through a difficult time together, and I had been less than pleased with her behaviour lately. But I wasn't ready to let go. I let her continue without interrupting any further.

'When we first met, I was just leaving Paris to visit my family in Bessiness. I told them all about you – that you were writing a history on Maurice, and that I thought you were charming and I intended to see you again when I returned to Paris. They told me to be cautious, that I was still sore from what happened with Edouard, that I was vulnerable. They advised me not to tell you about the painting unless I was sure you wouldn't exploit me. That was why I kept my connections to myself. I thought if we became... friends... then I would let you know about the painting. I keep it a secret, as I can't afford to insure it. Now your friends from London harass me every day about it. I told them its existence is to remain secret, but they don't listen. They have offered to insure it for me if I let them photograph it and give them sole pictorial rights. They assure me they will only acknowledge that the painting is in a private collection. I'm not sure what to do. I know it will help your book if I say okay. You will have to speak to them for me. I will only do it if you make the arrangements.

'Everything was fine with us and my life in general until Edouard came back from Africa. He now says he wants me back. At first I hated him for leaving me and ruining my life, and then I hated him for coming back and ruining it again. It was Edouard who showed me the photographs of you and Thérèse. He got me so mixed up I didn't know what to believe.

'It was Edouard who sent the men to attack you. They were men who he had stitched up from their drunken fights in Saint Denis before he went to Africa; the ones he called 'les mauvais'. He only told me of this earlier today, when we met to discuss our divorce. It was then that he told me he wanted us to get back together again. I said I was seeing you and that I had no intention of getting back with him. We then argued about you and he let it slip that he had done something to sort you out. When I pressed him to tell me what he had done, he eventually confessed that he had phoned a man he knew whom he had helped a few times when he turned up injured at the hospital's accident and emergency unit. This man owed Edouard a favour for not reporting his injuries to the police. If I had known about this, I would have stopped it straight away. I would have come to the hospital if I had known sooner. It was only when Pascal arrived at my flat, an hour ago, that I knew where you were and what you had done. If you don't believe me, check your phone's answering machine. You'll find a message from me telling you this. Will you report Edouard for this? He said he tried to stop it but couldn't get in touch with the guy. He assured me he just wanted you roughed up. He thought you might leave Paris more quickly if you felt unsafe. I think I believe him, John. He wouldn't be so stupid to do anything more than that.'

So there I had it. It was her loving husband, after all. I doubted whether I would be able to prove any of this if I went to the police, and Yvette was clearly not going to report Edouard. What concerned me more was her defence of him. She obviously still had some sort of feelings for him. Her tone of voice gave that away.

'I thought he wanted a divorce,' I said. 'Why has he changed his mind? Are you sure you are not getting back with him?' I asked as matter-of-factly as I could. There was nothing else I wanted to know at this exact time.

'He says he now wants to get back together; that he's sorry for what he did and that it was all a mistake. He says he regrets what he has done. But it is too late for him and me. What went before was bad enough, but all this mess makes me realise that I could never trust him again. No, Edouard and I will never be together again. I've told him this.'

'What about us? Do we have a future?'

I don't think Yvette was expecting my question. She looked uncomfortable the moment I had said it. I sensed this had been a question she had been thinking about too, but didn't anticipate it coming up today.

'I'm not sure. Some days I want you so badly; other days I just want to be on my own. I have so many mixed feelings about so many things – all the things that have happened to us. Sometimes I feel the fates are conspiring against us. I'm also really not sure if you love me. Something in me tells me you still have feelings for Thérèse. She is a beautiful woman, full of grace. You know I think she is still in love with you, even after what you put her through. I need a man who needs me as much as I need him. I'm not sure you need me. I know you want me – I can understand that in a man – but I'm not sure you need me. I think you need a different kind of woman from what I am. I think you need Thérèse.'

What I needed there and then was a Scotch, and couldn't get one. I lay on the sofa, wanting to get up, but I couldn't. I had just been told who was behind the attack on me, and I could not have cared less. Yvette had just closed the book on us, more or less. But more than that: she had just told me what I needed, and it wasn't her. Was this her way of letting me down lightly, by giving me something else to think about, to ponder on, while she slipped away to get on with the rest of her life?

'Are you telling me this is it, that it's finished between us, all because you think another woman still fancies me even after all the terrible-things-I-am-supposed-to-have-done-to-her. Did she tell you that? Did she say, "I still love John"? Or is this just a clever way of you getting back with Edouard – who is still your husband, remember? I'd rather you were honest with me and just say it's over. Don't bring anyone else into the equation. That's a cheap trick.'

'I'm sorry, John. I didn't mean to hurt you. I'm not playing any tricks on you or anyone else. I genuinely believe that Thérèse still loves you. Call it women's intuition; call it what you like. And, yes, I think you still love her. It just hasn't dawned on you yet. Let's not end fighting. Think about what I am saying. Try and see it from where I'm standing. Both our pasts have come back to haunt us, and we need to deal with them differently. But not together.'

That was it. I suggested she leave; that I would be okay. I assured her that, if I needed help, I would call her. This was the end, and I couldn't even demonstrate how I felt. What I hoped

239

was going to be a new beginning in my life had ended right in front of me, and I couldn't do anything to stop it. I knew it was over. Every bone in my body ached.

39

It's an ill wind

Paris is most beautiful when one is about to leave it.
Robert Brasillach

Yvette had walked out of my life, leaving behind the debris of a failed romance. Was I getting a taste of my own medicine? Maybe not. I have known failure before, even tragedy, but now my perceptions were being challenged in a way I had not experienced before. What Yvette had done, whether consciously or not, was to leave me with a number of unanswered questions. I wanted to phone her to ask what she meant about me still being in love with Thérèse. Surely this was only a convenient speculation on her part. She had no real grounds to base her comment on, that I was still in love with Thérèse. I had been entirely honest with her, but I knew in my heart that she would say it was her intuition and that any phone call would be a waste of time. Her mind was made up, and I would have to live with the consequences.

I didn't report Edouard to the police. My physical pains came nowhere near the emotional ones I was feeling. Any revenge would only be petty and spiteful and, more importantly, nor would it affect Yvette's view on these matters. It happened and I survived. I played the message Yvette had left on my answering machine. Sure enough, what she told me was in her message. I couldn't bring myself to delete the message and found myself listening to it over and over again.

For a few days after our break-up, I pondered on the

question – 'What if...?' What if Edouard had never come back to Paris? What if Pascal and I had hit it off? What if Thérèse and me had never met on l'île des Cygnes? Would any of this have changed the final outcome? I doubted it very much. All I was doing was keeping something alive that was causing me pain. It would be better for me if I concentrated my thoughts on something more tangible than the fallout from our failed relationship.

Something more tangible was indeed on the horizon. The Open Day at the Institute was only a couple of days away, and I had decided to go along and see what happened. I was hoping Thérèse would be there, and Frieda too. What my role would be on the day was up to Emile. But he had given me the impression we would have ample time to 'catch up'.

I spent the intervening days revisiting galleries and places of interest, in between talking to Fiona Shaw, my editor in London. She was delighted with my written material and only had to make a page or two of changes – which wasn't too bad, considering she had almost re-written some of her other clients' books. It transpired that Yvette had taken up her offer to insure the Utrillo painting and had agreed a tidy sum for the pictorial rights. When I told her that I was no longer seeing Yvette, she was neither here nor there. 'Plenty more, boy,' was all she said. 'Plenty more.'

My body was healing fast, and I was slowly coming to terms with what had happened between Yvette and me. I was going to miss Paris too. In some ways I thought of myself as a Parisian. I probably knew more about the city than the average citizen. I had certainly walked along more streets and visited more bars in a year than most would do in a life time. In a few weeks' time all of this would be behind me. I wasn't sure if this pleased me or not.

40

The pieces fall together

There are three things I have never understood – painting, music, women.
Bernard de Fontenelle

It had to rain on the day the Institute had its Open Day. It couldn't have rained harder in Manchester or Glasgow as it did that day in Paris. I was bemused. How could Emile Renouf let this happen? He couldn't have been involved in selecting the date of the Open Day, otherwise the sun would be shining. Emile would have consulted metrological records, shamen and fortune tellers to make sure it was the best of the weather on the day in question.

I decided to walk to the Institute despite the downpour. I recognised I was still, to some degree, in victim mode; a state of mind that in more severe circumstances could lead to self-harm. My level of despair was far from such a nadir that I would expose myself to anything more than a drink too many and a walk in inclement weather. A little rain would do me no harm at all. And anyway: we Northerners were used to it.

As I approached the Institute, I was surprised to find the streets busy with all sorts of people heading towards the entrance of the main building. It crossed my mind that the occasion was more important than I had given it credit. This wasn't a fun day out but, rather, a day when families, in the most part, would make important decisions about their children's future.

Rather than go into the main building, where the

dignitaries would be welcoming the intellectually curious, I decided to walk over to the lecture rooms where the 'Foreign Legion' spent most of its time during my twelve months as a post-graduate. This would give me time to collect my thoughts and, hopefully, a chance to dry off my hair and face before venturing over to the official proceedings.

I passed a number of familiar landmarks on my way to the grassy knoll where the almond trees blossomed a decade or so earlier. I never considered that the door to the annexe might be locked. Thankfully it wasn't. I entered as if I was a burglar entering a home where a family slept, not sure what to expect, but ready for the unexpected. What I found was not what I expected under any circumstances.

The room was poorly lit. I stood still, waiting until my eyes adjusted to the available light. I didn't want to put on the lights in case I attracted the attention of any staff wandering around. As I stood there, I became acutely aware that I was not the only person in the room. I could hear the breathing of someone else; I could smell the scent of a woman. As my sight adapted to the room's dimness, I saw my shadowy companion.

'Thérèse, what in... what are you doing here?' Her presence threw me off guard. I stammered, 'I mean, here in the annexe? Shouldn't you be in the assembly hall?' I was certainly not expecting to find her here.

'No doubt I am doing the same as you. I wanted some time to myself before the festivities began – and a place to dry myself.'

'Of course. Ditto. It's good to see you. I hadn't expected it to be here, of all places. I don't know why I came here. It just seemed the right thing to do. Checking up on the past and all that. I miss the grassy knoll and the almond trees.' I heard the words leave my lips before I could register their meaning. 'I miss you too.'

'I miss you too. Isn't that strange? And here we are in the room where it all started. Isn't this an odd coincidence?'

I walked towards her, my eyes fixed on hers, looking for a sign, any sign, that would tell me not to proceed a step further. None came. I took her in my arms and kissed her. She kissed me right back. We clung to each other for a few moments. I could feel the heat of her body. I could feel her womanly shape. I wanted the moment to last forever, but Thérèse pushed me away.

'We should go over to the main lecture hall, John. We're being foolish...'

'Maybe so, but it was nice to be foolish – if only for a moment.'

'Dare we be foolish again? Maybe you can, but I can't.'

When we got outside Thérèse noticed that my face had the marks my attackers left as a souvenir.

'What happened to your face? It's bruised. Were you in a fight?'

'No, nothing like that. I was mugged. It serves me right for being in the wrong place at the wrong time.' I lied. I didn't want to drag Thérèse into the events of the last week.

'It still looks quite sore. Are you sure you are okay?'

'Nothing a kiss couldn't help.'

'You've had your quota for today. Think yourself lucky. You caught me off guard.'

We both laughed.

When we arrived in the main hall, the Director was just finishing his speech to the assembled crowd. Emile, who was standing next to the Director, nodded in our direction, acknowledging our appearance. We nodded back.

A polite applause greeted the Director's closing remarks.

Emile left the podium and joined us.

'I see you have already managed to find each other' He said this with just the slightest hint of sarcasm, implying more than was deserved. 'Have you had a fight already?'

Thérèse came to my defence. 'John was mugged,' she told him. Emile hardly registered what she had said.

'I have to go over to the faculty to speak to the prospective students, but it would be helpful if you both could wait here. We are assembling some stalls that will have literature for each of the faculties. You could lend a hand at the microbiology stall, speak to anyone showing an interest and maybe even send them over to the faculty rooms. After that, it would be good if we could meet for lunch in the refectory.'

We all agreed to meet for lunch. It wasn't what I wanted to do but, under the circumstances, I felt I couldn't decline.

As we waited for the technicians to assemble the stalls (which they did in a matter of seconds) we stood in a corner, keeping out of the way. I'm sure we were both thinking about what had happened a little earlier. I certainly was. Did our kiss mean something? The moment my lips touched hers, my heart was fit to burst. Did she have the same feeling, or was she just caught in the heat of the moment? Thérèse didn't look my way as the men assembled the stalls. Was she looking away deliberately? After all, it was she who brought us both back to reality in the lecture room.

As the stalls were erected, a range of materials were brought out of boxes and placed on the tables: brochures, leaflets and magazines; everything and anything to do with the Institute's microbiology department. Then staff appeared out of nowhere, or so it seemed, and stepped behind the tables. I introduced myself to a young and rather earnest young man. He was in his final year and had been roped in to assist. When

Thérèse introduced herself (by her married name) the young man immediately smiled and took on a different posture.

'We have all heard of you, Dr Dumard. Professor Renouf said you might be here today. He told us you and your husband were the main reason the faculty's research reputation is so highly regarded across France. It is a pleasure to meet you.'

You had to hand it to Emile; he could charm anyone, anywhere.

As we spoke to the young student, we were joined by Frieda Pechstein. At first Thérèse didn't recognise her and asked her if she was interested in one of the courses. Frieda and I burst out laughing, much to the bemusement of the young student and Thérèse's consternation.

'Don't you remember me, Dr Dumard? I was in John's class. Frieda Pechstein. I was your German student, from Düsseldorf!'

The morning passed quickly enough. We said goodbye to Jules, the young student, and made or way to the refectory. It was still raining. Thérèse and Frieda had reacquainted themselves and formed an immediate friendship, and largely ignored me. I had no idea what they talked about. Every time I tried to break into their conversation, I was steered back out of it. I was told it was girls' talk. I knew my place and walked behind them smiling.

Emile was already in the refectory. I had to look twice when I saw where he was sitting. It was the very seats that Thérèse and I had sat on all those years before as we planned our first evening together. Even the décor was the same. I wondered if she noticed. If she did, she never let on.

We ordered food and drinks and kept our conversation polite. Emile made a joke about my work as an art historian, claiming he didn't understand painting or, for that matter, music. It was all a bit abstract for him. Some older lecturers that were there recognised Thérèse and came over and paid their respects. Thérèse accepted their acknowledgements with grace and dignity. Time had worked its miracle. Whatever sentiments her former colleagues had harboured before, none materialised today. I felt relieved.

'I think today has been a success, don't you agree? We have had some very good enquiries from some very able students, and even your rehabilitation seems to have worked out for you Thérèse, judging by how well you have been received.'

There was a stifled silence between us. My first thought was that I had misheard what Emile had said. I looked quickly at both Thérèse and Frieda. I could feel their embarrassment.

'Excuse me, Emile, but did you say that you thought Thérèse had been rehabilitated? Was that the word you used, r-e-h-a-b-i-l-i-t-a-t-e-d?' I was becoming angry and wanted him to apologise for his crassness.

'Leave it, John. I'm sure Emile didn't mean it like that.'

'Like hell I'll leave it. He meant it all right. He has no right to speak to you like that. If I was anywhere else other than this refectory, I would break every bone in his body.' I leaned into his face.

'Apologise to Thérèse. You have no right to say what you did.'

Emile looked indignant. His normal state of smugness had evaporated. Not only did he appear indignant about my demand, but there was anger in his eyes. A raging anger that was about to erupt.

'I will certainly not. I may not have meant to say what I did in the manner I said it, but Thérèse was elemental in bringing this Institute into disrepute, and her sordid little affair with you ruined one of the finest men I knew. She deserved everything that happened to her. If you act like a whore, you'll get treated like one.'

Emile was leaning into the centre of the table. He tried to keep his voice low but, as he spat out his words, the volume rose. I looked around. Others had heard his venom. His anger was not replete.

'Look at both of you! You turn up here today as if nothing had ever happened. But a man died because you couldn't keep your hands off each other. He was a brilliant man, one of the finest academics this country has produced. He had everything to live for. We were working to put this Institute on the world map – a centre of excellence, second to none. But, no – oh, no – you had to ruin everything. You couldn't even stop yourself from getting pregnant. Was that too much to ask? A stupid teenage girl could have done better than you.'

He was looking directly at Thérèse.

'That was the final straw. Yes, Claude knew you were having an affair. He didn't care. You meant nothing to him. And just in case you haven't worked it out yet, it was me whom he loved. Not you! You were just the mother of his children, nothing more than that. You could have your affair. Have all the affairs you wanted. He thought you would be discreet. You had far too much to lose to be stupid. We even planned our times together knowing you would use Claude's absence as an opportunity to meet your Scottish lover. While you thought Claude was giving a lecture at some university or college we were at his summer house toasting you and lover boy here.'

Thérèse was in a state of shock. Her face turned paler and paler with each of Emile's revelations and accusations. My own anger had subdued and turned to incredulity as he mouthed his spite on Thérèse. We had no idea that he and Claude were lovers.

'Don't look so surprised, Thérèse. Did it never really cross your mind that Claude didn't love you? Well you've now got the rest of your life to think about it. He loved me. He was the man I loved. And you pair of rutting rabbits killed him. Believe me, I'm glad that you suffered in the way you did. You deserved every minute of it.'

Thérèse stood up. At first I thought she was going to slap Emile, but she walked right passed him. Frieda and I quickly followed her out of the refectory. I would deal with the little rat later. When we caught up with her, we could see the tears streaming down her face. There was no way she could hide her hurt and pain. It had stopped raining.

Frieda suggested we go to her car. We could gather our thoughts once inside and decide what to do then. Frieda was as shocked as I was about Emile's outburst. We were both quite disorientated by what Emile had said. A million thoughts were going through my head; none made any sense. I had no idea what Thérèse was thinking. All I knew was that she was hurting, probably more than at any other time of her life.

Once inside the car Thérèse looked at me. Her expression was of someone who had just been stripped of all dignity, all humanity. Her eyes cried out for love, for some kind of affection to help ease the pain she was feeling. She looked like a little girl lost in a vortex of hate. I took her in my arms and held her close to me. There was nothing I could say at that moment that would diminish how she felt. Enough words had been said.

41

Facing up to the facts

Misfortune has some purpose.
Noël du Fail

We drove Thérèse home to Issy-les Molineaux. She sobbed most of the way there. Frieda and I kept our own counsel. Even in death, Claude still had the means and the ability to hurt Thérèse. I cursed Emile Renouf in a way I had never cursed anyone before. What he had done earlier was unforgivable – to be so cruel after all these years had passed. He must have been waiting for the day when he could deliver the final blow. Was he happy, now he had got his revenge?

When we got to Thérèse's block of flats, Frieda helped her up to her apartment. We hadn't discussed what we would do when we got there, It just happened. I suppose, in my mind, it was better if Frieda went with her – someone impartial, someone who wouldn't remind her too much of all the trials and tribulations she had faced today and for the last twelve years.

I took myself off for a walk. It would take Frieda some time to calm the situation and hopefully get Thérèse to rest. I found myself at an outdoor market that ran a half mile or so along rue du Général Leclerc, before it culminated in a triangle of landscaped concrete that seemed to be the centre of Issy-les Molineaux. I rummaged about the bric-a-brac that was on display. Nothing caught my eye. The quality of nick-knack was poor. The market was no Marché aux Puces de Clignancourt. In fact it was just a cut above Paddy's Market back in Glasgow, which specialised in circulating domestic debris to the down-and-out.

On my return to the car, Frieda was waiting inside.

'She's sleeping. I gave her a sedative I found in her medicine cabinet. It'll help her sleep for the rest of the day. The poor woman was really distraught. She obviously never suspected a thing. It wasn't a nice way to find out that your husband was gay and thought so little of you. Do you think Emile Renouf planned to tell her all of this today?'

'I wouldn't put it passed him. The man is a rat. But let's not talk here. Can we go back into town? I feel I need a drink.'

'Where do you want to go?'

'Back to my place, if you don't mind. It's near the Institute. I'll direct you from there. I feel I need some privacy. We can talk there.'

When we got to my flat, I made some coffee for Frieda and poured myself a large whisky. We had been quiet on the journey back from Issy-les Molineaux. This pleased me. I didn't want to have to make quick assertions about Emile's revelations, and my part in it, for the sake of conversation. I needed time to think through what had been said, and to analyse all that I remembered from the time Thérèse and I first met. I was looking for clues and didn't want to be disturbed needlessly. The journey gave me that opportunity.

'Sorry about the state of the flat. It looks a bit empty. I've been packing my things away, getting ready to go back home. My work here is finished, but I managed to squeeze out a couple of weeks extra from the publishers so that I could wind down. It's been some couple of weeks!'

I took a large gulp of The Glenlivet. It worked its miracle.

Frieda sipped her coffee.

'Tell me, John. Did you know any of this? What Emile Renouf said today?'

'No, none of it. And I don't think Thérèse did either. We always thought that Emile was homosexual. Most of us did back then, if you remember, but we never had any proof that he was. We never saw him with a boyfriend; only Professor Dumard. Now it transpires that the professor was his boyfriend. What baffles me is how they found out about Thérèse and my affair.'

'I don't think that would have been too difficult. There was a fair bit of talk back then, between us students, if you and she were an item. Some of the boys were quite open in their speculation. I suppose some of this could have been overheard. Some may even have joked to Emile Renouf about it. I promise you, John, I never said a word.'

There was no point in mulling over what was spilled milk. The professor did find out and used it to his advantage.

'I suppose our affair was a mere detail to Emile and the Professor; a convenient one all the same. Everything would have been fine if Thérèse and I hadn't messed it up. It's the hypocrisy of it all that gets me – and I include myself in that too. Everything was acceptable, as long as certain lines weren't crossed. But we stupidly or accidentally crossed the line.'

'What are you going to do? We can't leave Thérèse to cope on her own. She'll need a friend to help her get over this. Someone needs to visit her tomorrow and see how she is.'

Frieda was right. Someone should check on her. I offered a suggestion.

'I'll phone her tomorrow and find out how she is. We can decide then if she wants me to come down. She has an old friend, a woman she used to lunch with. She might contact her.

But I'll phone tomorrow morning and see. There's nothing more we can do today.'

I poured myself another whisky and topped up Frieda's coffee. Our conversation turned to other matters. We talked about our meeting in Luxembourg Gardens, how we had enjoyed each other's company. I told her about Yvette and how another romance had reached a sorry end. I didn't change my story about being mugged. It was better left that way. I didn't want to encourage alternative opinions of what I should have done or not done about the attack.

'So, you're a free agent again,' Frieda stated with a knowing look.

'I suppose I am, on the face of it. But I don't feel free from my feelings for Thérèse. Yvette is convinced that I am still in love with her, and that was one of her reasons for breaking off our relationship. I'm not so sure if my feelings for her have more to do with guilt than love.'

'Do we ever truly know if we are in love? Love can mean different things, depending on the circumstances. We have a passion for love and a love for passion. Somehow we get mixed up about how we feel. Do you feel a passion for Thérèse?'

'If you mean do I want to make love to her, then the answer is yes. I still feel a longing for her. But I've been trying to suppress those kinds of feelings because of what happened in the past between us. She needs more than physical love or passion. She needs... she deserves absolute love. Love in all its facets; the full faculty of love.'

Frieda got up from her chair and picked up the bottle of whisky and topped up my glass. She then placed the bottle back on the table and sat down beside me on the sofa.

'Do you think I need love, John? Do you not think I deserve absolute love too?'

At this Frieda put her arm around my shoulder, inviting me to caress her, easing her body closer to mine. The tension between us was tangible. Here was a beautiful woman, offering herself to me. All I had to do was reach out and take it.

'Is this all it takes Frieda? Is this the love that you want – just the passion? If it is, then I'm sorry. Right now I want more – I need to give more. Today I saw a woman cruelly hurt, all because she fell in love with me. I might regret my decision tomorrow, but right now I think it best if we don't do anything we could both regret in the morning.'

'Damn you for being right, John Gil-Martin. I throw myself at you like a common whore, and you turn me down – again. Your friend Yvette is right: you have to sort out what it is you need from Thérèse before you can move on. Have you ever thought that all this talk of Thérèse could simply be theoretical, that she is not thinking along the same lines? What will you do then?'

'You're right. This may all be empty talk. But I need to sort out my heart before I start losing it to someone else.'

Frieda stood up and pushed her skirt down over her knees. Our adventure was over for the day, with no damage being done. As she said her goodbyes she promised she would phone to find out how Thérèse was coping. I promised I would not leave Paris without speaking to her one last time.

42

A final judgement

It's because everything must end that everything is so beautiful.
Charles-Ferdinand Ramuz

The trial of Magdeleine Dupré for the murder of Rene Rousselier was due to start later that morning in the Paris Criminal Court. I had planned to go to the trial as my final 'act of involvement' in the great city. From what I had read in the newspapers, the outcome was a foregone conclusion. The poor woman was guilty of murder. The only question in anyone's mind was what the punishment would be.

I telephoned Thérèse as early as I thought befitting under the circumstances, and was glad when she answered straight away. She had got herself up an hour earlier and made some coffee. She said she was fine and coming to terms with what Emile Renouf had said. She thanked me for getting her home and asked me to thank Frieda on her behalf. I assured her I would do so. She sounded so formal and defensive, as if speaking with me would expose her to the haunting feelings she was trying to suppress. Her formality frustrated me, and I found myself becoming agitated by it.

'Thérèse, listen to me. I know you are hurting and trying to cope with everything that happened yesterday. But please don't keep me at arm's length. I want to be part of the solution, not the cause of the problem. I'll kill the little rat if you just say the word. I've been meaning to do it for years. Can I come and see you? I need to know that you are all right. I can't leave Paris again with unfinished business between us.'

There was a silence at the other end of the phone. 'Are you still there' I asked.

'Yes, I'm still here. Do you think coming here is going to change the way we are? Is it going to alter what's happened? Will it make my pain go away? Come if you like, but not this morning. I am going to meet a friend for lunch. I have much to say to her, and no doubt she to me. Give me some time to myself first. Come later. Tonight. I'm sorry if I sound distant. I don't mean to be. Come later, John. Later.'

Thérèse's decision to meet her friend allowed me to attend the trial after all. It would be a good diversion for me. From what I knew of Thérèse's friend, Colette – if it was Colette she was meeting – she would be in safe hands. I felt better, now that I knew Thérèse had some purposeful activity to her day. I only hoped I could make matters better when I visited later that day.

As I got ready to go to the trial, the phone rang. I half expected it to be Thérèse, or maybe Frieda to find out how Thérèse was feeling this morning. I picked up the phone to be asked:

'Hello, is that you, John?'

'Yes.'

'It's me, Yvette. I was hoping you'd still be here – in Paris, I mean. Can I talk?'

This was completely unexpected. I didn't know what to think. Why phone now? Had something happened to her deal with my publishers? I didn't want to sound cold, but I was still irritated by how she brought our relationship to a close.

'I thought you'd said everything you wanted to say to me.'

'That's why I'm phoning. I might have been a little hasty

257

in some of the things I said to you. I've been giving it a lot of thought recently. I was upset with all the events that were happening around me and reacted badly. I suppose you got the brunt of it because I associated you with all of it. I'm sorry, John. Is there any way I can make it up to you? Maybe we could meet for a coffee later and let me apologise properly.'

'And what about Thérèse?' I threw this at her. 'You seemed pretty convinced I was in love with her, and she me. I thought that was your main reason for bringing our relationship to a close – that I was in love with someone else.'

'I know I said that, but I was angry with you. I don't know why. I just thought that she had a hold over you. I was jealous that she could still snap her fingers and you would go running. Can we not do this over the phone? Can we not meet up and talk this through face to face? I don't want you to be angry with me. I said some stupid things that I now regret. I can be in the corner café later today, when I finish my work at the hospital. We could talk then.'

I didn't say no, but I didn't say yes either. What I did say was that I was busy, but I'd see how I got on. She said she would be there waiting. We hung up.

Once again Yvette had knocked me off my equilibrium. She had been good at that from the first day we met, right up till now. I didn't want to think about it. She had the potential to make me happy, but I didn't need her baggage. I had enough of my own. I grabbed my jacket and left for the trial.

The metro journey cheered me up. There was the usual entourage of puppeteers, singers and beggars hustling their way across town. For a while I studied how passengers reacted to them, when the tin cans were proffered in front of their faces. The indigenous population tend to ignore them and find something to scrutinise in their reflection on the train's windows, or a mark on the ceiling that captivates them for a few seconds. Mostly it's the tourists who pay up, unused to this type of activity. I always keep a few centimes handy for this very purpose, but only for those who perform in some way. Direct begging usually gets a cold stare.

I don't profess to know much about the French legal system; in fact, I find what I do know quite baffling. But if it is good enough for the French, it is good enough for me. I was allowed to sit at the back of the court, well away from the main players. When the gendarmes brought in the accused I was surprised to find that Magdeleine Dupré was indeed the woman I saw Rene Rousselier with outside Montparnasse Station – the blonde with the white PVC coat and red scarf.

It never occurred to me that she was his nemesis. I had always assumed that they were lovers – she looked his type. I was conscious I was stereotyping her and rebuked myself for doing so. I was convinced the woman in the park was his killer. Now I had two mysteries: who was the woman in the park and why was Rene Rousselier murdered?

I would never get an answer to my first question, but my second question was quickly answered as the prosecutor laid out her opening argument before the judges. Her case was simple: Madame Dupré acted solely out of revenge. She killed to avenge the murder of her husband. She had confessed as much. To contemplate any alternative was a waste of the court's time. The prosecutor went on to detail the events of the day of the murder: that Madame Dupré had attended to a number of routine chores that day, paying bills and doing a little shopping before going to the park. Such actions signified someone in a rational frame of mind. Witnesses would testify that, as she entered the park, she showed no signs of distress or agitation; that her every move was coldly calculated. The prosecutor went on in this vein for some time. The picture she painted was of a woman who had waited her time to exact revenge on the man considered to be responsible for her husband's death. The fact that she did it in broad daylight, and in plain view of witnesses, was neither here nor there.

The defence put forward the argument that her actions amounted to self-defence; that the deceased had terrorised the defendant over a protracted period of time, demanding sexual favours and making her fear for her life. When the now deceased turned his attentions to her twenty year old daughter, the defendant, in fear for her daughter, took the only course of action she could to protect both of them from Rene Rousselier, who was known in the underworld as an enforcer. In fear for her life and that of her daughter, she had shot him when she was in a fugue of terror.

Rene Rousselier was described by both the prosecution and the defence as a man feared within the Paris underworld. There was no dispute that he was one of life's undesirables, a man who would not think twice before sticking a knife between the ribs of some unsuspecting opponent. It was acknowledged by both parties that Rousselier was suspected of the killing of Henri Dupré, the defendant's husband and known associate of Rene Rousselier. The prosecutor argued that the defendant had enjoyed the spoils of her husband's criminal activity with the deceased for many years, and therefore should not be seen as a victim or attract anyone's pity.

The arguments went back and forth for most of the day. I discovered that my knowledge of the French language had its limitations, as terms and phrases were used by counsel and witnesses that were not in my vocabulary. When I left the court later that afternoon, I was none the wiser how the judges would determine fact from fiction. I had had enough. The outcome no longer seemed important. My sympathies lay with Madame Dupré, and I hoped they would accept her version of events. Whatever the outcome, I had my own decision to make that afternoon – a decision that would affect me for the rest of my life.

I came to Paris looking for Utrillo and found him. My search took me into the shadows of despair, as Dr Bricard warned it would. Maybe he was right, and Utrillo should be left in the darkness of his distorted life. What I do know is that I found more than what I was looking for. I found a meaning to my life that I thought I had lost forever. I had found love again. Or maybe love found me. Now I had a purpose in my life that transcended books and the writing of books. I had a destiny to meet.

Outside the court, I watched the ordinary people of Paris going about their business. They looked content. I hoped they were. I waved for a taxi to stop and pick me up. It had begun to rain again. The driver pulled over and I got in. I was just another fare in his daily routine.

'Where to, monsieur?'

'To a new beginning,' I said quietly to myself.

'Pardon monsieur!'

'I'm sorry. Excuse me.'

I had my decision to make. My choice was simple: Thérèse or Yvette. My heart was telling me one thing, my head another. This time I was not going to overrule my heart. I had done that before and paid the price. Nor did I know what to expect when I got to my destination. Would I find the love I wanted to receive and to give? Either way, I could be making a mistake, a big mistake. But then, as Romain Rolland once said of love: *One makes mistakes; that is life, but it is never a mistake to have loved.*

My year in Paris was over; one journey completed. A new journey was about to begin.

'Take me to Issy-les Molineaux, please. That's where I want to go.'

The End

Postscript

When I was asked to write a postscript for this story, my first reaction was to refuse. Why was a postscript needed, the story was there for all to read? It was put to me, by the editors of the publishing firm that secured the rights, that Gil-Martin had left a few loose ends; that readers would be interested to know what happened to some of the characters after the story ends. Eventually I agreed. Much of what I write I obtained from personal contact with the characters; other information I got from second hand sources and can't vouch for the veracity of the information.

Not long after the publication of *Utrillo: The Man Who Loved Walls,* John Gil-Martin wrote and fronted the television documentary on Irish painters: Milo Marsh, Luke Sweteman and Narcissus Netterville. When the programme was broadcast it was considered a success by the critics. The Irish Times thought it one of the most intelligent and watchable art retrospectives ever shown on RTE.

Thérèse Dumard accompanied John during his stay in Dublin. On their return to Paris they married. To everyone's surprise Thérèse's daughter Clara turned up at the registry office. Sadly, Thérèse and her son Marc remain estranged.

John and Thérèse are still together and now live in New York City where Thérèse runs a small but successful gallery in Manhattan's Lower East side and John writes for a number of American journals. He has just published a book on the Scottish abstract landscape painter and sculptor, Findo Gask.

Interestingly, when John completed his third draft of *Looking for Utrillo,* he included a poem which he subsequently removed from the final manuscript. I include this poem here, as it gives some insight to what his thinking was when he met Thérèse on l'île des Cygnes, or shortly afterwards.

Re-Union

On Pont de Bir-Hakeim
We cross into each other's time zone
And walk beneath the arching branches
Along l'allée des Cygnes.
Each step brings us closer to a time
Once shared. We recognise our
Past; its little histories,
Passions, betrayals, the regrets?
We keep our silences and
Wait for opportunities to share
What is harmless and need not be said.

Like small dark darts, starlings swoop
Down at us along the leafy archway.
Across the river on port de Javal
Barges unload the day's cargo.
Black smoke billows up aimlessly.
We hear men's coarse laughter.
At pont de Grennelle we hold hands,
Smile with our success, make more promises.
I turn towards the laughter, walk out of reach again.
Liberty's shadow falls like a cloak on the river.

Did John think he was walking out of Thérèse life at that time? It would seem so. Was this the reason he didn't include the poem in the final manuscript? John made no comment when told I was going to include the poem in my postscript.

Yvette Carné continues to live and work in Paris. She has moved from the apartment she lived in on the Left bank to a town house in the Marais district across the river and now works as a GP in a nearby practice.

I met Yvette on two occasions only. Both were to make arrangements for her painting, Rue Francoeur, to go on tour in Britain and North America. She had agreed thereafter that the painting would be hung in The Musée de l'Art Moderne de la Ville de Paris.

It was after business on my second trip that we got around to talking about her relationship with John. Yvette told me she bitterly regretted what she had done and had finished their relationship while under considerable stress. She realised too late that John was the victim of circumstances and not the perpetrator of them. She also told me she no longer keeps in touch with Pascal and, as promised, her husband Edouard moved to the south of France. They are now divorced.

Frieda Pechstein has re-married and lives in Poitiers where she spends most of her time looking after her children and step children. Her new husband is, believe it or not, a Scotsman from Glasgow by the name of Rutherford Jack. I make no further comment. She remains on good terms with John and Thérèse.

Emile Renouf remains chair of the Microbe Research Department at the Pasteur Institute. He took a year's sabbatical on the pretext of writing a paper he and Claude Dumard had been working on. I am told the real reason behind his year out was 'stress related'. On his return to the Institute he was passed over for the position of Director. He lives alone.

Magdeleine Dupré was found guilty of second degree murder and sentenced to five years. She has subsequently been released.

After my second visit to Yvette Carné I found myself near the Square Saint Lambert, off rue Lecourbe. I recognised the park immediately as the one John Gil-Martin frequented. I ventured in and sat on the bench where he met Emile Renouf and Thérèse Dumard. As I looked around at what John would have looked at I saw on the far side of the park, sitting in the shadow, a woman reading. I wondered if this was the same woman that bemused John so often; the woman he thought was the killer of Rene Rousselier.

Curiosity got the better of me. I picked up my purse and made my way along the path that runs along the curvature of the garden beds and out of sight of the far gate. I was going to find out who the mystery woman was once and for all. When I got to where the path straightened I quickened my step. I was only a few steps away; only a few shrubs blocked my view. Imagine my surprise on reaching the bench only to find it was empty, she was gone! I ran on to the gate, she was nowhere to be seen. She had vanished in broad daylight.

Much happened when John Gil-Martin started out on his journey looking for Utrillo. Much has happened since. Change is inevitable. I no longer work for Reid and Seymour but have taken up a post with a rival publisher. On occasion I would drop into the bar that John, Gillian and I visited during one of John's visits to London. Jeff, the gentleman who provided protection that first visit, was a regular imbiber. I discovered he wrote a regular column for a well-known magazine. I became a subscriber to his monthly outpourings. Sadly, his years of enlightenment caught up with him and he is no longer with us. London is not the same place without him.

Today there are streets, schools and hotels named after Maurice Utrillo. You can even visit the Maurice Utrillo

Museum in Sannois. His paintings hang in the best art galleries in the world. This, from a man whose housekeeper put a dog collar round his neck and chained him to a tree for fear that he might escape her supervision. She even kept the chain on him when she walked him in the garden. That such a man could produce such masterpieces may beggar belief, but he did, and John Gil-Martin captured that genius for all of us to know.

Fiona Shaw,
Soho, London
2011

Maurice Utrillo: The Man Who Loved Walls

BIOGRAPHY

1830 Madeleine-Célina Valadon (Utrillo's grandmother) born in Bessines-sur-Gartempe, a small market town in the arrondissement of Bellac in the department of Haute-Vienne.

1865 Marie-Clémentine Valadon (Utrillo's mother) born in Bessines.

1869 Madeleine and Marie-Clementine move to Paris. Eventually settle in Montmartre.

1871 First day of the Paris Commune.

1883 Maurice Valadon born at 1am in * rue du Poteau, Montmartre. Dec 29
Birth registered at the Mairie of the 18th arrondissment.
Father unknown.

1886 Maurice, his mother and grandmother, move to N° 7 rue Tourlaque. **Toulouse-Lautrec has his studio in an upstairs apartment. Vincent Van Gogh visits Lautrec most Sundays during his stay in Paris. Around this time Marie-Clémentine changes her name to 'Suzanne Valadon'.
Maurice attends elementary school in the Place Saint-Pierre, later moving to the Institut Flaisselle in rue Labat.

1888 Maurice, as a five year old, meets Renoir in the Lapin Agile.

1891 Maurice officially adopted by Miguel Utrillo y Molins at the Mairie, on rue Drouot, 9th arrondissment.***

1893 Moves to the suburb of Pierrefitte - Montmagny.

1896 Maurice attends Pluminard Boarding School.
Suzanne moves in with Paul Mousis.

1897 Maurice leaves his private school in Pierrefitte.
In the autumn he is enrolled in Collège Rollin on the Avenue Trudaine in Paris.

1898 He is awarded second prize in mathematics and an honourable mention in French.

1899 He wins a mention for ethics. Ironically, he has to leave the school as he is already an alcoholic and his teachers consider him unfit to continue his studies.

One of his first jobs is with Dufayelle, an emporium selling cheap furniture; he is fired. He then works for a milliner, a shoe-cream manufacturer, in a lampshade factory, a publicity agent, as a mason's apprentice and many others.

1900 He obtains an apprenticeship in Crédit Lyonnais as an office boy. It lasts 20 days.

1901 Maurice gives up working and continues to drink heavily. He is committed to Sainte-Anne, an asylum and hospital for nervous diseases in rue Cabanis, near Santé Prison to undergo his first treatment for alcoholism. He stays two months.

Toulouse-Lautrec dies.

1903 Maurice takes up painting as a therapy to his drinking. He paints 150 paintings in his first year.

IMPRESSIONIST PERIOD BEGINS

1904/5 Maurice sells his first paintings to the picture framer, Anzoli, who hangs them in his shop at N⁰ 4 rue de la Vieuville. Signs his name Maurice Valadon.

1906 At the age of 23 Maurice returns to Montmartre and lodges in the family flat at N⁰ 12 rue Cortot.

IMPASTO PERIOD BEGINS

1909 At 26 he moves into lodgings at N⁰ 2 rue Cortot, before staying at the bistro Casse-Croûte at N⁰ 1 rue Paul-Féval. Invited to exhibit for the first time at the Salon d'Automne.

1910 Begins to sign name as Maurice Utrillo V.

Paints first still life.

WHITE PERIOD BEGINS

1911 Suzanne leaves Paul Mousis.

Maurice moves with Suzanne and André Utter and his grandmother to N⁰ 5 Impasse de Guelma.

1912 Maurice admitted to asylum in Sannois.

Makes a trip to Ouessant, Brittany.

First foreign exhibition held in Munich.

1914 Suzanne Valadon marries André Utter.

ARCHITECTURAL PERIOD BEGINS

1915 Maurice's grandmother Madeleine dies aged 85.

1916 Maurice is confined in the Villejuif asylum from August to November.

1918 From March 1st to August, Maurice is treated for alcoholism at Aulnay-sous-Bois.

1919 Maurice is hospitalised in Picpus asylum for the violently insane. He escapes to Montparnasse.

1920 He is recaptured and spends a further 5 weeks in the asylum. COLOUR PERIOD BEGINS.

1924 Maurice attempts suicide.

1925 Officially declared incompetent and all legal affairs transferred to his mother and stepfather, André Utter.

1926 Utrillo designs the scenery and costumes for Balanchine's ballet Barabeau, produced by Diaghilev.

1929 Awarded the rank of officer of the Legion of Honour.

1935 Utrillo marries Lucy Valore.

Utrillo baptised into Catholic Church aged 55.

1938 Suzanne Valadon dies. She is buried next to her mother in the cemetery of Saint-Ouen, Paris.

1940/5 During the German occupation of Paris Utrillo leaves the city and settles in Le Vésinet.

1950 The film, La vie dramatique de Maurice Utrillo, wins the Prix Lumière at the Cannes Film Festival.

1955 Utrillo dies at Dax. Buried at Saint Vincent cemetery, Montmartre.

1965 Lucie Valore dies. She is buried next to Utrillo.

Notes

Earlier biographers are inconsistent about many of the dates and addresses pertinent to the lives of Suzanne Valadon and Maurice Utrillo. For example:

*One writer places the birth at N⁰ 13 rue du Poteau; another records it as N⁰ 3.

**The same writers dispute whether Toulouse-Lautrec's studio was on the third or fourth floor at 7 rue Tourlaque. The painter's private accommodation was a flat at № 19 rue Fontaine.

*** It is suggested that a civil ceremony took place on Jan 27th. Other suggestions claim that Maurice was adopted on April 8, 1891.

21442099R00160

Printed in Great Britain
by Amazon